Shadow Games

Shadow Games

N. Penz

Dedication

To the bonds of sibling hood: may you fight harder than any war and protect one another no matter the cost. To the past you when you dreamed of the future and the future you dreaming of what could have been. To the present, where all the stories are unraveling before you, as infinite as the stars in the sky, this is what you are living for. Thank you, dear reader, for your time.

Imagined Worlds Publishing

Imagined Worlds Publishing supports the right to free expression and the value of copyright. The purpose of copyright is to encourage writers and artists to produce the creative works that enrich our culture. The scanning, uploading, and distribution of this book without permission is a theft of the author's intellectual property. If you would like permission to use material from the book (other than for review purposes), please contact n.penz9@gmail.com. Thank you for your support of the author's rights.

ISBN 978-0-578-91568-5

First Printing, June 2021
Second Printing, May 2026

{ 1 }

New

The young woman considered her unfamiliar home with thoughts revolving in a circle like a burning halo. With her ocean-blue eyes puffy and swollen, she examined her surroundings of unremarkable white walls, a small kitchen, and a shared living and dining area. The end of a short hallway led to a single bedroom and a bathroom with off-white linoleum floors, and beige carpet everywhere.

She should be gallivanting in and out of the bedroom and bathroom, but she couldn't dredge up an ounce of joy. Instead, she sat in the middle of all her worldly possessions that she could pack up in fifteen minutes, something she had done too often recently. Salty tears splashed onto the glass of the picture frame she cradled in her calloused hands, the water magnifying the face that dominated her teenage years. Unbidden, the memory of their last night together surfaced; her mind still coming to terms with the unimaginable.

"Sean, really?" She had asked, holding a fraying towel up with a hand on her bony hip. The towel may not have looked like much, but it was important when it was all you had.

He had snorted and, with an impish grin, had apologized, "Sorry Ciara." Then, together, they had scooped up their bags and left the studio apartment, tossing their keys onto the counter as they moved into the shadowed corridor.

Carefully, she hugged the picture to her chest and rocked back on her heels, choking down the howl she knew was coming, and shoved herself to her feet. She slumped to the kitchen peninsula and placed the picture at the end, brushing her fingers over the round, freckled face with wavy red-brown hair falling over his forehead.

A strike of lightning illuminated the near-darkness outside, even though her three-year-old iPhone 5c read that it was only eight in the evening. Ciara straightened, her muscles tensing, as her eyes narrowed on the man-shaped shadow lurking on her empty balcony. Fear drove her grief from her as she reached into her back pocket, knowing there was no one to protect her any longer. Anger at the cause for her forced move and sudden solitude burned away her fear as her fingers wrapped around her pocketknife, pulling it from her loose-fitting jeans. She prowled toward the sliding glass door, Ciara's dark brown hair and milky white complexion reflected back to her. With a clenched jaw and a steady hand, she raised the blade, refusing to let him escape her retribution this time. As another strike of lightning lit the sky, her balcony and the turbulent Atlantic Ocean beyond were thrown into stark relief – it was simply a shadow.

The fight drained from her as she closed the knife, and she leaned against the cool glass, taking a shaking breath and dragging her fingers through her tangled shoulder-length hair.

It isn't The Shadow; it was only a tree. You are in Pine Harbor, Massachusetts... alone. For the first time, she was alone, and all because of The Shadow and because she couldn't keep her mouth shut; the adrenaline drained out of her. Her limbs were left shaking as she shoved headphones into her ears, spinning her ancient iPod to her punk rock playlist. And a memory hounded her, pulling her back into its hold.

Ciara had squeezed his upper arm, unable to prevent the words from escaping her. "I want to take a semester off. It's getting into the final classes and it's hard jumping around."

"You take one semester off and then you never finish. Mom and Dad would haunt me from their graves if you don't finish college. Love you sis," he had stated.

"It's a long drive to Michigan, but I love you too." And then her eyes had blown wide, as a man clothed in black had melted out of the shadows between the two buildings, striking at them with a long-bladed knife.

She snarled in exasperation at the memory incessantly repeating and pressed the heels of her hands into her eyes. If she had only waited to talk to him and kept her mouth shut, so many things could have been different.

The man didn't have a name, at least not one the siblings knew, nor did they know what he wanted from them, because it was more than simply eliminating witnesses. When they were teenagers and first forced to flee, the man had blended into his environment so well that they named him The Shadow, and it had stuck.

Ciara opened her eyes and pushed away from the glass, turning in time to see the ocean lit up again as the mid-

May storm raged. Sluggishly, she stumbled into the bathroom and splashed her face with water, wishing her grief could slide down the drain with the water. Her big brother was all she possessed in terms of blood family, her foundation when everything else felt wrong. They were always there for one another; they never left each other. But that was a lie; she *had* left him.

Sean had grabbed the back of Ciara's shirt and tossed her behind him as he had ordered, "Go, get in the Jeep!"

"I'm not leaving you!" Ciara had dropped under Sean's arm, landing a blow to the man's ribs.

Four black sedans had squealed to a stop around them. Using the distraction, The Shadow had gripped Sean and forced him to his knees. Then had put the knife to his throat, using him as a human shield.

"Drop your weapon or we shoot!" A man had bellowed, climbing out of their vehicle with a gun trained on The Shadow.

He had simply laughed, "You wouldn't risk hitting these two. Now Sean, be a good boy, and tell me where your parents hid it."

"Where they hid what?" Sean had choked out as he shook his head, telling Ciara not to move.

"I know you're lying," the man had snarled, moving backward toward the alley, pulling Sean in front of him.

"Drop your weapon," a man with a black goatee had demanded.

Ciara had stood frozen, uncertain what to do because she knew their Shadow wanted an answer they were unable to give. And if they couldn't answer, they were dead. Sean had held Ciara's gaze, begging her to stay put.

The Shadow had made it to the mouth of the alley before a gun went off, and he had sinisterly teased, "Missed me." Then he had dragged the knife across Sean's throat.

She had run before she consciously decided, and Ciara had found herself kneeling in a pool of Sean's blood, with her hand shaking as she stroked his freckled face. She had stared into the lifeless eyes as her world shattered.

Tears strangled her, spilling out in tiny crystals that gathered on her thick eyelashes. She blinked, watching them fall into the porcelain sink. Sean put her first no matter what, and she had stood and done nothing as a knife was pulled across his throat. Someone had bound her in a blanket like a doll and then let them take her from him. Deep down in the functioning part of her brain, she understood it was shock which had allowed it. But it sickened her how readily she had let them take her away.

Two weeks had passed since then. In that time, her grief settled into her as a constant companion, but a boiling sense of anger and a driving need for justice warmed her like a cloak. Ciara splashed her face with cold water and let out a long-controlled breath. Then commenced stacking her vertebrae on top of each other until she was at her full, six-foot height.

She regarded herself in the mirror and said, "You can do this, this isn't the end; it's a new beginning, and you have the agency now. You have protection and the agency will find out who The Shadow is and what he wants," she said, and snorted at the thought. It took the agency six years to find them after

The Shadow murdered their parents, and they didn't seem to have a clue what he wanted from the siblings either.

"No, *I* will find out what he wants, and *I* will bring him to justice because he has *always* found me. But first, I need to get a job." After another deep breath, Ciara tied her thick brown hair up into a short ponytail and straightened her baggy black sweatshirt. She bit her lower lip, and her eyebrows contracted as she swiped under her deep blue eyes with the heel of her hand. "And I should also try for some new friends, so I stop having conversations with myself because it's probably not very healthy."

For the first time, she forced herself to take in the good things as she kept her breathing under control, just as she had learned from her various choir directors. *First thing, you are alive*, she told herself. *Second thing, you have a working bathroom for the second time in a row.* Ciara let out a slow breath, trying to remember the last time that had happened and couldn't.

Sean and Ciara had been on the run since their parents were slaughtered by The Shadow, because the cops refused to believe the orphaned teens that it wasn't a murder-suicide. Whatever information The Shadow failed to get from their parents, he was trying to obtain from them, stalking the siblings all over the country. Relocating often was the only way they stayed ahead of him, which often meant sleeping in abandoned buildings, living out of Sean's Jeep, and, when lucky, month-to-month apartments.

Ciara ran her fingers along the edge of the mirror, and her mother's charm bracelet jingled at the movement. She touched each charm until her fingers inevitably found the one that had always seemed out of place, before glancing at her reflection one more time. Her tall, lean form was swamped in the dark fabric that made the purple bruising under her eyes stand out. She could cover it up with concealer, but she didn't like wearing makeup.

With narrowed eyes, she promised herself, "I will find him and he will pay for what he's done." She strode out of the bathroom and flipped the light on in the only bedroom, shaking her head in disbelief that it was all hers. *Third thing, I now live in a mansion, but I have nothing to put in it.*

She sucked in her bottom lip, forming a mental note to look for a job first thing in the morning. The security of a job needed to come before either school or retribution, even if completing her degree was the only way she could honor Sean and their parents' wishes. She wouldn't sit idly while waiting for The Shadow to find her, despite the agency claiming they would keep her safe.

It was that thought – the need to take advantage of the brief respite the Agency had given her, the opportunity to have some semblance of a normal life – that had her moving toward the door. She wouldn't ruin her chance, but she could use it to her advantage. Learn about her new town, Pine Harbor, and force The Shadow to meet on her home turf for once.

Anxiously, she dug around in the front pocket of her jeans to make sure the Jeep keys were still there before walking to her door, wanting her things in place to feel planted somewhere. She stepped out into the hallway, shutting it behind her as the stairwell door opened and jumped.

"Hello!" An older man rasped out, his wrinkled face brightening with his gray hair stuck up in all directions. "You must be my new neighbor. I'm Nicholas Durand, it's a pleasure to meet you."

Ciara eyed him for a moment, taking his measure, letting her gut be her guide as it had never let her down before. "Ciara, pleasure to meet you Mr. Durand," she said, pronouncing her name in the Irish fashion of Key-Air-uh.

Her neighbor appeared both surprised and pleased with her manners as he took her hand while asking, "Are you all unpacked? It's late and you must have just got in, do you need any help?"

She felt her own smile rise to match his compassion, her hand instantly warming in his, drawing out her grief like poison from a wound, leaving behind calm. With a sigh, she admitted, "I don't have much more to bring up but thank you."

Mr. Durand met her eyes and held them, inquiring, "Are you alright? I apologize for the straightforwardness when we just met, but you look done up."

"I...no, I'm..." Ciara closed her eyes and gulped as the stinging behind her eyes started again. Two weeks. It had only been two weeks ago. *Fourth thing, extremely kind, if nosy, neighbor that reminds me of Grandpa.* It was impossible not to feel drawn toward the gentleman with his rain-spattered tweed jacket and wrinkled face; her longing for anything resembling friends or, better yet, family intensified.

"I'll make you some hot tea and leave you a thermos out here. If you feel like company, just knock, I love a good card game," he said as he began unlocking his door.

Ciara latched onto his last comment, grateful for the invite, and stated with a small grin, "I'll challenge you to any game you want tomorrow night, how's that sound?"

He nodded, appearing delighted, as she let a smile drift to the corners of her mouth before lifting a hand in farewell and progressed into the stairwell.

At the Jeep, she pulled a thick envelope tucked into a ziplock bag out from under the wiper blade and grimaced. Her worn-out senses prickled, and she glanced around her, taking in her surroundings of blossoming dogwood trees and flowering tulips. A pounding spring storm sent sheets of rain into her face, but nothing stood out in the parking lot. She climbed into the front seat, withdrawing the letter from the agency. Written in cramped handwriting, it told her to use the credit card to furnish the safe house they had placed her in. As she read on, it said they would be in touch, but not how, and to keep her eyes open for any sign of trouble.

She growled into the silence, knowing that was what had kept her alive for the last six years, and felt the anger bubbling inside her again. Anger that, only after having been forced to learn those skills, did the agency step in to help. Anger that it was after one of them died, they showed up. Anger that no one had believed them. She clung to that anger. She could work with anger; it was the tears she didn't know what to do with.

{ 2 }

A Helping Hand

"May I assist you?" A gravelly voice asked around the giant box Ciara laboriously heaved up the stairs. Sweat poured down her face in rivulets as her fingers began losing their grip. She clutched it tighter, struggling against gravity.

"Sorry, I didn't think anyone would be around right now." She grunted, pulling it onto the second landing. Then, she tried to open the hallway door with her hip; that's when she recognized her elderly neighbor.

He appeared unsurprised at her independent struggle as a delicate smile touched his lips. "I thought you said you were all moved in?"

She exhaled in a gust at his inquisitive prying and tried to remind herself he undoubtedly was attempting to be kind. Ciara simply didn't like requesting assistance, especially now that she was on her own, because usually when she needed it most, there would be no one around to depend on. The young woman regarded the few steps down to her neighbor's place and grunted as she replied, "From the stuff I had, yes."

"Would you like help now?" His eyes twinkled, and she got the impression that if she answered no, he still wouldn't permit her to continue on her own.

She shook her head and attempted it anyway, and attempted to kindly decline, "I'm fine, but thanks."

"Stubborn, is what you are, that box is bigger than you," the old man rolled his eyes in an excellent imitation of a young adult.

"I'm stronger than I look." Ciara dragged a hand across her sweating forehead, but laughed at the strangeness of his gesture, despite herself.

"Clearly, you already came this far without help. Unfortunately, for you I'm stubborn as well *and* I have more practice with it, let me help." Mr. Durand smiled, and it brightened his wrinkled face.

"I concede," she said with a glance at his barrel chest and arms muscled despite his advanced age. There was a point where independence became narcissistic and obstinate, and she refused to be either. "I guess if you don't mind, I could use some help, thank you."

He inclined his head and waved past her as he added, "If you give me a minute to drop this off in my room, I'll be back to help you." She nodded, and he dashed off to his room.

An hour later, the two were planted on her living room floor, building a wooden futon and a coffee table. They had already discussed the general topics of the weather, Mr. Durand's two children spread across the United States, and what Ciara had studied in college. With nothing more to talk about, Mr. Durand finally gave her a hard look and questioned,

"What brings you here to Pine Harbor?" He pulled his gray hair away from his dripping forehead while he methodically screwed a leg into the frame. When she had turned the ceiling fan on, only years of collected dirt had rained down on them, and she had quickly turned it back off. Apparently, her protection crew needed to hire a more capable cleaner, but she also needed to go back to the store to pick up more cleaning supplies.

Ciara smirked slightly as she completed putting together her end of the futon. Evasively, she answered, "Escaping, I needed to leave where I was." She tried hard not to think more on the reason than that and moved to throw away some of the trash which had accumulated from all the packaging materials.

"Decided to start completely fresh," he said, not pressing her further as he added, "I still can't believe you only have those two bags and a box of books." He shook his head, utterly oblivious that many of her belongings were still confiscated by the agents who had appeared five minutes too late. What she had were the items not under suspicion of whatever they were searching for, not that they would reveal more than that. "Most girls, no, most *people* would have three times this and more."

For the first time in weeks, a laugh bubbled up her throat, dissolving some of the weight pressing down on her heart. "I'm not most people, plus, I traveled a lot before."

"By yourself?" He observed her glance up at the picture and then down to focus on the leg she had just put together for the coffee table. "With him?" He guessed.

Ciara considered his attempting to piece together the puzzle of her life. Previously, Mr. Durand had told her she reminded him of his youngest daughter. And that he was a retired teacher, but the job had probably honed his instincts to notice the subtle warning signs of evading complete truths.

"Yes," she stated, and stood, pressing her hands against the small of her back, stretching. Everything was still too raw, and she didn't want to get into a conversation about it yet. Mr. Durand appeared nice enough, but Ciara didn't feel the need to reveal her entire life story, nor was he asking for it. She changed the topic. "How did you end up here?"

Mr. Durand helped her move a bookcase into a corner, clearly letting her steer the conversation back onto solid ground. The older man took a sip from his water glass and began to tell her of his wife, deceased for ten years, and how they ended up in Pine Harbor. Then moved to a humorous description of his oldest granddaughter's recent marriage while they moved the coffee table into the center of the room.

Ciara pointed to the glass door separating them from the balcony and asked, "Should I get furniture for out there?"

He pondered her inquiry before he responded with his own question, "Do you think you will be out there much?" He thought of his days spent reading outside, adding, "I have a chair, but I also have more time to sit and contemplate nothingness."

"I'll get a lawn chair." With a smirk at his dry humor, she ran her hands through her midnight hair. To sit and do nothing sounded like a lovely, unattainable dream. Ciara gazed around at her semi-furnished place and sighed before stating, "I didn't realize how much stuff it took to fill a place up."

He gave her a pointed look. "Why don't you join me for dinner tonight?"

She leaned against the door of her almost-empty bedroom. Her bed and frame wouldn't arrive for another week. It was one reason she had bought the futon instead of a standard couch. Ciara looked at him critically. "Are you sure you don't mind the extra company?"

He shook his head and smiled, waving his hand at her, dismissing her worry. "Not at all, as long as you don't mind playing a game of cards or chess. And if you like we can have a friendly chat about Irish history."

"I would appreciate it, otherwise I was just going to have cereal... again. I bought all this food but forgot that I didn't have anything to cook with, or any dishes other than a few mugs and bowls." But she didn't want to go out shopping again in the morning. "I do love history," she said without a trace of sarcasm, before adding, "Thank you for all of your help today." Ciara turned into her room and flipped the light switch on.

"You slept on the floor last night?" He questioned as he saw past her into the unfurnished room. Unconcerned, she shrugged but caught the wide-eyed shock and concern in his eyes. Horrified, it seemed that a young woman would be unfazed at the lack of commodities, as Ciara searched for her sketchpad in the pile of blankets.

She didn't see what the problem was, and if she wasn't being supplied with endless amounts of money, she still would be sleeping on the floor for months to come. Sean and her had slept in a barn for a month the year before while on the run and worse before that. In her senior year of high school, they slept in the back of his Jeep for three months and cooked over a camp stove. When she became malnourished from not eating right, they pooled their money and got extra jobs so they could afford a cheap place to live for a short stint.

>>>

"I didn't even know the place was being rented and you were there," Mr. Durand said, gesturing wildly with a potato on his fork a few days later. "And how old did you say you were?"

"It was a pretty quick decision and I'm 21," she explained, smoothly evading answering. Despite the man's prodding questions, she enjoyed Mr. Durand's company. Mr. Durand, in his grandfatherly way, had reached out to her tattered heartstrings.

Mr. Durand contemplated her new information, taking it all in for a minute before asking another one of his endless questions, "Do you have everything you need now? What else are you missing?"

"A dresser, bathroom stuff, and cooking supplies, and still waiting on the bed and frame to arrive... I also need a job. I looked some yesterday and the day before, but nothing really sparked my interest." She took a drink of her hot tea and added, "Not that I want to be picky. I'll take whatever comes, but it would be nice for a change to have something I really enjoyed, you know?"

Mr. Durand tapped his lip with a weathered finger, brow furrowed as he thought about her predicament. "I do know, let me think... I have an old friend down at the Children's Center, do you like working with kids?"

"I've worked at a few day cares and summer camps," Ciara said after swallowing a mouthful of potato and the mush her neighbor called steamed vegetables.

What she was beginning to really like about Mr. Durand was that he didn't pry. At least not in the way most people did. He would ask open-ended questions but never seemed to mind if she fleshed out her responses or not. It was left up to her to decide to talk or to change the subject; there was no pressure where there always had been before. People her age had this *need* to know, a need to understand and dissect and poke for good measure. She wondered if all older people were like this or if it was just him. But Ciara hadn't had the opportunity to meet many people outside of her age group and her teachers in a long time.

The older man folded his hands as he watched her watching him, the edges of his mouth raised up. "I can make a call if it's something you are interested in, she had an opening for an athletic assistant. If I am recalling our conversation correctly, she seemed a bit desperate as the summer session is about to start."

"I love sports, I could do that," Ciara said eagerly. Eager to both have a job and do something that sounded fun. "Thank you, that's very kind of you."

He chuckled and waved away her gratitude as he said, "Haven't gotten you the job, just the possibility of an interview." Mr. Durand pushed his chair back and reached for the old-fashioned phone attached to the wall by a spiraling cord. Quickly punching in a few numbers by heart, the way the new generation never had to learn, he waited for someone to answer. Before long, someone answered, and he spoke into the mouthpiece. "Cynthia, it's Nicholas, how are you?" A soft voice answered, and after a brief exchange of pleasantries, Mr. Durand responded, "Great, that is wonderful to hear. I'm calling to inquire about that assistant athletic position you had open." After a pause, while he listened intently, he let out a hearty laugh. "No, I'm not interested, but I do have a young woman here who is, new neighbor in need of a job. She has worked with children before. Seems capable, but I will let you be the judge of that." Another pause, in which he spelled out Ciara's name for her and then inquired if one o'clock in two days worked for Ciara. She nodded, and he told Cynthia it was acceptable and thanked her with a promise to have coffee together soon.

Smiling earnestly, he hung up. Ciara impulsively reached across the table to squeeze his hand. "Thank you Mr. Durand, I really appreciate this, and I know it's not a job yet, but the prospect of at least having an interview set up is a relief."

"Of course, my dear, you are very welcome." He smiled at her with a twinkle in his faded blue eyes.

Begin Again

Ciara pushed an already full cart through an emporium of home goods. She was nauseated at the idea of shopping before she ever dragged her feet in, but her new friend was right. It would be better to get it done now rather than later when she would have more problems to distract her. Ciara reprimanded herself for thinking of the large items she could live without instead of remembering the objects she needed in order to survive. She reminded herself it wouldn't hurt to get a handful of new things for the bedroom and bathroom. *Novel idea, I could put my toothbrush in one of those fancy toothbrush holders, is there an actual name for those?*

She was really beginning to enjoy his subtle humor and calm temperament after only a few short days of living next to Mr. Durand. She was too sporadic and quick to action, at least that's what Sean always told her, and having someone slow her down reminded her of what she had.

Sean, who could sit for hours contemplating a single decision, and whose movements, although mechanical, always held intention. Out of the two of them, she graduated high school with college credit and continued into higher education when they moved, not because he lacked intelligence. It was all because of Sean's self-sacrificing nature, and she even had scholarships to pay for all of it, and only because of Sean's methodical planning. Ciara sighed and stopped the cart in the middle of the towel aisle. That was the one thing Sean always wanted: to see her graduate from college.

Stop thinking about it, Ciara said to the vaults of her mind. *I can't, it's still too fresh,* she argued back. And arguing with herself made her laugh, and the wave of depression dissipated. *What I need is a nice cup of tea. Maybe Mr. Durand likes tea.* Reigning in her emotions with the ease of practice, Ciara locked them up tight and resumed walking. Stopping here and there to run her hands along the material. Over the years, practicing locking up and swallowing down her fear, grief, loneliness, and anger had become her only way to cope and had become second nature. She contemplated using her new phone to call her best friend, Lex, or her only other friend, KT. They were both overseas, though, and when she counted out the hours for the time change, she realized they would both be sleeping or getting ready for bed.

Lex graduated from college two years prior with a degree in journalism and multi-media. Always an overachiever, she had been taking AP and college classes throughout high school, leaving her to graduate college two years early. She entered into a severely underpaid internship immediately after graduating, but after six months was hired full time, with benefits, as one of their travel journalists. Lex had always loved traveling and exploring unknown places; so to get paid to do it was even better.

KT, on the flip side, was a year older than Ciara and Lex. He had spent his first two years out of high school taking pre-med classes and knocking out all his pre-requisites while working as an EMT. After two years living at home, and two years biting his tongue with his challenging family, KT had enlisted in the Marines. Both Lex and Ciara worried about him; they also knew he loved almost every part of it. Ciara did her best to send care packages with his favorite food, unscented soap, t-shirts, and pillowcases whenever he was deployed. He was the envy of all the other guys, but Lex and Ciara would try to send enough to share whenever they could.

Ciara frowned and shoved her phone back into her pocket, maybe she could finally get one of those fancy high-tech phones everyone else had. *I should talk to Sergeant Curry about that.*

The teal-colored towels stacked on the shelves caught her eye, and she studied the colors transitioning from light to dark before transitioning to blue. And then refocused her attention on the texture variations before picking the thickest and softest one out and setting it in the cart. About to move away, Ciara paused and strode back over. She snatched up two more to toss next to the first, then moved to the hand towels, taking three in a shade lighter, followed by washcloths and then dish towels. Ciara didn't read the price tag and forced herself not to cringe at what she felt was an unnecessary luxury. Instead, she let the voice of her best friend be her guide, and she knew Lex would be telling her she deserved it after all this time.

>>>

"Ciara, order up!" The cook hollered from the chaos of the dinnertime rush.

After quickly tucking her hair behind her ear, Ciara swiftly placed the plates piled high with food onto her tray. She shifted through the restaurant and served her hungry customers, while scooping up the cash they dropped on her tables. In her spare time, she relieved their high school bus girl who seemed overwhelmed by her first part-time job.

Ciara surveyed her area and exhaled as she leaned against the bar counter a few hours later, sweat coating her neck. Everyone was happily devouring their food at the moment. Her feet ached, and she rolled her stiff neck. Only two more hours left in her fifteen-hour day.

"Ouch, what happened there?" Her work friend asked, pointing to the bruise on her upper arm.

"Over-zealous kid with a hockey stick," she snorted out her response, before stating, "I used to love hockey. But now I'm beginning to wonder who thought giving children sticks and a hard object to hit was a good idea. Seems like a very dangerous combination to me."

Her work friend laughed before agreeing, "Yeah, I still don't know how you manage to run around with a bunch of preschoolers all morning. Then teach sports to kids, *and then* come here. I think you are crazy or perhaps your masochistic."

Ciara pushed off the counter with a shrug, followed by stretching her arms over her head with cracking and popping limbs. There hadn't been much of a choice in the past, and she learned to take money whenever she had the chance. Oftentimes, it had to be under the table, and those were not always easy to come by. They had needed to move suddenly, or go off grid for a few weeks, and then working wasn't really an option, and they needed to rely on their limited savings. Now that she was on her own, building up her reserves was important. She was preparing for the next inevitable move or the day when the agency decided to pull out its support. "I don't mind, I'm off the next two days. Haven't had two days off in… I don't know, since September, I think."

"You should come over on Friday then. A few of us are having a girl's night in," she offered.

Ciara looked over her tables to stall. It wasn't that she didn't want to, but more that she was used to not letting herself get close to people, and sleeping over at someone's still seemed risky. Ciara fiddled with her apron strings, but what would a few hours of hanging out hurt? A nod, and then with a tentative smile, Ciara answered, "Sure, I'll bring some guacamole and chips."

"Great!" The other girl exclaimed, not fully able to contain her surprise. Ciara had only accepted her invite two other times in the almost year that they had worked together. Ciara watched her surprise turn into a grin as the girl said, "Your guac is delicious, but don't worry on the chips, I already have two bags."

Ciara nodded and began to walk over to one of her tables, saying, "Thanks, it's my best friend's recipe."

Two hours later, Ciara's stomach rumbled as the smell of popcorn wafted down the hall. She pulled her keys from her messenger bag and began to unlock her door when Mr. Durand's was suddenly thrown open. Without saying a word, he shook a large bowl and smiled, making the young woman groan and salivate. "You're the best neighbor any girl could ask for."

He held up a finger and declared, "Proper food first, but I'll put on a movie."

Ciara acquiesced with a glance down at her smelly waitressing clothes, "Deal, let me go change and shower first."

>>>

That first Christmas in Pine Harbor was more dreadful even than the one right after her parents' death. Not only was her birthday only weeks beforehand, but the absence of Sean emphasized the vacancies of her parents even more. The thought of her grandmother in Ireland made her frown deepen, and she wondered if she was even still alive. But Ciara had no way of knowing, and trying to contact her would be dangerous. Even Mr. Durand had departed to be with his children and their families for a few weeks. She didn't want to admit how much she had grown used to his presence.

Their weeks had become very routine over the past months. Saturday was their set day for a late game of cards once she finished her most recent sports camp. Then Sunday they had dinner; it was supposed to be promptly served at six, but that never actually happened. Mr. Durand provided the majority of their meal, and Ciara brought a side dish of vegetables, determined to get him to eat them without being cooked to mush. On her late nights during the week, Mr. Durand would greet her with a snack, and they would sit down to watch movies, usually something in black and white. He told her it was educational, but Ciara knew it was nostalgia. His late wife had adored Audrey Hepburn, and it was his way of holding on to her. Ciara understood it was why she seldom took off her mother's charm bracelet and why Sean had constantly worn their father's watch.

Mr. Durand's absence left Ciara to roam her apartment alone. She had finally purchased a TV, but she didn't have much in the way of movies or shows. What she had, she had already watched and was reasonably sure the last Blockbuster had closed a decade ago. Ciara regretted her decision of not signing up for a streaming network, but she ingrained fear kept her from putting any of her information online. She glanced over at her stack of books from the library and scowled, not in the mood to curl up with a good book and read. She was feeling too restless for that. Her fingers were still sore from playing Sean's, no, *her* guitar. Ciara had already spoken to both Lex and KT the day before, and she knew they were busy with family.

That had been a disappointment because Ciara hoped she could have them visit, but Sergeant Curry put a kibosh on that the moment she asked the question. She groaned in boredom, wishing the restaurant wasn't still on a limited holiday schedule and the Children's Center was open, but she still had five days of a barren schedule.

As the hours crawled by with only her progressively more miserable thoughts for company, Ciara frowned. Yes, she missed the hustle of working, but she didn't want to be a waitress forever, nor did she want to work with kids the rest of her life. Both were wonderful options, but they weren't the right ones for her. She admitted to herself that she had already been growing restless before this week. It was being alone with her thoughts that brought them out and into the open. She eyed the guitar in the corner of her living room once more. That's what she wanted to do: music, or even better, music and history. Perhaps together, or perhaps separately, but the beauty of her new life was that she wasn't trapped. She could change her mind and become something else entirely.

With a new sense of purpose, Ciara strode over to gather her laptop from her kitchen table and moved it to the futon. It was time to go back to school. Fulfill Sean's wish and her dream. She pulled up an online application to the university in her area and began the process.

$$\{\,4\,\}$$

Let It Out

Ciara gazed out at the pounding rain, smelling the wet pavement and earth as a boom of thunder shook the surrounding air. She imagined herself with a cup of steaming tea and lounging on Mr. Durand's cozy couch with a hand of cards in front of her. Part of her regretted picking up the extra hours, but the manager was desperate when two of the wait staff called off only hours before their shift.

With a furrowed brow, she watched people running through the storm, umbrellas clutched tightly against the rain and wind. Raincoats wrapped protectively across shoulders and heads bowed against the wind. Ciara questioned her judgement about not purchasing either over the past year, but a few months ago it hadn't seemed quite so necessary. Snow clung to clothing; it didn't drench like rain did. *Oh well, it's your own fault,* she scolded herself while striding out of the restaurant and into the howling storm. As she waited for a pause in the storm, she untucked her faded black shirt from her thrift store slacks, then pulled her hooded sweatshirt on, eyeing the streaming rain with annoyance.

And then she ran into the maelstrom, attempting to stay below the awnings, although it didn't appear to be doing her any good as the rain continued to pelt her in the face. A car raced by, momentarily submerging her in a tidal wave of filthy water, drenching her. Ciara growled indignantly at herself while thinking, *it was your own stupidity to walk to work today. Get some fresh air, clear your head; well, is it clear now?*

Her neighbor watched her splash through a puddle and lingered with his liver-spotted hand on the door. Swiftly, she sprinted into the alcove and halted, expelling a breathless thanks as she wrung out her short hair. She shook her body, dislodging fat drops, and stomped her feet, attempting to bring sensation back to them after the icy rain. Numbness seeping in from the freezing water, Ciara looked at him with a worn smile and repeated louder to be certain he heard her, "Thank you."

Mr. Durand eyed her with the gaze she supposed he gave his daughters, once upon a time, when he caught them making less than perfect choices. "Anytime Ciara, but you are soaked to the bone, what were you doing out in this weather?"

Ciara wrinkled her nose at the kind old man as she tried to rationalize her poor decision, "I didn't think it was going to rain. It said clear skies this morning before I left, although that was seven a.m."

"It always rains this time of year, at least once a day, but I haven't seen you all week, how are you?" He smiled at her briefly and gave her appearance another quick study, as if to make certain all her appendages were still intact, before continuing up to the next floor.

Gently, she patted his shoulder as he puffed up the staircase, and explained her absence, "I've been interviewing at the university, or rather their scholarships and some on campus jobs. I also had to cover for a co-worker this week at the restaurant, because some stomach bug is going around." She paused so as not to get too far ahead of him, even though he was in decent shape despite his age. But Ciara had several inches on him in height, making her climb much easier as her long legs mounted the staircase. She tilted her head at him with a question in her ocean-blue eyes, "Did I miss something while I was away?"

"You did," he said with a grin as he began climbing the last set of stairs before their landing; his eyes twinkled as he watched her mount the last stair. "Someone moved in across from you and they seem to be a better candidate than the last tenant."

Curiosity aroused, Ciara raised an eyebrow at him, silently requesting additional information. She had barely spoken to the last person who had lived across from her, because not only had they appeared uninteresting, they had even more reclusive than she was. The person lasted in the apartment for merely eight months before vacating unexpectedly while she was at work. And then it sat vacant for over a month. "Hope this person lasts longer or we are going to have to start referring to it as the Defense Against the Dark Arts room."

Mr. Durand chuckled at her reference to the *Harry Potter* series he had been hearing way too much about from one of his granddaughters who recently discovered the books. "Hopefully this tenant does, he's a young man about your age and is just beginning graduate school." He winked at her slyly as he added, "Music and business."

"Did you ask for his credit report too?" She teased playfully, but from experience understood her neighbor undoubtedly had only been making friendly conversation. It was hard not to open up to the former high school teacher with his warm and welcoming aura. In some ways, the ease she experienced around him seemed dangerous, but he had been a balm to her broken soul the past year as she discovered how to heal.

Mr. Durand snorted good-naturedly, clarifying, "No, but you both like music, so you should meet him."

"You are not setting me up with someone, so get that thought out of your head." She laughed, the joyful sound echoing in the stairwell, a sound that had been appearing with greater frequency in the past months. "I'm sure I will meet him soon; our paths will have to cross in this tiny apartment." They both moved to their own doors and shoved the keys in the locks in synchrony as she waved at him. "Let me know if you need anything else for dinner and I'll see you in a little bit," Ciara said before pulling open her heavy powder-blue door.

He nodded as a smirk creased his face, and he stated, "6pm sharp, dinner will be ready."

She smiled and closed the door to her spotless apartment, with the knowledge that dinner wouldn't be ready until 6:30, even if she came over to help him cook. She found it exceedingly humorous that he always believed dinner would be ready at 6pm. Ciara shivered as she moved through her kitchen and into her small living room to set her bag down and launched her laptop. After turning on the music, she sluggishly walked into her bedroom to discard her wet clothes and slip into a hot shower.

Several minutes later, she towel-dried her hair and put on a pair of sweatpants and her brother's old t-shirt. It was one of those days, and she knew the rain always brought it, like the sky was sobbing with her. Quickly, Ciara placed a personal pizza in the oven for a late lunch just as a knock sounded on her door. She opened it just enough, so that she didn't have to undo the chain to see a stranger peering down at her.

"Hi, my name is Ash. I just moved in…" his voice trailed off as she closed the door in his face. Ciara detached the lock and opened the door, running her fingers through her wet pixie cut with a bright blue streak at the bangs that matched her eyes.

With a hand on her narrow hip, she eyed him up and down and introduced herself, "I'm Ciara, Mr. Durand mentioned someone from the university had moved in earlier today."

"That's me," he said in a low baritone as he paused and shifted uncomfortably, before he seemed to remember why he had knocked on her door. "Do you have any tea? Mr. Durand said you were a better bet and I can't find mine."

Ciara rolled her eyes and stepped out of the doorway, and the shadow he cast over her. "Come on in and pick what you want," she said, closing the door behind her. Ciara walked around the tall man with broad shoulders to her kitchen cabinets before opening the one by her sink. "Take your pick," Ciara added with a wave as she gazed at him, realizing he must be about six foot seven, and she marveled at it. Usually, she was on a level with men at just under six feet, and Sean had only been a few inches taller, but Ash had her by at least a head.

His eyes widened at her selection as she ogled his vertical advantage. He looked overwhelmed at the cabinet filled with tea boxes and jars of loose leaf as he stated the obvious, "You really like tea, but just plain is fine."

She nodded and pulled herself onto the counter to reach the top shelf, clarifying, "My best friend travels for work and she sends me fresh teas all the time. I think I have plain back here, are you sure you don't want to try one of the others?" She looked over her shoulder at him and noticed his strong jawline and high cheekbones.

"I guess, if you don't mind," he hesitated, and she watched him glance around her apartment as he answered with his hands shoved in his pockets. His cheeks looked a bit red under his slight scruff of facial hair.

"Ever had Darjeeling?" He shook his head, and she expounded on her selection, "This is a first blush from Berlin; it's really good." After handing the small package down to him, she jumped to the floor just as the oven went off. "One minute," she said, snatching up a hot pad, pulling her cheese pizza out of the oven and setting it on the stove. Then she opened a drawer and handed him the tea strainer.

Ash raised an eyebrow and looked at the gadget as if it should come with instructions as he asked, "What's this for?"

Ciara laughed and explained, "Your tea. Give it here." She set water to boil and took two mugs and placed them on the counter. "Would you like lunch?" If she learned anything over the past year, it was that inviting people to share food was the first sign of acceptance. To bring people together, it seemed, all she needed was to have food or a meal together; somehow it leveled the playing field. Ciara also enjoyed sharing meals with people since she hadn't been able to before. Even if she never invited people over to her apartment, she always made sure she brought something to share with her. But since Ash already knew where she lived, it didn't matter, and it felt novel sharing her kitchen table with someone her age for once.

"I have some made, but I can bring it over," he said in his soft way and slipped out the door with a tentative smile on his stubbled face.

From the table, her phone began buzzing, and she flipped it open with a glance at the caller ID. Her best friend's voice crackled over the connection, "Ciara, how are you?"

The young woman's shoulders slumped, and she let out a gust of air as she said, "It's one of those days Lex."

"Did I get the day right? I hope I didn't miss it," she said in a rush, her low voice made higher over the phone.

Her eyes filled up, and she wrapped an arm around her stomach with a pizza cutter in her other hand. "You're right, he died today, last year. I can't believe it was only last year."

"You should go do something, because sitting home won't help," Lex promptly advised, and Ciara could hear one of their favorite bands playing in the background.

"It's raining and I was already out all week," she said with another sigh. "I'm having lunch with my new neighbor and then dinner with Mr. Durand. He seems nice; a grad schoolboy and he likes music apparently."

"Good, go watch a movie or write a song together. Just don't be alone, okay?"

A tap sounded on the door, and Ash came back in at her call. She smiled slightly at him before answering Lex, "Okay."

"Promise me."

"I promise," Ciara said with a watery chuckle at her persistent friend.

"You know I'll question you on it later for vivid details, so, you can't lie," Lex half threatened, and Ciara felt the smile in her voice.

Ciara let the corners of her lips shakily turn up as she responded, "I know, I'll tell you and thanks for calling and remembering."

"How could I forget, he meant the world to you. Take care sweetie, I'll give you a call tomorrow," Lex said, waiting to hear Ciara's farewell before hanging up.

"Are you alright? I can leave if you want to keep talking," Ash said, shifting uncomfortably as Ciara blinked damp eyes and drew herself up, finding her steel once more.

"I'm fine, today is... it's just a rainy day, that's all. Water's done," she commented while ignoring his worry. She made the tea before taking her plate and mug to the table, apologizing as she sat, "Sorry it's such a small table, but I don't have people over... ever."

"That's alright," he acknowledged and set his nachos down and pointed at the picture in the middle of the table as he sat. "Boyfriend?" Ash questioned as he looked between the two faces in the picture.

Ciara shook her head and tried to hold back the tears again at the innocent question. Without intending to, he had asked the worst possible question, but she also knew he would have had no idea. She took a steadying breath before stating, "He was my brother."

Instantly, Ash froze, balancing a loaded nacho just before his mouth and his eyes wide. It dripped salsa in big splats onto the plate; he looked horrified and uncertain what to say in response.

"He died a year ago," her voice sounded vacant even to her own ears. She looked down at the pizza she was cutting as she added in a minuscule voice, "He was all I had for years." Inhaling slowly and deeply, she stilled her mind and then started again, "What kind of music do you do?" He gave her a questioning look, and she forced a smile. "I ran into Mr. Durand earlier."

He swallowed a bite before answering, seeming grateful for the change of topic. "Composition mostly, and I play piano and violin. Do you do anything?"

"Guitar and I sing." She wrinkled her nose as she continued, "I'm not very good at guitar though, self-taught."

"Do you go to the university?" He questioned shifting his feet under the table.

"I start in the fall, as long as these scholarships go through." Ciara pulled a piece of pizza from the small round and sighed.

"How old are you if you are just starting?" He shifted his eyes onto her with a slight blush at the directness of the question, and she noticed for the first time his eyes were a striking yellow-gold. "That was rude, I'm sorry."

On a shrug, she explained, understanding it was a question she would probably be getting a lot soon, "I'm just starting *there*. I didn't say I was just starting school, but I have enough college credits to be a junior. I'm almost finished with one of my majors and I'm enrolling in the honors college *and* I'm twenty-two."

"Where did you go before here and what's your major?" He questioned, a curious look in his eyes.

"Sean and I moved around a lot, so mostly community colleges. I want to major in Music and history with a minor in English." She tore off a chunk of pizza before asking, "What about you?"

Ash shrugged, looking down at his plate as he answered, "Nothing too exciting. I have a younger sister and an older brother." He fidgeted with his nachos, and Ciara held back a smile, noting his tiny, anxious quirks. She guessed he was probably an introvert. "My parents travel a lot, but we rarely go with them."

As he continued to fidget with the remains of the food on his plate, Ciara bit her lip, understanding some topics were difficult to dissect in company, especially new company. She tried for a topic that maybe wouldn't make him feel so ill at ease, "Where did you get your undergrad?"

"Same place, but I lived in a dorm apartment, but grad students aren't allowed. I have a group of friends who also got into grad school or are finishing up their undergrads this year. They all went home for the summer and I, well, I obviously didn't. Got a job on campus at the music department and they offered to keep me on over the summer." He shoved one of the remaining chips into his mouth, but it cracked and spilled salsa and cheese down the front of his shirt.

Unable to stifle a chuckle at the poor giant in front of her, face flaming as he tried to scoop up the mess, Ciara grabbed a hand towel from her counter. "Here, it's all good; happens to me all the time." Not meeting her gaze, Ash mopped up the salsa from his shirt, his face the color of a cherry. "Ash, seriously, it's not a big deal. You should see, actually you shouldn't, see my sorry attempts at drinking water in the middle of the night. Or chicken wings, barbeque ribs, I'm a mess, and trust me, not a hot one. Shit, I should have a caution sign set out when I eat loaded burgers, or tacos. I'm sure I've given many a child a nightmare from watching me eat tacos."

That made Ash smirk and rub the back of his neck as he shifted the conversation, "Tell me about this friend who sends you tea, ever gone with her?"

"Sadly no," Ciara said with a smile, at ease with this topic of conversation, and began the attempt at describing her eclectic friend, Lex.

{ 5 }

Ash

After a month of running into Ash at the grocery store down the street from their apartment, Ciara told him they should just go together. That was how she found herself pushing her cart halfway through June next to her neighbor, having an increasingly easier conversation. She wasn't surprised when their topic shifted back to college. It was one of the common grounds that they had unearthed between them, which seemed to be expanding with every passing week.

Ash placed a box of cereal into his cart before surveying her and inquiring, "What do you want to do when you graduate?"

Ciara knew her answer: she planned to go on to graduate school and then possibly teach, compose, or write, but that wasn't what she thought of. As usual, her thinking shifted back to Sean; he had so desperately wanted to see her graduate and discussed it more than she did. Whenever she questioned Sean about it, he would simply grin and tousle her hair, as it was the only sense of normalcy Sean could give her. It was her way out into a better life, a life as close to ordinary as she would ever have.

After a few steps, Ash realized Ciara was no longer directly behind him. He saw her face pale, and her ocean-blue eyes looked like the turbulent sea as she clutched the handle of her cart as if it were a lifeline. Hesitating for only a moment, he quickly strode over and studied her expression with genuine concern painting his voice, "Ciara, what's wrong? What happened?" She bit her lip and refused to look at him. "Ciara, look I know you don't know me that well, but I would like to help. What is it?" She shook her head, unable to speak as she struggled to compose herself. "We don't have to finish," he proposed, transferring his weight from one foot to the other.

"I'm starting school in the fall, real, normal college," she breathed, her throat feeling thick as molasses.

"That's a good thing, isn't it?" Ash questioned, brows contracting in uncertainty.

In a strangled voice, she gasped, "Yes," while squeezing her arms against her slender chest.

"I don't understand, why are you sad?" Ash slipped a hand into his back pocket and the other by hers on the cart handle, the muscles lining his arm flexing from anxiety.

She could tell he didn't know what to do to comfort her, and she wasn't sure either, as there had rarely been anyone outside of Sean. The tears leaked over in small silver streaks, and she furiously swiped them away as she clarified. "Sean always wanted to send me."

"Your brother wanted to send you," he slowly echoed while realization flying across his face and his sentence freezing in its tracks. He cleared his throat and scratched the deep brown scruff on his jaw.

"Yes, but he couldn't. We didn't have the money and with my parents gone, what were we supposed to tell the schools?" She wiped her cheeks, regaining control of her emotions. "I'm sorry, I'm not normally like this. It's just, there's no one..."

Ash awkwardly wrapped his arms around her. She clutched his green t-shirt and sniffled, pressing her forehead into the hard expanse of his chest. He rubbed her back, and Ciara could tell it wasn't a practiced motion, but she savored the soothing motion, anyway. It wasn't comfort she was used to receiving. "Would you like tea or ice cream? Really anything that would make you feel better."

Ciara gave a watery chuckle; she hadn't cried like that in a year. She gave the offer some thought, thinking about what she would like more, but wasn't sure. Out loud, she voiced her thoughts: "I love mint ice cream, and you know I like tea."

"We can get both," he said with a smile as he gazed down at her, surprised to see her peering up at him with wide, grateful eyes.

"Just tea," she decided, thinking it was still too early to be eating ice cream. She sniffled and wiped at her nose with the collar of her shirt. Ash nodded, and Ciara tossed her short hair back, rebuilding the steel in her spine with each fresh word spoken, "Okay, we can finish, it's just a little bit more." She gripped the handle on her cart again and led the assault against the fruits and vegetables.

An hour later they relaxed at a wrought-iron table at a coffee shop, clutching hot mugs of their chosen beverages to warm their hands against the chill of the morning. She watched Ash hesitate over the topic he wanted to bring up.

But she understood the subject needed to be broached if they hoped to move past this. Ciara waited for it, debating how to answer, and whether she wanted to answer with the entire truth or not. She recognized that she would need to if they were actually going to become genuine friends. Something that she hadn't had since KT. It was exciting and intimidating at the same time.

Finally, Ash cleared his throat and jumped in. "I know this is a tough subject, but why didn't you just go home after your brother died? And if you weren't home, where were you, where were your parents?"

Ciara frowned and glanced out the window at his series of hard questions. Mr. Durand knew something of what had occurred, but he wasn't aware of everything. She hadn't been in a place psychologically where she could elaborate on the incident. And when she finally believed she could, she didn't know how to initiate the subject. Ciara twisted her teacup in her hands as she croaked, "No home to go back to. My parents died when I was fourteen and Sean and I left that same night."

He narrowed his eyes in further question, "Will you give me more to work with than that? I mean, you don't have to, but I'll listen, if you want to."

She blew at the steam rising from her mug and took a sip, beginning her tale, "I don't want to drag you into it, but we *were* home. At least where we called home at the time he died; it was Seattle." She watched a family ordering at the counter. They looked so happy, so normal; she wanted to feel that again. "I like this place." Ciara inhaled deeply the bergamot-scented steam from her Earl Gray tea, letting it settle her tightly wound muscles.

"I play here sometimes. I'm surprised you've never come in before; the people are always great, and it rarely gets over-crowded." He followed her gaze to a group of teenagers.

Cautiously, Ciara examined the surrounding shadows, despite her mind mangled by her emotions. It had been over a year since she had last seen The Shadow, and despite the promises from the agency that she was safe, she didn't absolutely believe them. There was too much at stake now for her to get out of practice, and there was no way he had given up the hunt.

>>>

Ash appeared to fit in seamlessly with Ciara and Mr. Durand, who made it a point to invite him over as often as possible. Although Ciara was busy with her two jobs, their schedules always seemed to align in the mornings. And as long as she wasn't at the restaurant, they returned home within half an hour of each other, which often led to long stairwell conversations. Gradually over the hot summer weeks, those conversations transformed into hallway chats and then long discussions and laughter over more hot mugs of tea at one of their kitchen tables. Their friendship came with an ease Ciara hadn't felt since she was fifteen and met KT. It was something seamless, as if he were always there, just waiting for the right moment to remind her she was only as alone as she let herself be.

Once Ash discovered her movie and television education was severely lacking, he began a habit of appearing with giant bowls of popcorn and movies weekly to catch her up. Of which Ciara was more than happy to partake in as she relaxed from her busy days. He appeared to have everything in the form of motion picture and the few he didn't, they accessed on one of the streaming networks he subscribed to. Ciara was surprised at how comfortable she was in his presence, snuggled up under a blanket with Ash a few feet away, laughing and joking as the movie played. Despite having always been more of a bookworm, she had to admit the movies he had her watch were all reasonably good. KT made her watch a few, but she hadn't liked his taste; he was more of a horror movie buff, and she had enough of that in her real world.

Ash, on the other hand, once she mentioned she liked detective shows, was lining her up with a new education of the BBC series *Sherlock*. At first, she didn't want to like it, as it was one of the few books she had carried with her when Sean and she escaped. It was one of her most prized possessions, a collector's edition of Sir Arthur Conan Doyle's *Complete Works of Sherlock Holmes*. However, once she saw the attention to detail the producers and writers put in, Ciara was intrigued and then in love with the show.

Her favorite thing about becoming friends with Ash was by far when he invited her onto campus on one of her days off. Ciara packed her messenger bag with a book, notebook, and a sandwich for lunch before driving over to meet him in the music department. Ash greeted her with a wide smile and a wave of his hand.

"Thank you for breaking up the monotony of my day. When school is in session, it isn't so boring. There are always students asking questions and professors needing help, but not in the summer," Ash explained with a shrug and waved his hand around to encompass the completely empty department.

"What do you do with all your spare time then?" Ciara asked.

Ash pointed to the note on the desk stating to go to practice room one and ask for Ash if they needed anything and said, "I go practice or read."

"Does that mean I finally get to listen to you play?" Ciara's eyes widened in excitement, and she bounced on the balls of her feet.

She watched his cheeks heat before he nodded. "If you want to."

"Is it one of your pieces?" Ciara asked hopefully.

"I was going to practice a piece I'm considering for the fall recital actually." Ash waved her over to a practice room and propped the door open, with sheet music waiting on the piano.

"Dang, I was hoping, but I am excited to finally get to hear you play," Ciara stated with anticipation before setting her bag down on the floor. She watched people shuffling by with briefcases and backpacks and realized it was hard to tell if they were professors or community members, but she enjoyed trying to guess. Eventually, she shifted to the other side of the room to get a better view of the hallway, not liking the surprise every time someone shifted into view without warning. Feeling more at ease and with the sound of Ash's playing encompassing her, Ciara fell into her book.

{ 6 }

Friends

In record time, the summer vanished with Ash part of her little circle, and Ciara eyes widened in shock when she scanned the calendar to see it was the last weekend of summer. That was how she found herself trailing after Ash on a bike, questioning what she had signed herself up for.

"Where are we going again?" Ciara asked as her blue and silver bike leapt beneath her like a well-bred stallion.

Ash swung his head back and called, "A few friends of mine just got back in town. They are usually a couple of weeks early, and I thought it might be nice for you to meet someone else from school."

Ciara nodded, inspecting a car flying by next to them as she hollered back, "I understand that part, but I asked *where*."

He snorted and shouted to be heard over the traffic noise, "Water Street. Turn left here!" He swung his bike to the left and swerved to dodge a lamppost. "Nate, he's a percussionist, and a whiz at math. This is his second senior year."

"You've told me about him, but it's hard to keep everyone straight, not used to the million friends most people have. I have two friends and both are far away and I mostly just have work friends, not hang out friends." Ciara frowned from be-hind him and thought about KT, currently deployed with the Army and out of contact for almost a year now.

She hadn't talked to him for over a month, but Lex, she had talked to a few days ago. She was always good for a laugh, but Ciara hadn't seen her since she moved to Pine Harbor. Yet, Lex knew Ciara so well that, a few days after getting her address, she sent a box full of Ciara's favorite loose-leaf teas, funny mugs, and a tea ball. She did all of this at regular inter-vals and had since they were fourteen whenever Ciara could safely divulge her address. While Ciara had made 'friends' in the past year, she didn't hang out with them much and no one ever came over. The truth was that most of the people she had met in the past year didn't even know where she lived.

"Here," Ash yelled as he came to a stop in a short driveway with cracked cement and weeds springing out of it. "Just be prepared, it isn't just Nate who lives here. The others showed up yesterday and they're probably going to interrogate you because I don't have many friends who are girls." When he chewed the inside of his lip, Ciara grinned at his anxiety sud-denly showing through.

"If they don't like me, then don't worry about it, we can still hang out," she said with a slight grin. And tossed her short blue stripped hair in an imitation of Lex as she climbed off her bike and pushed the kickstand down.

Ash flashed a nervous smile at her jest and turned as he climbed the stairs, calling behind him, "Watch the third step up, it moves." He rapped on the chipped paint of the door as Ciara hopped up onto the porch.

"Ash, hey man, it's good to see you!" Nate exclaimed as he leaned his dark head around Ash to see Ciara. He considered her as she leaned against the railing and clapped hands with the much taller man, a broad grin crossing his face. His eyes appeared to twinkle as he took her in and asked, "And who is this?"

"This is Ciara, I told you a bit about her, she lives across from me," Ash said, shifting over for Nate to get a better view of her.

She stepped up to him and extended her hand to the young man, barely taller than her. She noticed the way Ash stuffed his hands into his pockets, his broad shoulders hunching minutely as he watched their exchange. After a suspiciously long pause, Nate spoke in his deep voice, "Good to finally meet you."

Nate smiled, his teeth vibrant white against his dark complexion. "Ash has told me about you, not quite what I expected."

"Is that good or bad?" Ciara took his hand, her eyebrow raised in question. She tried hard not to look him up and down, to size him up.

Ash shook his head with a chuckle, the tension withdrawing from his muscles. "Coming from him, probably a good thing." Nate bowed his head and signaled them into the small house. Apparently, she had passed the first test.

"Jared and Tyler are back, but I think they went to get pizza and most likely a movie too."

"So, they should be back in about an hour?" Ash ducked his head as he entered to prevent hitting it on the low frame and glanced around at the pandemonium already rising in the living room.

"Or maybe sometime next week," Nate said, scanning around. "They haven't seen each other in a week or two and were being obnoxious about it all morning. Air isn't on yet so if it's too hot, we can grab drinks and go outside." Ash's friend wiped at the sweat beading on his forehead and opened the fridge. "We have Bud, Sam Adams, and Corona, but no clue who drinks the Corona, but it's here."

After considering for a moment, Ciara said, "I'll take a Sam, don't know if I like it, but we'll see."

"I'll drink it if you don't," Ash offered while pointedly staring at a burn mark on the floor instead of at her.

Nate raised an eyebrow pointedly at his tall friend when he thought Ciara wasn't watching, but was disregarded as they strolled out onto the porch. And then moved out onto the lawn where chairs had been set up around a metal fire circle.

While listening to the straightforward conversation, Ciara ran her hands through her short, spiky-backed hair with no desire to partake. She didn't know the people and didn't have any context for the jokes, but it felt pleasant just to listen to their light talk.

In Ciara's world, people didn't stay friends for long; they were just acquaintances who were fun to be around for a little while. But they couldn't understand what she had gone through, and she never knew when she would have to disappear again, which made it easier to keep people at a distance. Meanwhile Lex had been there from the start, though, as it was her mother's house they hid at when it all began. And eventually even there became unsafe, and they had to run. Her mother had given them money and a burner phone with the promise that if they ever needed anything, she would be there for them. Lex and her mother had understood the risk and their need for secrecy. As for all the others from her past, Ciara never knew what to tell them and was worried what would happen if she tried to reach out.

KT was just different because he didn't pry about her history. Calm, levelheaded, gentle, and protective about those he cared about, KT constantly stood by her. When Ciara was almost sixteen, he took her out in his truck. Taught her how to drive a manual on the back roads of Jackson, Michigan, during a very wet spring with beer cans in hand and ACDC on his CD player. Thinking back, Ciara remembered how they met in Spanish class when they had to make a family tree. Still feeling too raw after her parents' death, she ran out of the classroom sobbing. KT didn't even know her then, but he followed and pulled her long hair out of her face and offered to take her to lunch. She accepted hesitantly, but from there it was just a blur, and when she left unexpectedly, he stayed in touch, unlike all the others.

She pulled out her phone and sent him an email, hoping he would get it despite being almost half a world away.

"Earth to Ciara," Ash said, touching her shoulder, and she flinched, nearly dropping her bottle. "You were completely zoned out."

"Sorry, what's up?" She questioned, dragging her mind back to the present.

"How do you like it?" He inquired, inspecting her bottle.

Ciara smiled and took another swallow before asserting, "Not bad, tolerable, but can we switch after half?"

His face brightened, and he nodded his agreement as a door slammed at the front of the house, followed by loud singing and the smell of pizza.

Nate opened the back door as he called out to his house-mates, "Out here and bring the food!"

A few moments later, two men ambled out of the back door and into the tiny yard. The shorter, burly one walked over with a rolling gait, balancing the pizza boxes, while the other glanced from Ash to Ciara with complete confusion. Ciara snorted and introduced herself, "Ciara, Ash moved in across from me in May, I am woefully friendless, so he took pity on me."

The wiry male with long legs and a tie-dye shirt waved enthusiastically as he introduced himself in return, "Jared, nice to meet you!"

The other said more stoically, "Tyler. Pizza."

"Thank you," she beamed as her stomach suddenly growled. Then watched as Jared dragged over an abandoned and worn-looking table to hold the pizza boxes while Tyler set the paper plates down next to them.

Tyler glanced over at Ciara, and this time he spoke with the addition of multi-syllable words. Ciara realized he must be the type that needed to warm up to new people. "What kind? Pepperoni, cheese, or whatever weird combo Jared ordered?"

"Just cheese, please and thank you," Ciara said as she examined the new people and took in a deep inhale of the unique smell of pizza. Her mouth began salivating as Tyler turned to dish up her food without another word.

"You never bring me my food," Jared complained as he took three slices and set them on his own plate.

"Not true at all," Tyler quietly responded, leaning over to hand Ciara her plate.

Ciara took the offering and watched as Jared sat on the ground instead of in the empty chair. Ash stepped around her to access the table, adding his own commentary, "I'm with Tyler; he brings you food all the time, because if he didn't you would just eat his. Really not sure where you put it all."

Nate grunted his agreement, "Yeah man, I've seen you eat an entire box of cookies in one sitting and then devour two orders of Chinese food."

"Cookies and Chinese food?" Ciara asked with a raised eyebrow and a smirk.

"We try not to question his strange food choices," Tyler lamented as he scooted behind Jared to drop into the chair.

Noticing the slight flush on Jared's cheeks, Ciara struggled not to smile as she abruptly realized the two men were a couple. She focused her gaze onto Jared again, as she requested, "Now I *have* to question though, when they say weird food choices, what does that mean exactly? While cookies and Chinese *is* a bit strange, I can at least understand the sweet and salty."

"Thank you, see? I'm not crazy," he exclaimed, batting Tyler's knee.

"Not true," Tyler argued around a mouthful of hot pizza and tapped Jared back with his foot.

Jared rolled his eyes in response and explained, "I just like a lot of food." He looked back over to Ciara and elaborated, "I'm a military brat. We lived in a lot of foreign countries, and my mom loved making whatever the traditional cuisine was, except she always added her own flair. Made for some really strange meals, but I'll eat just about anything you put in front of me because of it."

"Still doesn't explain why you *purposefully choose* to put artichokes, black olives, spinach, *and* pineapple on pizza," Nate tossed in.

"He also put mushrooms and I think there's anchovies and pepperoni on it," Tyler helpfully said.

"Alright, that's strange," Ciara chuckled her agreement, before adding, "And that's coming from a girl who lived off Spam and oatmeal packets for weeks at a time."

Ash raised an eyebrow at her but didn't press for the reason. Instead, Jared interjected, "I'm not the only one whose had Spam anymore! I like this girl, nice find Ash."

Flushed by the comment, Ash shook his head as Tyler gently pressed his foot against Jared's side. Softly he reminded his partner, "Remember how we talked about thoughts that are supposed to stay *in* your head? That's one of them; people aren't objects."

Jared just laughed good-naturedly with a wave of his hand as he said, "She knows what I mean, right?"

Ciara laughed in response, almost choking on her bite as she agreed, "I know what you mean and it takes a lot more than that to offend me."

The conversation shifted, leaving Ciara to her pizza and listening to the light conversation about their summers and people she was beginning to want to get to know. She was happy that the three boys treated her as if they had been friends her whole life. The inclusion gave her a warm feeling, and yet, in the back of her mind was the dark thought that she would eventually have to leave again. Maybe not tomorrow or the next day, but Ciara still wasn't convinced she would be safe. Nothing was ever that permanent, and this was as close as she had gotten in eight long years.

She let their talk surround her in a cloud. She listened and participated as much as she could, but mostly enjoyed the noise as fireflies drifted by. The night passed into darkness in a haze of laughter and a few yard games, lulling Ciara into peace until she got the call. It was an odd number which gave her two options: the agency or KT. The look on her face immediately made Ash raise an eyebrow at her and pause with a beer to his lips.

After pushing her bangs out of her face, she answered with a tentative, "Hello?"

The phone crackled a response, "Hey, what's getting you down?"

"KT, I didn't recognize your number," she said, beaming, and moved away from the guys to hear better with a nod in Ash's direction. "I'm better now, I was just missing Sean, Lex, and you earlier, that's all. How are you?"

"I'm alright. This last mission took forever and can't leave base right now either. Heat index of a billion... yeah. It's a bit rough and missing you, of course." She heard a smile in his voice through the wavering connection.

"You probably can't talk for long either." Ciara sighed and asked, "Need anything?"

There was a pause before he answered, "Raspberry lemonade and if you can send some mint cookies, I would love you forever." He laughed, as in true KT style, he worried only about his stomach. Then added, "Maybe a pillowcase, these ones are so itchy."

She sensed her muscles easing at the sound of his voice and hearing the proof that he was alive and whole. "I can do that for you, just email me where to send it."

"You're the best. What's been going on there, any sign of your Shadow?" He asked cautiously, and she could hear the worry in his voice.

Ciara looked around to make sure no one was listening as she softly said, "Not yet, which kind of worries me. The Shadow always shows up eventually and he hasn't ever been this long in-between, but Maybe these guys really will keep him away."

"Just breathe and keep your eyes open. I will be home soon, and you will be the first I visit aside from the family, of course, promise. Hang on a sec..." he paused and listened to loud chatter on his side. "Damn, I gotta get off, sorry Pea Pod, but I'll send you an email later. Miss you and *stay safe!*"

"You too, on all of the above," she expelled a breath as the line clicked and moseyed back over to the group.

"Everything alright?" Ash questioned with genuine concern in his eyes.

"It was KT, my friend in the Middle East, just checking in."

Ash nodded and looked up at the dark sky with a frown as he said, "We should probably get going, it's late and we rode are bikes over."

She peered at the boys and waved as she said farewell, "Thanks for letting me hang out."

"We'll see you soon," Jared said with an excessive amount of energy, and Tyler hit his arm, telling him not to sound so ominous. Nate rolled his eyes and waved with a smile, showing just the hint of his straight white teeth flashing.

Ash opened the gate to the front of the house where their bikes stood next to the front porch.

Closing In

When Ash and Ciara strode into the apartment building, they halted on their floor, somewhat out of breath from the ascent and their late-night ride back. Ciara leaned against the wall and looked up at Ash's face with a raised eyebrow as she pressed, "What did they think, do I pass the friend inspection?"

Ash snorted and combed his fingers through his hair as he answered with a grin, "You passed with flying colors."

"Why did they seem surprised you were hanging out with me?" She questioned, her curiosity getting the better of her.

Ash chewed his lip as he strained to think of how to respond before explaining, "Girls, well, I *usually* have trouble talking with them, but not you, anymore."

"Anymore?" Ciara regarded him with her wide blue eyes in confusion.

Ash blushed and rubbed the back of his neck as he confessed, "Yeah, I was a little nervous at first. But then, well, sorry if this is awkward, but you just seemed so lost and in need of a friend, I forced myself to get over it."

Ciara watched him soundlessly for a moment, noting his signs of anxiety, before acknowledging, "I'm glad you did."

Ash smiled, almost shyly, and shoved his brown hair out of his tanned face before saying on a yawn, "I need to see Mr. Durand still before I head in."

She waved and unlocked her door as Ash tapped on their neighbor's and stepped through into the dark. After placing her bag on the counter, she immediately recognized something was wrong as her bag crashed into the picture of Sean and her, which was supposed to be in the middle, not on the edge. Her heart pounded as she flipped the light switch and saw her apartment was in disarray.

Scattered across the floor with spines bent lay her precious books, and her futon was flipped over. The TV stand was moved, pots and pans were littered everywhere, and her pantry stood open with food crushed and spilled over every surface. However, the worst was that the glass covering the picture of her brother and her was cracked, with the shatter mark bisecting Sean's throat. By accident or by intention, she couldn't tell, but the meaning was clear.

Leaving the door unlocked, Ciara grabbed the picture and her bag before running over to Mr. Durand's, knocking frantically.

"Ciara, what's wrong?" He asked as he threw the door open, studying her features intently.

Ciara examined every corner and shadow on their landing with paranoia; contrasting her actions, she explained in a calm voice, "My apartment was broken into."

Ash immediately emerged around the door frame, apprehension on his face as he asked, "Are you okay, was anything taken?"

Mr. Durand pulled her in and closed the door, locking it before turning around to see her repeating her attempt to soothe Ash. He couldn't seem to comprehend how or why her room would be broken into, as he knew she didn't have much.

"Have you called the police yet?" The old man asked. When Ciara shook her head, he began dialing 911, but she hung up the phone before he could complete the three numbers.

"No, no police," she said, sounding frantic for the first time, before taking a steadying breath.

"Why no police?" Ash asked, bewildered, before pressing further, "Ciara, what's going on?"

"I need to make a phone call first then," she hesitated, feeling doom settle around her, realizing it was time to tell them. They had been nothing but kind to her – friends, and they deserved to know the truth about how dangerous it was to associate with her. "Then I will tell you everything," Ciara said, pulling out her phone and dialing a number she had been forced to memorize the night her brother died.

It buzzed once, before a stern and sharp male voice answered, "Sergeant Frederick Curry."

"This is Ciara Fitzpatrick, my apartment was broken into, but I don't believe anything was taken."

The voice grew strained, "Are you hurt, where are you now?"

"I wasn't there at the time and I'm at my neighbors," she said with her eyes closed; icy frustration crawled through her veins. This is what KT told her to be watching out for only an hour ago. She slumped, and powerful arms wrapped around her petite waist and held her up as Sergeant Curry's voice said her name. Faintly, she asked, "What?"

"I will be out there in a half hour, stay there," the voice repeated.

"Okay," she murmured, annoyed both at Curry for telling her what to do and at herself for reacting the way she was. Evidently, she wasn't as strong as she believed without Sean by her side; she mumbled a thank you and placed the phone back into the receiver. Safety began to set in, but with it her adrenaline faded, and she leaned against Ash, letting his heat bring warmth back into her frigid extremities.

He wrapped his arm tighter around her, rubbing small circles on her arm, as Mr. Durand boiled water for tea. "Ciara?"

She tilted her head back to study him and saw his yellow-gold eyes staring at her with concern. "I'm alright, I need to sit down," she said, needing to regain control of her emotional state before the completely dissolved into pieces.

Ash helped deposit her into a chair, just as Mr. Durand set a piece of pie in front of her. "Eat all of it," he commanded as she stared at the crumbling on top of the raspberry pie for a moment before picking up the fork in shaking fingers.

She began her story after the second mouthful, even though neither male had asked her for an explanation, but she knew it was coming. "Sean and I never really knew what our parents did, but now I know, they worked for a special research and defense branch of the government, but we were a happy family, normal." She paused and took another mouthful, trying to figure out how to explain the next part of her story, and felt the backs of her eyes begin to burn from the salt of unshed tears. "Until the night my parents were killed, when a person broke into our house in the middle of the night. Sean is the one who heard the noise and stopped me from going into our kitchen, but whoever it was beat my mother to death. And then poisoned my father to make it look like he beat her, then killed himself."

Ciara swallowed down the sob threatening to suffocate her and pressed on, needing to get the words out before her courage failed her. "We weren't supposed to wake up apparently, but we did and so we ran before the man could catch us. We were in Sean's Jeep and gone before he had the chance; Sean had just turned sixteen thankfully and I was fourteen. We hid out at my friend Lex's house and called the police, but they didn't believe us, thought we didn't want to see the truth or whatever. We saw their killer three days later when we were at the park by her house and Sean realized it was safer to run. We snuck back into our house, gathered some belongings, and left. We ran for six years until the killer caught up with us again and killed Sean."

She ate another shaky bite of pie before continuing, "That's when Sergeant Curry showed up. Curry had been looking for the killer, who KT calls my Shadow. Curry never explained why but believed my story when I told him and said he had heard of my parents and told me what their job entailed. Although I think he still left some things out, because it wasn't just a murder, the man had been hired to kill them." She swallowed and shoved another bite of food into her mouth before adding awkwardly, "There wasn't much opportunity to make great friends where we went. The longest time I ever remember staying anywhere was four months and that was in my senior year. Lex visited me when I was there with her mom, but I always had Sean to take care of me. He was steady and grounded me," Ciara hesitated and looked up at Mr. Durand, before focusing to see Ash next to her. The stunned look on his face made her internally cringe until she saw his arm twitch in a gesture that seemed like he wanted to put it around her.

When a tear dripped into her tea, and an arm went around her shoulders, the residual anxiety of laying her life out for examination and judgement faded somewhat. "So that's my story, what I have not been telling you."

Neither man responded immediately as they soaked in her words. But then, Ash scooted his chair closer, the sound of the wood on linoleum grating in the silence. Finally, after a minute passed without a word spoken, Mr. Durand crackled a reply, "You have had a very hard life and have been very blessed. Your brother must have been one incredible person, as you are one incredible young woman. No matter who is after you, I will always protect you so long as I have life in these bones." Ciara looked up at him and smiled as her eyes filled with unshed tears.

"I agree," Ash said quietly, "All you have to do is call, and no matter where you are, I'll come." He leaned towards her and with the pad of his thumb wiped away her tears. "I wish I could have met Sean, but I will get to know him."

Another tear dripped down in a pearly streak, but Ash wiped it away too as she choked out, "How will you do that? He's gone and even the picture frame is cracked."

Softly, Ash explained with a gentle smile, "Through you, with your memories because he is still living in those."

She thought about his words and solemnly nodded as she whispered, "I guess you're right, but you both believe me?"

Mr. Durand chuckled and questioned, "What reason have we not to? I've heard stranger tales in my life."

"Why would you lie about that?" Ash commented as a knock sounded on the door.

The old man got up and straightened his shoulders as he looked through the peephole and questioned, "Are you Sergeant Curry?"

"I am, you must be Nicholas Durand." Curry waited for him to open the door, then held out a rough hand. They shook before Mr. Durand moved sideways to let him enter. Quickly, he scanned the space, taking in everything from the photographs and boat paintings on the wall to the bookcase filled with bird manuals and sports biographies. Satisfied with the fast search, Curry turned his black-bearded face to the single woman in the room. "Ciara, what happened, are you alright?"

Murderous in her fear and anger, Ciara scowled at Curry as she snapped out, "I'm fine, thankfully, he wasn't there when I came back. I don't care about the destroyed apartment, but I thought you were supposed to be watching for this, so how did he find me?"

Accusingly, Curry narrowed his black eyes and chewed out, "You are not the only one we have to worry about."

"I realize that, but I may have been better off on my own since he still found me. I may not be the only one, but I am the one you ignored for seven years that ended in my brothers' death. If you aren't going to protect me from him, then do something to stop him." Fear, anger, and grief had her shaking so severely that Ash laid his arm around her shoulders. When she continued to vibrate, he tightened his embrace. He didn't bother holding back his own glare at the smaller male.

"You think you could live on your own? Go ahead, you'll just go the same way as the rest of your family and in record time!" Curry snarled at the young woman, his cheeks transforming into a ruddy red.

Ciara narrowed her eyes at him with tears tumbling over her sun-kissed cheeks. Only then did Ash thrust his chair back and step up to the sergeant, who instinctively shrank away. Ash cast a very imposing figure, and it didn't matter that he had never been in the military like Curry. His striking six feet and seven inches of height gave him an advantage over the lesser man. "Do *not* speak to her like that, she has been through enough without you acting like a jackass."

The sergeant pulled himself up to his full height and gripped Ash's wrist hard enough to leave a mark as he snarled, "You do not tell me how to act."

Ash let him pull his wrist in, his threat failing. And then twisted to grip Curry's and knock him to his knees in one smooth, practiced motion. "You should do better research on people before you think yourself their better. I'm a second-degree black belt in Tai Kwan Do and a black belt in Teng Su Do."

Curry bit his lip in pain as Ash released him and stepped away. As he sat, he took a deep breath and reigned in his anger; his cheeks turned purple under his dark beard. But he mumbled his excuses, "I'm sorry Ciara, it's not you, it's been an endless week. It's Asher, right?"

"Yes, Ash Callaghan," Ash responded, crossing his arms over his broad chest, feet planted firmly on the ground.

"My apologies to you as well," Curry said, rubbing his forehead as he closed his eyes in embarrassment. "We will work harder from now on to keep a better watch over you and your place."

Running her hand through her dark brown hair, she watched Curry's face, looking for signs that he was just trying to appease her. She didn't see any, and after a moment nodded her assent.

Curry rubbed his wrist and tried to soften his voice as he asked, "Ciara, will you take me to your apartment?"

Slowly, Ciara pushed her chair back and said in a steady voice, "I'll take you over and Mr. Durand, thank you for letting me come here." She stood and gave her elderly neighbor a quick embrace before guiding Curry to the door.

"Do you mind if I tag along?" Ash softly inquired, pausing several feet from the exit.

"No, please come," Ciara stated, straightening to her full height, rebuilding her steel on the spot as she opened her own door and let the two men in.

After examining every room for signs of what the assassin was searching for or even where he had come from, the sergeant discovered nothing in the way of a clue. He even tried dusting for prints, but everything came back frustratingly clean.

Steadily stroking his perfectly trimmed black beard, Curry exhaled loudly after almost an hour of searching before proclaiming, "It's clean, nothing to go off. But I'm going to send a couple of people down here to stand guard at the entrance and under this side of the building from now on. Sound alright to you?" He questioned, directing it both at Ciara and Ash. With Ciara's nod of approval, he carried on, "I wish I could do more, but with nothing to go on." Curry shook his head in annoyance. "I had better get back and make a few calls; there are going to be some very angry people in the next couple of hours. I will keep in touch, try and stay safe." With that, he opened the door and disappeared into the stairwell.

Ciara looked around her place, clutching her tea mug closely between her hands. "Honestly, I don't think he was searching for anything tonight; I believe he was just messing things up. This is the first time my stuff has ever been gone through like this. And it's the first time I have ever been anywhere that seemed slightly secure, he was trying to get to me." She closed her bedroom door to conceal the mess inside so Ash wouldn't see her ancient underwear strewn about the room from where Curry had left it open.

"Why don't you stay with me tonight?" Ash blurted and rubbed the back of his neck with a flush rising in his cheeks.

Ciara eyed him with surprise in her dark blue eyes and said, "Really?"

Ash nodded, staring at the floor as he spoke. "I can't imagine you would want to stay here, with your bedroom a disaster and everything else. I can help put everything back together tomorrow. Could probably at least get Nate or Tyler over to help, Jared said he had to go into the lab tomorrow."

After surveying her rooms one more time, Ciara acquiesced, feeling utterly defeated. "Let me grab pillow and pajamas – oh, and my toothbrush," she said with a sigh as she sluggishly moved through the chaos.

{ 8 }

A Start

Ciara was pleasantly surprised by how comfortable Ash's couch was, especially to sleep on. Although she had slept in numerous stranger places before, it was uncommon that she felt so at ease so quickly. With exhaustion setting in, Ciara snuggled under the extra-long blanket and inhaled deeply; it smelled good, really good. She pondered what laundry detergent he used as she inhaled again, before pulling the blanket up to her eyes, curling her toes into the space between couch and cushion. Then wriggled into the perfect sleeping position, her thoughts raced, but Ciara didn't try to catch a single one. If she did, it would stem the flow and take her longer to cope with what was happening again, and this time alone. She didn't want to think about that most of all.

Roused to the same thoughts flying through her mind the following morning, the birds at least added a pleasant trill to dissipate the dark of the night. More than anything, she wished Sean were there; he always knew the right thing to say and do to cheer her up. *He would have made...*

"Coffee?" Asked a deep baritone voice from behind, interrupting her reflections. "I have to have coffee in the morning and not the pod stuff."

Ciara smiled under the blanket, realizing it was exactly what Sean would have done. Coffee with cookies. "I would love some," she said with a yawn as she sat up and tugged the blanket around her. Gradually, her thoughts grew less turbulent, and she questioned, "What are your plans for the day?"

Ash ambled into the kitchen in gray sweatpants and the plaid shirt he wore two days ago. Ciara presumed he usually walked around shirtless in the morning, but tossed something on for sake of modesty. "Going into the university, I need to practice my violin and I was supposed to be practicing percussion a little more frequently than I have been. What about you, did you have any plans for today?"

"School supplies and books. Plus, I wanted to walk around campus again before classes start to get a feel for where they are located." With the smell of coffee grounds hitting her nose, the lingering tension in her body relaxed, and she rubbed the sleep from her. "My last day at the Children's Center was on Friday, so no work, remember?"

He nodded and pointed at the coffee cup as the stream dripped into the pot. "What do you want in it?" He questioned and added, "I have sweet cream."

"Two splooshes," she said with a grin and a twinkle in her eyes.

"Splooshes?" He asked, a tilt to the side of lips as he watched the humor on her face.

After a brief attempt to appear solemn, Ciara realized she was failing when he rolled his eyes at her and pulled out the creamer.

"Right," he acknowledged and attempted her request, before he advised, "You can order the books online, it's cheaper than the bookstore." With a steady hand, he poured the coffee in before it was done brewing and walked carefully over with the hot beverage in his large hands.

"I know, but I have a full tuition with a stipend that covers books, but only if they are from 'The Official' university bookstore." She made air quotes, then added, "I'm going to be working in the library once school starts." Between her hands, she clutched the cup, inhaling the aroma and noticed Ash hadn't buttoned his shirt all the way. And was slightly surprised to see how built he was until she remembered him saying the night before that he was a double black belt. She dragged her eyes away from the sight with more difficulty than she wanted to ruminate on and inquired, "Do you mind if I tag along?"

He leveled his yellow-gold eyes at her. "Nope, I was planning on leaving in an hour, is that enough time for you to get ready?" The look she gave him made him rumble out a laugh as he answered himself, "Of course it is, you aren't like most girls."

"Can I take this cup with me?" Carefully, she stood, trying not to spill her coffee and waited for his nod while leaning back on his chair. "Thanks, I'll be back in an hour."

She left with a cup in hand to her room where she withdrew her red berry cereal and milk, before sifting through the fallen dishes for a spoon and bowl. Gently removing her brother's picture from her bag, she placed it back in the middle of her table and began eating as she turned her phone on.

Unlike normal, Ciara chose her outfit with care, wanting to make a good impression. She put on a blue and green halter with dark blue Bermuda shorts. The young woman even wore a necklace Lex had made for her a few years before. She looked in the mirror and smiled, commenting to herself, *I don't look that bad.* With a final fluff to her hair, Ciara turned the light off and swung her messenger bag over her shoulder. She locked the door behind her as Ash stepped out of his apartment.

Ash locked his door and then turned towards Ciara who I watched his Adam's apple bob as he swallowed. He had never seen Ciara dressed in anything except a boy's t-shirt or loose tank top and apparently it was having an interesting effect on him. Slowly, a grin spread across her face as she watched his cheeks redden and the corner of her lip curled up when he stuttered out, "Wow, you look really nice."

"Thanks, it doesn't happen very often, but I wanted to make a good impression for my work study." She brushed at a speck of lint on her shorts and asked, "Ready to go?"

Ash nodded and twirled his keys, questioning her back, "Who's driving?"

"I'll drive," Ciara said, pulling her keys from her dark green bag.

On the way to school, Ash pointed out some favorite stops and told stories about what him and the boys did on their class breaks. Ciara laughed as they easily chatted and hoped they would let her be a part of their group once everyone was back on campus. Ash rubbed his smooth chin and asked, "How long are you planning on being here?"

Ciara spun the wheel, "I wanted to print off my class schedule, walk around, then the library to meet the professor I'll be working with, and get my student ID. And then to the bookstore, so at least few hours, but maybe longer."

He tilted his head, causing his hair to fall out of his eyes, revealing the flecks of yellow amidst the dark gold star. "Okay, I need to do a bunch of things as well. Come with me and I can give you a tour of the music department, so then you can find me when you're done. If you are willing to wait for me, I mean, but I can catch a ride with Nate if you don't want to wait."

Ciara turned into a parking spot, cut the ignition, and said with a laugh, "I'll wait for you, you giant oaf. Lead the way so I know where I can come find you when I'm done."

Campus was eerily deserted as Ciara wandered both the winding twisted paths and the wide straight ones heading towards doors of different buildings. Excited, she followed one of the longer paths up to the library and paused to gaze at the immenseness of the building made entirely of brick and windows. Then, serenity passed over her as she strolled slowly under the ivy-covered arch guarding the knowledge within the walls. Ciara trailed her fingers along the stone and green leaves, before pushing the glass door open to feel the carefully maintained air in the building move in to surround her. Libraries had always felt like home to her and the smell sent memories of strong arms holding her in their lap and a manicured nail trailing along an inky page. When her parents were alive, they had a small library and she could always catch her mother there in the golden dawn and her father in the inky blue of twilight. She let a breath out, feeling like she was home.

Once inside, she lingered in the halls, taking in all the study carrels and rows, upon rows of books. Home. She smiled widely to herself before beginning her wandering through the shelves, feeling like she was being welcomed by old friends.

There were quite a few computer rooms hidden around the library and tucked away in corners with doors closing out any sound, and it was the same for group study rooms. Despite the immense size of the building, it seemed very comfortable. Ciara sighed in relief and ran a hand through her hair as she hopped down the stairs of the stacks, to head back to the front desk to meet her new boss.

He was a shorter man with a round face, very white hair, and gave her a kind smile as he waved her into his office. "Ciara, it's good to meet you! I've looked over your school transcripts and am very impressed, although you haven't been in many places for long; I hope that will change and you stay with us longer. Come on in and take a seat so we can talk about what our expectations are."

Ciara gave him a cursory smile and sat in the only empty chair in his book crowded office. "I am Professor Austin and I teach creative writing and am the head librarian here. Tell me about yourself, I know you are a music and history major, so why did you choose to work in the library?"

The girl sighed, and the answer came as easily as breathing as she said, "I love books. They have always felt like home, The smell, the feel, the sight."

Professor Austin nodded with complete understanding and said, "I am so glad to hear that." They chatted for a bit longer before he let out a heavy sigh and pressed to his feet. "Let me give you a tour and show you where your study room is; all the students who work here have one as sometimes the work demands it." He smiled kindly, and it brightened up his round face as he waved to her to follow him out of his office.

Half an hour later, Ciara's head reeled as she tried to remember all the descriptions and names of the people she met and the ones she still needed to meet. She placed sunglasses on her nose to guard against the brilliant summer sun and jumped down the stairs, with a feeling of being watched tickling the back of her neck. Quickly, she glanced behind her but perceived nothing, although she knew better than to dismiss the sensation from experience it always meant something.

She quickened her pace and continued to the music building, using her peripheral vision to monitor the shifting shadows around her. Outside the door, she paused to take off her glasses and froze as a darkness passed over her. Her shadow blended with someone else's, and she peered back to watch a person disappear around another building. The woman smacked into the well-built arms of Tyler and Jared.

"Ciara," Jared caught her arm before she fell and questioned with a hint of laughter in his voice, "Are you okay?"

"You look like you saw a ghost," Tyler commented studying her face.

She shook herself, realizing Tyler and her were the same height. "I'm fine, I just thought I saw something but thank you for catching me."

"Pretty lady like you can run into me anytime you like," Jared joked with a wink.

Tyler rolled his eyes and stared pointedly down at their linked hands as he asked, "Something you need to share with me?"

Jared rubbed his thumb over the back of his partner's hand with a grin, before stating "I can appreciate feminine beauty, even if it doesn't do anything for me, no offense, Ciara."

"None taken," Ciara responded with a chuckle at the two, then for simple curiosities sake inquired, "How long have you been together?"

"Almost two years, I wasn't exactly out when I started school and it took a bit of convincing on Tyler's part," Jared said fixing his tie-dyed shirt.

Tyler amended Jared's statement, "That's a bit of an understatement, but I hope it's, well, that you're okay with it, I kinda thought you'd maybe figured it out last night."

"I'm totally fine with it," Ciara reassured, before pointing out, "And you weren't extremely subtle."

Tyler loosened his grip on Jared's fingers as the other man began to settle and asked, "Where were you headed?"

"To find Ash, he told me to find him once I finished all my stuff."

Tyler promptly turned around and said, "Follow us, we can take you there. He's in a practice room with Nate."

The two boys walked on either side of her and she, unexpectedly, felt safety seep into her like a calming wave. These two hardly knew her, but they were taking the time to walk her to Ash, instead of simply pointing the way. She smiled at the simple kindness and thought about all the different types of people she had met over the years. But Jared and Tyler's type were scarce, because people rarely liked to go out of their way for others, even those they termed friends.

"What are you two doing after this?" Jared questioned, pulling at the hem of his tie-dyed shirt again and she wondered if it was something he did when nervous.

Ciara shrugged and explained, "I need to get my books, but then I'm not sure."

"We should all grab lunch at The Pita, they make really good food, have you tried it?" Jared interrogated.

"We just ate an hour ago, but he is always thinking about the next meal." Tyler chuckled and Ciara shook her head with a slight smile, because she did the same.

Tyler opened a door to her left and waved her in as noise rapidly assailed her ears. Ash stood with his back to her, bobbing his head along to the beat he rolled out. Nate played another measure before noticing the recent additions to the room and stopped, waving his arm to cut off Ash.

"Hey guys, and Ciara, I thought you two were going to find Leah and Maddy," Nate said, his deep voice rumbling.

"We got distracted when we ran into Ciara," Jared said with a shrug and added, "We can meet up with them later."

Ash looked over at her, asking, "Finished with everything?"

"Just need to get books from the bookstore," she said with a light smile and saw Nate frown and open his mouth. She guessed he was going to tell her to get them online like Ash had when she spoke with him earlier and beat him to the punch, "I have a book voucher."

"Gotcha, lucky you," Nate commented, sighing dreamily. "If only we all had those. What classes are you taking and do you know the books? I might have some of them and then you could save the voucher for the other books."

She pulled out her list and told the boys the titles and classes. Jared, being a science major, had her beginning biology book with his own notes in the margins, while Tyler had a few of the English books. And between Ash and Nate they owned most of the music books, and all she had left were the workbooks and normal school supplies. She was taken aback by their generosity and thoughtfulness.

Jovially, they trampled from the music department to the bookstore and from there to The Pita for lunch. Through a mouth filled with sprouts, Tyler interrogated the group, "So when did Darren and Maddy start dating and what happened to Sara? I thought they had a thing last year."

Nate grunted his response as he explained the gossip, "I told you over the summer he broke it off with her during exam week. Something about him getting sick of the way she acts when she drinks, not that I blame him, Sara is kinda crazy. And Darren and Maddy both went on the same study abroad this summer, must have been a wonderful summer," he added while wiggling his brows dramatically.

"I am so glad I don't have a girlfriend, that all just sounds way too complicated," Tyler admitted with a heavy sigh.

Nate shrugged in response and Ash patted his shoulder, before saying in a teasing voice, "Unless it's Jez, but she is different."

"So sweet and wonderful, she's perfect," Tyler and Jared intoned together as they batted their eyelashes dramatically.

Ciara started laughing and asked, "I take it Jez is your girlfriend?"

Rolling his eyes at his friends, Nate nodded, giving a brief explanation, "We've been together since Freshman year, but they *are* right, she is all those things and more."

{ 9 }

Normal Life

Ash and Ciara roamed the park by their apartment complex, enjoying the cool evening breeze after the sweltering day. As another gust trailed by, Ciara ruffled her hair, letting it dry the sweat beading on her neck. Weightlessness filled her as her worries seemed a world away with the pleasure of the warm summer evening surrounding her. She wrapped her forearms around the chains of the swing before sitting in the cracked rubber seat. Swiftly, the tall woman began swinging her legs and pumping the swing into action.

Ash settled against a pole of the play structure and watched as the motion pulled her short hair away from her lightly freckled face. He smiled at the sheer joy illuminating her eyes from this simple thing; it was extraordinary seeing Ciara let go and be at ease. After a long moment, Ash cleared his throat before rumbling out, "Are you ready for classes?"

Ciara dipped her head back as she hit the top arch in the swing. "I think so, I just can't wait to go to classes as normal; I never thought I would be able to." She smiled and glanced over at the young man who had become such a powerful presence in her life in just a few short months. When she gave it more than a passing thought, it reminded her of how quickly KT had become a part of her world. Ciara chuckled to herself because she knew that was the reason she had always got along with boys better than girls, except for Lex. It wasn't that they didn't care about her life or past, but they didn't, usually, pressure her for every detail. Instead, they waited for her to be ready to talk, and that made all the difference. "Are you ready for classes to start?" She questioned back.

For a moment, Ash stayed quiet, appearing to be carefully calculating his response. "I believe so, all of my books came in and Nate and I are sharing the Western Music book. I told you I was taking an undergrad class just to fill things out, right?" She nodded and smiled, having noticed Ash liked to double-check things multiple times before executing anything. "I just have trouble wrapping my head around the fact that I am no longer an undergrad. I'm glad I had room to take it though because it always sounded so cool."

Ciara dragged her feet against the wood chips, slowing the swing as she inquired, "But the others are staying in the area for graduate school, aren't they?" As she spoke, she remembered him talking about this before, but couldn't quite put all the details in order.

He shook his head and explained, "Most of us are, but Jared is studying Bio-Chem something or other and he's in grad school already. Tyler is in music, but, like Nate, he is on the five-year program and there are a few others staying in the area, because of graduate school or jobs." Ash sighed again before continuing, "A lot of our friends graduated last year, so it's kind of a big change."

"Change can be good though and I think you will be just fine. I would know, and you can make new friends and stay in touch with the old; you have the means and ability." Ciara watched him and, over his shoulder, she saw the shadow of a person lurking by a tree in the distance. She couldn't be certain, but she recognized that balanced stance and the slight tapping of the hand on the thigh. The Shadow was watching. A kid cried on the play set, reminding her he wouldn't try anything in plain view. For now, she was safe.

She stood and leaned on the pole opposite Ash, ignoring her feeling of unease and trying not to alarm Ash. It was something she was used to, something that always set her apart from others. Ciara had carefully cultivated the ability to let fear work its way through her system and then move forward. KT, adrenaline junkie that he was, said she would have been perfect for the military, or as a first-responder. Ciara said she had enough thrills in her life without that, too.

"Of all people, I shouldn't be complaining about things changing." Ash frowned at her and looked her up and down, tilting his head to the side as he asked, "What's wrong?"

Ciara eyed him with narrowed brows, surprised that he had noticed the minute change and questioned back, "What do you mean?"

Ash shrugged and explained, "Something is bothering you and you look like you are getting ready for a fight."

She stared hard at Ash, trying to hold eye contact. "Don't look, whatever you do, don't look, but The Shadow is over there by that tree," she said on a mere breath of air. "Maybe we should go but try to act normal." Ciara sighed, increasingly surprised that he had picked up on her subtle body language that only Sean had ever noticed. She wished her peace hadn't been broken, that she could travel back to an hour ago when they'd strolled in the sunshine.

The tall young man nodded and followed her directions not to look. "Okay, we can go back to Mr. Durand and talk him into some popcorn and a movie perhaps?" Ciara bit her lip and then smiled as he stepped closer to her. "Sounds like a good plan, did you keep in touch with anyone other than KT and Lex?"

Slowly, they began to follow the winding cement path out of the park. Ciara glanced up at his scruffy face with her hands tucked into the pockets of her loose jeans. "Not really, I tried at first, but my friends back home just didn't understand why I couldn't tell them anything. They believed what the news said – that it was suicide and abuse and Sean and I couldn't handle it so ran off. My friends didn't get it, and some tried to convince me to tell them where I was to tip the police off, and I finally just gave up caring. I later realized people enjoy and are drawn to those who seem mysterious, but when that person leave's they are just gone. The draw is no longer there, because of that, I at least almost always had friends, but could never keep them. Except for Lex and KT, they are special."

Ash nodded as he pushed the gate open and held it for her to pass through, as he commented, "That's really strange, but I can understand it. I'm sorry for that."

Ciara just shrugged and asked in return, "What about you? Did you keep contact with anyone from high school?"

"No, not really, I didn't want to. I was always in the shadow of my older brother in school. He was a basketball star, and I was a band geek who did swimming for fun. I liked basketball, but only playing with friends, and I guess I didn't live up to the Callaghan name. My brother was always invited to stuff because he was popular, but I was always invited because my family has money. The few close friends I had went off the deep end freshman year of college, but they stayed closer to home. One is in rehab, another has a kid, and the last one flunked out and spends his time high at home all day every day." With a frown, he unlocked the main door to the apartment complex and realized he had just given a small monologue, and a blush rose in his cheeks. "We just have nothing in common and to be honest, never really did."

"That's sad, I'm sorry for you too. I guess I never realized your family had that much money, you don't talk about them a whole lot. You video chat with your sister and talk to your brother, but that's all I really knew. So, what do your parents do then?" Ciara looked up at him and saw a thoughtful crease on his forehead before the breeze blew his hair over it.

For a moment, she wasn't sure he would keep talking, and watched his face, appearing to struggle with what to say or if to say anything at all. She slowly began climbing the stairs, hoping that he would continue. After several more moments of silence, Ash answered, "My dad is the head of a law firm and my mom is a neural surgeon. She gets to pick who she treats and all that." Ciara's jaw dropped at the admission, and she didn't have time to monitor her reaction before he glanced over at her. "We have a giant house and a barn out back so my sister could have private horseback lessons and people always picked up after us. We even had our own cook, but the other side of it is my parents hired nannies to take care of us and watch us. They never knew what was going on and would leave for weeks here and there for conferences but would tell us by leaving a note. It wasn't until I graduated that they saw me as a person to take interest in really and things have gotten better since then, sort of."

Ciara paused a few steps ahead of him and turned to face him when at eye level. The look on her face was neither pitying nor sympathetic. Instead, his expression was caught somewhere between empathetic and anger as she said, "I'm sorry, my parents had money too. I know that, but they were still around and we lived a normal life. I wish you could have had that too," she said and wrapped her arms around his neck in a tight hug for the first time.

>>>

Finally, classes began, and so did Ciara's job at the library, which became her saving grace. She had always been smart, and she believed this would help her fit in at college. Instead, her love of learning and asking questions caused the other students to groan and roll their eyes whenever her hand went up in the air. After a week of this, she stopped asking during the lessons and learned to wait until everyone else filed out. And then she would interrogate the professor with all the other students possessing the label of nerd. If that failed to satisfy her curiosity, she would borrow another book to add to her growing stack in her private study room to consume in her dwindling free time.

She rapidly discovered a few of the people also hovering after classes happened to be friends of Ash's or the other guys. Thankfully, the boys had readily accepted her into their fold, and within the second week, she no longer sat by herself in most of her classes.

Ciara tapped her foot on the bar of the stool as she sat logging a stack of returned books at the library check-out counter in the second week of school. As she took a closer look at a book that appeared interesting, one of the most gorgeous women she had ever seen walked in. She wore bright red heels, a short black pencil skirt, and a tight plaid blouse. Her dark hair hung to her middle back in lustrous brown waves. Everything about her screamed popular queen, right down to the slow swagger of her hips, except she held Nate's hand and Ciara thought she knew Nate. Tentatively, Ciara smiled at him and watched as a grin slowly crawled across his dark face.

"Ciara, hey, I'm glad I ran into you." He glanced at the other woman and back to Ciara and introduced the women, "This is Jez."

Ciara held out her hand and wasn't surprised to see her nails were perfectly manicured in a deep red. "It's nice to finally meet you, I've heard a lot." Ciara suddenly felt underdressed in her baggy Ramones t-shirt and loose-fitting dark jeans. And was infinitely glad her ratty Converse couldn't be seen by this perfect image of a girl, right down to her dark eyes and caramel-colored skin.

"It's good to meet you too, I love your t-shirt. Ramones are good, but I prefer punk, post Ramones. The Clash are my favorite and I've want to go to Brixton, so I can say I've been in the same town they lived in, but it isn't a safe area." Dismissively, Jez turned to Nate and waved her fingers at him as she declared, "You can find a study room, I need to get a book and Ciara can help."

Nate nodded and left the two. "Of course, what are you looking for?" Ciara asked, stunned at how friendly Jez seemed to be despite the glamour. It contradicted everything she knew about every girl Ciara had met who looked like her. And with that thought, guilt rose in her belly, and she determinedly began altering her perception.

"A book on Roman Law, my professor was talking about something that intrigued me. It was about the treatment of slaves, and I didn't want to question him about it in class, but he disappeared before I could ask. I hate it when they do that," Jez said, flicking her hair over her shoulder.

Ciara smiled as she swiveled to the computer and began typing into the search bar as she asked, "You do that too?"

Jez laughed, showing slightly crooked teeth. "Of course, even at graduate level, the idiots seem to run the show. Almost everyone who cares does it, because it's the only way to survive if you actually care about learning."

"Aha! I think I found something," Ciara exclaimed and turned the monitor to show her a list of books with a proud grin.

Pulling pen and paper from her large leather purse, Jez copied down the numbers that would lead her to the books and said, "I heard you're close friends with Ash?"

Ciara tilted her head, wondering the purpose of this line of questioning as she answered with a hint of hesitation, "I guess so, is that a problem?"

Jez threw her head back and laughed before explaining, "Not at all, but I kind of wanted to warn you. The other girls the boys hang out with tend to be a bit crazy, the jealous and possessive type. They hang out with them only around campus or at parties, they are awkwardly territorial but just ignore them. I don't mean to scare you or anything, but half of them tried to date Ash, while the rest try to have a ten-minute conversation with him on something other than music." Jez sighed and carried on, "But if Ash and Nate like you, and you like the Ramones, then I like you and I don't want them running you off."

Ciara stared at her with wide eyes and tried to process whether the girl was trying to help her, as every mean girl movie seemed to start in this way. But then she reminded herself that she had already made an erroneous judgment on Jez and told herself just to take the advice for what it seemed to be: advice. "Thanks, I think."

Jez smiled and picked up the paper. "We are meeting over at the coffee shop by Ash's tonight if you want to come and some guys are playing."

"Jez!" The woman turned to see Ash and another girl stride into the library. He walked up and half-begged, "Nate somewhere?"

"Somewhere on the second floor, care to join?" She asked with her skin somehow appearing radiant despite the fluorescent lighting, a feat Ciara hadn't realized was humanly possible. A small part of her wanted to ask, but Ciara had never worried about what she looked like and was determined not to begin caring now.

Ash nodded, but amended, "In a few, will you take Mary up with you? I wanted to talk to Ciara."

"Come on Mary, let's go," Jez commanded and took the other girl by the arm, leading her away and asking how classes were going. Ciara didn't miss the glare from the other girl as she was forcibly steered towards the steps.

I guess it really was just a friendly warning. Ciara thought to herself with slight surprise before she turned to look at Ash expectantly and inquired, "What's new?"

"Other than being scared by a tiny female, because I think she is mentally deranged or maybe just has amnesia, nothing. How is work going?" He smiled and leaned his long frame against the counter, the tension visibly draining away as the other girl left.

"Quiet, until you lot showed up," she said with a quick smile as she dragged her eyes from the firm line of his jaw to the tiny crinkles at the corner of his yellow-gold eyes. "I like working here, but you seem like a giant from this angle, and I'm not used to it."

He laughed quietly while watching one librarian push a cart into the elevator. "A couple of us are going to the coffee shop by our apartment tonight, if you want to come along."

She looked up from typing a book into the catalogue. "Sure, what time? Jez already told me but didn't say when."

"Eight, at least that's when open mic night starts," he explained with a glance down at her, watching her fingers dance lightly across the keys of the computer.

"Are you playing?" Ciara mentally crossed her fingers as she tried not to physically show her hope. She loved listening to him play, and it had become one of her favorite things about living across from him.

Ash shrugged his broad shoulders, the motion pulling his t-shirt up to reveal the worn leather belt holding his jeans to his narrow waist. "Probably, I know Jared and Tyler both are."

"You should," Ciara encouraged, turning her head as Professor Austin called her name. "Sorry, I need to go, but I'll see you later."

10

Girlfriends

The noise level in the coffee shop aggravated her ears. The pair performing had no concept of the difference between meaningless sound and magnificent music, and the chords clashed in ways that made the four music majors at their table cringe. They attempted to communicate, but it was next to impossible with the noise. Still, Jez leaned over, screaming her question of if Ciara wanted a refill for her tea, and Ciara nodded. Finally, the employee in heading open mic night stood up and called Ash's name after the polite applause stopped.

He afforded a nervous glance towards the table, but everyone beamed at him in encouragement as he shouldered his acoustic guitar and strode to the front. They adjusted the microphones to accommodate his height and, before long, his melodic voice began shaping a beautiful melody with his guitar. His fingers danced across the strings as he sang a song of his own creation, the first time Ciara had never listened to one of his own compositions before.

The change in music was so drastically different compared to the previous performance that the entire crowd was instantly mesmerized, and a few people even stopped on the street to listen. Ciara couldn't take her eyes off him, not wanting to acknowledge that she enjoyed having an excuse not to. When Ash finished, he stood up and awkwardly waved to everyone before marching back to their table, like he was desperately trying not to make eye contact with anyone.

"How was it? It still needs a little work," Ash started the moment he returned to their table.

Tyler cut him off before he could get going on his self-critique and said, "It sounded awesome, shut up."

Nate bowed in agreement before adding, "You got your rhythms down, that was excellent."

"Harmonies fit seamlessly," Ciara said, thoughtfully considering what she had just listened to.

A girl in a black leather jacket moved to the center of the stage and began singing a cover of a pop song as Jez smiled in reassurance to Ash. The boys began to discuss the differences in harmonics, so Jez turned to Ciara and asked, "What landed you here as a Junior?"

Ciara chewed the inside of her lip, contemplating how she should answer, but something about Jez told her just to be as honest as possible. The woman's eyes seemed to see more than the average person, and while she had heard Jez could let loose, so far, Ciara had only experienced the business side. For some reason, though, Ciara was drawn to her, and she felt this need to get Jez to let her in, to consider her a friend. So, she confessed, "My brother Sean always wanted me to go to college and he died a year ago, so I decided I would complete his wish."

Sympathy entered Jez's dark eyes, and she reached across the table and clasped Ciara's hand, attempting to sound sympathetic while yelling over the music, "Oh sweetie, I am so sorry."

Ciara strained to plaster a smile on her face, but knew it fell flat. She hadn't experienced much pity or awkward sympathy before, and she was discovering she didn't like it. "This was the school I always wanted to go to and Sean left me money." That was technically only a half-truth; she couldn't be fully honest with it. Sean *had* left her some money, but their combined 150 dollars in savings would have bought her only one and a half books. Jez didn't need to know that, though, nor did she want to unload her entire tale on someone she had just met.

"Did you live with him or something?" She asked curiously.

Ciara felt her stomach squirm, and she shifted her long legs before feeling Ash press his knee against hers, giving silent support as she said, "Yes, he was my guardian." She left it at that, and thankfully, Tyler was called up to the front, cutting their conversation off. They all listened as he played a beautiful song on the piano from a movie Ciara had not yet watched. Apparently, though, everyone else had, as she saw the peaceful smiles on the crowd's faces and many lips softly mouthing the words.

Ash leaned over and whispered into her ear, "Are you okay?"

Ciara squeezed his arm and nodded, responding, "I'm okay, still hard to talk about though."

When Tyler finished, and the noise from the applause died down, Ash turned back to her. "On the way over, didn't you say you had something exciting to tell me?"

She set her mug back on the table, and a genuine grin lit up her face. "Lex is coming to visit at the end of September! I haven't seen her in so long, I can't believe it, but she is going to be here! I already checked with Curry too and he said he will help arrange everything. It's going to be awesome."

Ash and Jared chuckled at her excitement before Ash added, "I can't wait to finally put a face to this girl I've heard so much about."

"That's homecoming weekend; you should bring her to our party. We always have one for all the music students because the concerts They get out with barely enough time to make the tail end of the fraternity parties. So, we have our own the night before," Jared added with a wink at Tyler and Ash.

Ciara glanced around at each of the people at the table, experiencing a small sense of belonging. "That sounds like fun and I've never been to an actual party before."

Jez stared in shock and gasped out, "How is that possible?"

Rubbing the stubble on his chin, Ash answered for her, "Ciara's brother was protective."

She smiled at him in gratitude as Jez, still seeming incredulous, commented, "*Over*-protective, I mean, I'm sure he meant well, but seriously?"

With a shrug, Ciara steered the conversation back to safer ground about the coming party and what was to be expected at homecoming. The group obliged her with enthusiasm, and it quickly became obvious to Ciara that homecoming was a tremendous deal at the university as the night wore on.

>>>

"Ciara! Ciara!" a low female voice called, and the sound of clicking heels echoed behind the voice, breaking through her musings from her last lecture.

Ciara turned in the middle of the courtyard and smiled. "Hey Jez!"

Jez strode toward her, today in blue heels and skinny jeans with a pale blue tank top and a thick belt accentuating the curves of her body. Ciara wished she had the confidence to pull an outfit like that off and draw the eye of people like Jez did. Jez, like Lex, simply ignored the attention as she twirled a lock of her shiny brown hair. "Hey, so, a bunch of us are getting together at my place tonight for a movie and study session. Wondered if you wanted to come."

Ciara attempted to hide her smile and readjusted her faded messenger bag, giving her time to contemplate the offer. Jez had invited her to one of her movie and study sessions the week before as well, and she had gone, but she felt out of place. They hadn't been outwardly mean, but their lives were so different and their experiences a world apart from each other. While the girls had giggled and gossiped about their summers abroad, vacations with families, or volunteering, Ciara had listened and added details about places she learned about from Lex's travels. When they had asked her when she went, she had explained that her best friend had visited, but that she wanted to. An awkward silence followed her statement, and then they turned away from her to continue their conversation.

After that, Ciara struggled to join another pair that had been talking about going camping with their family. She explained how much she loved cooking over a fire and sleeping in a tent as well. This got her a little further along in the conversation, but then when the girls asked her how long her family usually camped for and where. Ciara didn't know how to answer and, not wanting to lie, explained it was just her and her brother and sometimes they would camp for over a week. After that, she pulled herself out of the conversation, not ready to give an exposé on her past with this group.

Finally, she had focused on her required reading and stopped trying to understand how to connect with the other girls. Especially when the only answers they seemed to care about were how she had met the boys and if she were interested in any of them. When Nate had shown up, Ciara perked up, but when none of the other guys followed, Ciara turned back to her textbook. That was when Leah slipped in silently next to her.

Leah was very quiet at first, but once Ciara got her talking, she discovered she had a very effervescent personality, unlike the other girls there. One of Tyler's best friends since high school, Leah appeared more content to watch the drama unfold around her rather than participate in it. While Ciara respected that, she also didn't quite understand why someone would even want to be near those other girls.

Despite her ill feelings towards the other women, Ciara wanted to have friends like a normal person again, and rejecting invites wouldn't get her anywhere. "Sure, but I will be running a bit late because I work at the library until nine," she answered.

Jez smiled brilliantly, her whole face brightening, and excitedly ordered, "Great, bring Ash with you. I'm sure he will probably still be in the music department, and I know he has other homework besides practicing."

Obediently, Ciara nodded before adding, "He does, I'll make sure he comes along." With a start, Ciara glanced around the perfectly trimmed and hedged courtyard and jumped. Only a few people strode with purpose towards the doors of the academic buildings, making Ciara panic and squeak out, "I need to run, class is about to start."

The other woman wiggled her fingers in farewell as she watched her run off to class before striding purposefully into the science department.

Just as the clock hit nine, Ciara plunked down the keys on the library computer to log out of her shift and switch over to the next student on duty. After bending down to pick up her bag from under the counter, she headed off to the music department to find her exceptionally tall friend.

Shadows followed her in the dark as she ambled towards the building on the far side of campus, still glowing and filled with students practicing late into the night. Ash was in his normal practice room with his back to the door and startled as she pushed it open.

"Didn't you get my text?"

Ash shook his head as he pulled his earplugs out. "My phone is in my bag, which I haven't opened in a while, sorry."

"Jez invited me to a study-movie night and told me to bring you along. If you wanted to go that is," Ciara explained as she leaned against the closed door, gazing up at one of the few men who dwarfed her.

"Sure, let's go," Ash said and took his violin from his shoulder and gently laid it in the velvet inside of the case. As he loosened the hair of his bow, he glanced at her with the hint of a frown and asked, "Unless you wanted to go alone."

"Not a chance, those girls are like hyena's," Ciara said, shaking her head.

"Hyena's?" Ash laughed, the deep sound vibrating through his chest, as he stood up and inquired, "How are they like hyena's?"

"They group up like a pack and if they find one person who is different, they circle around them and pounce when no one is looking. It's terrifying; girls are crazy," Ciara faked a shiver. "You're a boy, so it's something you may never understand."

"You're right, I probably never will," he said, swinging his bag over a broad shoulder and clutching his violin case. "I won't let them attack you, lead the way."

Ciara smiled and opened the door.

11

Lex

Bouncing around by the exit doors, Ciara could barely contain herself as Lex's flight number had changed to arrival almost ten minutes ago. The airport wasn't very large, and that should have been more than enough time for Lex to appear. A blonde head surfaced at the top of the escalator; she held her breath. But a second later realized it wasn't the yellow head she was watching for; the hair was to fly away, and a little too bleached.

Ciara let her breath out and bounced some more, to the amusement of her guards standing obtrusively behind her. When her eyes scanned back to the escalator, a grin spread across her face, matching the one already plastered on a young woman who appeared as if she had just walked off a movie set. She had a careless appearance about her, as if she realized she was gorgeous without trying, which Lex was extremely aware of. Her hair lay in perfect golden waves with natural white-blonde highlights, tousled from traveling, but that only made her appear more desirable to the eye. Her milky white features were interrupted by a red flush to her cheeks and the pink of her smiling lips. Meanwhile, her eyes were accentuated with a hint of mascara to make her already full lashes and vibrant cornflower blue eyes stand out.

They ran at each other, colliding in a tangle of arms, appearing like the perfect opposites of dark and light. They spun in a circle with their necks tucked together and tears running down their cheeks. When they finally parted, Ciara snorted as she gave her a once-over and said, "You are dressed nicely today."

With a dramatic smirk and an eye roll, Lex squeezed Ciara's shoulders as she said with a snort, "You know mom, so old fashioned. She made me dress nicely for the trip." She plucked at her loose-fitting emerald-green blouse before looking down at her dark-gray skinny jeans and slouchy gray ankle boots. "Now that you mention it," Lex said with a devilish grin as she dropped her oversized backpack on the floor, "I've got a shirt on top." She unzipped her bag and tossed a Clash t-shirt, with a band member flicking off the camera, at Ciara. She snorted as Lex pulled off her blouse in the middle of the airport, revealing her light green tank top, to replace it with a punk band shirt.

Lex tugged her long hair out of her shirt and piled it on top of her head with a hair tie and asked, "These are the bodyguards?" Ciara nodded, and Lex looked them over with narrowed eyes. "They seem... *buff*, what are their names?"

"Chuck," Ciara said flatly with a glint in her eyes, before explaining, "It's hard to remember who they all are since they rotate so much, so I started calling them all Chuck."

Lex laughed again and smiled at the guards who didn't seem the least bit fazed by Ciara's comment. Instead, they gave her the same stare every man always gave her: stunned and slightly dazed. "Hey Chucks, how are you?" She questioned politely, but they only smiled vacantly at her.

"The Lex Effect, it can't be helped," Ciara commented and snickered, patting her shoulder, feigning sympathy.

The other woman raised an eyebrow at her and tossed her hair dramatically, stating, "It's not *my* fault I'm flawless." Her lips twitched, and suddenly she burst out laughing with Ciara because Lex was not an arrogant person, and she was bad at playing it too. With a sympathetic sigh, she patted the guard's arm in the same way Ciara patted hers. "You get used to it, especially once you realize I may be a bit untamed." Then she linked her own arm into Ciara's, despite being almost five inches shorter. On a deep breath, Lex started in on one of their long-overdue conversations that were best had in person. "I can't wait to see this Ash friend of yours. I have never seen a veritable giant before, and he sounds like a hunk." Lex winked.

Ciara blushed as they weeded their way through the airport and to the waiting car with an exclamation, "Don't even start that with me."

"Start what?" She grinned innocently, and Ciara rolled her eyes, recognizing she was done for at the plotting gleam dancing in her eyes, but it had been years since she could be so light and free.

The drive back to the apartment seemed quick to Ciara with Lex's chatter as the bodyguards got used to the way the two girls stayed linked arm in arm. They waved goodbye at the door to the Chucks before climbing the staircase up to Ciara's blue door right when Mr. Durand closed his.

The older man smiled at the girls, his face the epitome of grandfatherly affection as he inquired, "This is Lex?" He held out a hand for her to shake as he added with a chuckle, "I can see why you are friends; you have the same taste in clothing."

Lex shook his hand with a grin and waggled her eyebrows. "Ciara said I would like you and she was right. By the way, I challenge you to a game of Bridge while I'm here; I've been looking for a tough opponent for years."

He raised a bushy eyebrow daringly and stated, "I accept the challenge. Have a good night girls and don't cause too much trouble." His laughter followed him into the stairwell, echoing out until the heavy door clicked shut behind him.

When Ciara opened her blue door, she ruffled her dark, spiky hair as anxiety suddenly spiked through her veins. "So, this is it, it's huge for me and I know I've shown it to you when we video chatted, but I even have my own shower and bathtub! Curtains and my own kitchen and a bed – an actual bed!"

The shorter girl enveloped Ciara's waist as she softly said, "It's wonderful Cia, absolutely wonderful." A crystalline tear slipped out of Lex's eye, unable to settle on an emotion. On one hand, Lex was beyond ecstatic for her best friend, but on the other, she was also desperately sad that she had lived for so long without any sense of home. "I want to see the whole thing before we make lunch. Show it to me!" Lex pronounced with building excitement as she squeezed her eyes tightly. She had wanted to come the moment she heard about Sean's death, but Sergeant Curry had forbidden it, and her time-off requests had been denied. It constantly seemed like one thing or another blocked them from each other, but no longer.

Gleefully, Ciara took Lex's hand and gave her the full tour before ending up back in the combination kitchen/living room. They started talking about lunch when a knock sounded at the door. Lex raised an eyebrow as Ciara looked through the peephole. "It's okay, just Ash, don't know why he's here now though."

Her best friend waggled her eyebrows and brushed her hands together as she eyed the door with eager anticipation and said, "Let him in, I'm ready."

"Lex, if you don't watch your mouth," Ciara started.

"I'll be good," Lex interrupted with a wave of her hand, "but you better let him in, or he will think you don't like him anymore." She crossed her arms and popped out a hip as Ciara sighed and turned to the door. Lex loved playing matchmaker, even if the people involved had no romantic interest in each other, and it was something she hadn't been able to do for Ciara since they were fourteen. Although she still had attempted from afar to set up KT and Ciara, until she realized they were more suited to almost sibling status.

With a suspicious glance at her oldest friend, Ciara pulled the door open and greeted her neighbor, "Hey Ash, what's up?"

"Let him in," Lex harrumphed from behind Ciara's tall frame.

"Sorry, I know Lex just got here, but I was trying to make cookies for Nate's party and ran out of flour and eggs," Ash said apologetically as Ciara stepped aside. With a bashful smile, he asked, "Do you have any I could use?"

"Course, you know where it is and we were trying to figure out lunch," she explained while watching his eyes land on Lex.

Shyly, he held out a hand as he greeted her, "I'm Ash, It's good to meet you."

Ciara surveyed him closer than she wanted to admit and was surprised when he didn't get that same haze in his eyes that other boys did when first meeting her oldest friend. Lex put her hand in his, giving him a firm shake with a wicked grin spreading across her face that made Ciara nervous. "Same, you are *quite* tall. Cia, I finally met a giant, and you finally have to look up to someone!" She began cackling.

Ash chuckled at that and dropped her hand as he looked back at Ciara, who was snickering as she observed from the doorway. His yellow-gold eyes seemed to soften as he looked at her, and she raised an eyebrow in confusion but pleasure washed through her as she watched his anxiety melting off him. Lex sucked in her lower lip and grinned impishly.

Ciara stuck her tongue out at the girl and strode into the kitchen as she read her best friend's reactions like an open book. She approved of him, at least as far as appearances went. "Should I make anything for this party? I can make some killer chip dip, if that's a good thing to bring."

"Sure, but you don't have to bring anything. I'm only because it's my friend's house and I'm one of the senior music students," Ash explained, opening a cupboard and snatching up a bag of flour as it started to fall out. "They wouldn't say no though. It's food and, well, boys like food."

"So does Ciara," Lex added as she moved to the fridge and conspiratorially whispered, "One way to win her love is to feed her and feed her often."

Ciara widened her eyes at her friend in warning, but had to acknowledge the truth, "It's true, I do love food. It's why I love going to your house; Her mom is a gourmet chef. Lex, you eat as much as I do, so, you can't really talk."

"On the contrary, I am talking right now." She smirked, and Ash held back a smile when she agreed with Ciara, "I do eat a lot, I will admit... so, for lunch." She opened the fridge and eyed the insides.

Unsure of what to do, Ash began backing up to the door, ready to take his leave, but Lex snatched his shirt unexpectedly, making him freeze. "I was just..."

"Trying to leave, which is unacceptable because deciding lunch is crucial and you are a vital person involved. Stay put," Lex ordered and returned her attention to rummaging for ingredients. "Pasta, pizza, Mediterranean, salad, mac n' cheese, stir fry, sandwiches... ideas? Come on people, I'm hungry and clearly Cia is too. I just heard her stomach growl and Ash you are huge so you're probably always hungry."

Ash rubbed the stubble on his chin and shrugged as he tilted his head in acknowledgment. "That is an astute observation, I *am* always hungry. Cia?"

She glanced over her shoulder at him and clarified, "Lex has an obsession with shortening names. I like it though, KT always calls me Pea Pod, but that's because the two of us have so many similarities we felt we must have been separated at birth."

Lex leaned over and flipped her head upside down, pulling her loose waves back into a ponytail. "So, Large One... what kinda party is this tomorrow night?" She popped out a hip again and grinned at him with her eyes dancing mischievously as she prompted, "Dancing, chatting, drinking, or all of the above?"

Ash looked like he was at a loss for what to do with Lex or how to react to her. He opened and closed his mouth several times, looked over at Ciara and then back to Lex before saying quietly, "A little of both."

"So, if I get this half boy here all glammed up for once, she won't seem out of place?" Lex waggled her eyebrows at him.

"Lex, behave," Ciara admonished without turning around and stated, "Mediterranean, I think. Pull out the Tzatziki sauce dear."

After ignoring the first order, Lex obeyed the second as she eyed Ash. With her cornflower blue eyes holding a hint of a plea, she questioned, "Don't you want to see her look like a girl?"

Sighing in distress, he looked between Ciara and Lex as he asked in return, "Why does it matter what I think? I have a feeling you will do as you please either way. If it matters though, you won't look out of place. Jez always dress up and some of the other girls do too. What is it you went to college for again?" He inquired of Lex, with the appearance of having been run over and backed up on as he set the bag of flour next to the eggs on the counter. The cookies clearly would have to wait as it seemed escape was impossible.

Lex smiled as brightly as the sun when she replied, "I'm a reporter and journalist, naturally pushy. Do you even have nice clothes?" She asked, suddenly turning her attention back on Ciara. Then she shook her head, answering her own question, while Ash struggled to follow the conversation that continued to jump back and forth between several topics at once. Lex didn't wait for Ciara's answer before she said, "Probably not, doesn't matter, I brought stuff. Now, food." Lex pretended to push sleeves up and started bustling around the kitchen to feed her oldest and newest friends. "Dinner is with Mr. Durand tonight, right? Then a movie here after I demolish him at Bridge?"

Ciara threw her arms up in laughter, wondering at what point Lex had memorized her schedule. "You are already thinking about the next meal, and we haven't even made this one yet!" She rolled her eyes as she calmly let Lex direct her around her own kitchen.

Ash grinned at the two women because he knew if Lex hadn't asked, Ciara would have mentioned it. They were so alike, and yet so different; it gave him the sense of unbalance, but he could feel the love they had for each other. Finally, he understood why Ciara had never been bothered so much about a lack of friends. Why should she be? She had Lex, who filled that gap enough for ten.

{ 12 }

Homecoming

Ash tapped against the counter a day later, with nervous anticipation overflowing every pore. Lex had greeted him at the door with a coy smile and promptly told him to wait, that she was almost done with Ciara. He had a sister, but that didn't mean he understood women. The absurd desire they seemed to have to remake themselves, when to him Ciara always appeared fine. *I guess it wouldn't be terrible if she wore girl clothes occasionally;* he thought silently to himself, but understood it didn't make a difference to him either way. Ash stared at the living room with his mind vacant in the way only men seemed to be capable of doing.

Thus, Lex caught him off guard when she dragged Ciara into the room in the most unexpected outfit. He had seen her 'dressed up' before, but only her version of it, where this time Lex had done the makeover. And she had meant something else entirely while still managing to keep something's, like the make-up, subdued. She put Ciara into a plaid mini skirt of blue, black, and gray with a black lacy halter top. The outfit showed more skin than he had ever seen on her and hugged her tightly in all the right areas. Instead of her typical beat-up Converse, she wore Lex's gray slouchy boots.

Although he realized Lex would probably get more attention at the party, Ash barely noticed her strapless shirt and jean skirt or her green two-inch heels that made her walk like a model. His throat went dry as he looked at Ciara and the curves he knew were there but had never fully appreciated before. Ciara bit her lip, in self-consciousness, but couldn't deny she enjoyed the way Ash was gazing at her. With a force of will, she forced herself not to wrap her arms around her middle.

"Told you," Lex grinned impishly at Ciara and, eyes smoldering at Ash in his jeans and green shirt, said, "Keep it in your pants boy, we have a party to get to."

He blushed and promptly turned, nearly running into the door before getting it all the way open in his attempt to flee. Ash didn't talk again until they were in the car and on their way over to Nate's, and only to briefly answer the questions Ciara or Lex aimed at him. His anxiety rose at what he knew would be a house packed with people. He didn't mind the occasional party, but he still had to prepare himself for one. And then a light, calloused hand touched his wrist, and he glanced over to see Ciara watching him closely.

"You good?" She asked.

"Yeah," Ash said before letting out a slow, measured breath. "There's gonna be a lot of people."

"I was a bit surprised when you seemed excited about the party," Ciara admitted and asked, "Do you actually like parties?"

"Sometimes but mostly I like the end of parties," Ash admitted with a shrug as he parked down the street.

Lex snorted and unbuckled to lean between the front seats and prodded, "So, you don't actually like them."

"No, I do but at the end there is just a chill vibe, like the feeling you get after a hard swim practice, you know?" Ash said, struggling to explain.

Ciara seemed to ponder this for a minute, before inclining her head in agreement. "I get that, it makes sense, the endorphin rush. Well, are you ready?"

Ash took another steadying breath and watched the crowd of people milling on the sidewalk and said, "Let's do it."

>>>

Louder than she had ever imagined, Ciara watched in awe at the number of students milling about all over the front lawn, spilling onto the steps, or leaning against the railing. Ash waved at a few but didn't stop to talk as he carried his contribution of food into his friend's shared home. The two women trailed him into the house, surveying the masses with sharp eyes.

Lex strode into the house with her hips already swaying along to the music and paused to survey the people and front room. After the brief observation, she dragged Ciara by the hand into the fray and passed her bowl of chip dip over to the man. Ash followed, wading through the sea of seething bodies with ease, continuing to nod to some and exchanging brief hellos with others.

The living room, normally filled with two couches and armchairs, was filled with people, a stereo and three speakers, and a couple of small tables. The couches and chairs were pushed against the wall by the stairs leading up to the second story. People in varying levels of dressed up or dressed down stood talking or dancing. Some lounged against the wall with drinks in hand, while others munched on food. Lex wandered through the living room for a moment and poked her head down the hallway, to get the layout of the house. Finally, she headed towards the lighted kitchen where Ash had deposited their food donations on one of the many folding tables holding all the treats.

Jez waved from behind the open fridge as Nate took the cold beer she handed him with a smile. He turned to face them with an excited exclamation, "Hey, you finally made it! This must be Lex." he held out his free hand to her, introducing himself, "I'm Nate and this is Jez."

Lex and Jez eyed each other as almost natural enemies before smiling, instantly seeming to recognize they would get along fine.

"Dancing?" Jez questioned as she stood and tossed her glossy sheet of long brown hair over her shoulder. Her bright red dress clung to her body like a second skin as she began to walk toward the darkened front room.

Lex grinned at her new friend and said, "Of course, lead the way. Come along Cia and leave the men to ogle us."

A little tentatively, Ciara followed, not having felt safe enough to be in such a crowded place in almost ten years. She either recognized or knew all the people, though, with Lex within arm's reach, she thought nothing could go wrong.

Lex and Ciara danced for what seemed like hours, with breaks only for drinks and briefly chatting with the boys. Leah and Jez joined into their pairing with ease, dancing and talking as if they had known each other for decades instead of minutes.

As one in the morning approached, Ciara decided it was time to join the boys by the fire behind their house. She skipped up the stairs for their jackets piled in Jared's room with a bounce to her step. She waved at Leah as she walked out of the bathroom.

"Going outside?" The quiet girl inquired as she began to move past her and down the creaking stairs, a flush still on her cheeks from the heat of so many bodies in the small house.

"Yep, the last few people holding out on the dance floor finally left," Ciara said, trying to hide her yawn. "I'm glad, my legs are exhausted. I didn't realize dancing was so much work."

Leah laughed softly and agreed, "Mine too, I will meet you down there then." She walked down the wooden steps and out of sight.

Ciara pushed open the door and entered the dark room. and quickly dug through the remaining pile of sweatshirts and jackets, finding theirs on the bottom, but then the hair on the back of her neck rose. Something was off. *Maybe I drank too much and am being paranoid,* she thought, but then countered herself, *No, you made all your own drinks. You know what this is; you just don't want it to be true: he's here.*

A slight creak sounded behind her, and the door slammed shut. Then, the Shadow stepped out of the dark into the sickle of light filtering through the window. Time seemed suspended as they stared at one another as if in greeting. Fear began to rise in Ciara's chest, but it quickly gave way to anger and vengeance for this man who had killed her entire family and disrupted her whole life. He was not going to kill her too; he would die before he had the chance to murder her, even if she had to be the one to perform the atrocious act.

A slight twist of his body warned her of his action before he followed through with a dagger aimed at her body. She leapt to the left and rolled nearer to him, flicking her feet up into his stomach, propelling him into the wall. Pictures fell onto them as their limbs tangled together, and she attempted to rip the mask from his eyes and fend off his dagger simultaneously. They slammed to the ground again, and this time, the noise aroused the attention of others.

Voices carried up the stairs, along with the sound of stamping feet. Realizing his target wouldn't be alone for long, he made one more swipe at her and cut her across the shoulder. In retaliation, she gouged his neck with her nails, tearing a chunk out of his flesh. He dodged toward the window right as the door opened, flooding the room with light, and The Shadow jumped out onto the edge of the roof without looking back.

Lex flung herself toward Ciara and the open window, swearing like a sailor before wrapping her arms around her best friend. "Are you hurt? I'm gonna rip that assholes head off and feed it to the sharks! I swear, but torture first, bamboo growing through his body. To The Pain with the bastard!" She screamed through the open window as she quoted a punishment from one of their favorite movies, hoping he could hear her.

"Just a cut, it's not too bad and I got him back right across his neck." She attempted a feral grin, but her limbs were already beginning to shake. "He won't get many dates in the next few weeks."

"How did he find you here?" Ash questioned from the window where he tried to glimpse the man already lost to the dark.

Ciara shook her head and said wearily, "He always finds me Ash, everywhere I have ever been, The Shadow has found me, nowhere is safe." She shook her head, mentally berating herself. *I shouldn't have let my guard down. I should have known better.*

"But why, why do you matter to him so much?" He questioned, but it wasn't Ciara who answered.

"She has something, information in physical or intellectual form, we have never known for sure, but that's what we think he wants." Lex sighed and frowned, rubbing Ciara's back and trying to give her a semblance of comfort. "Whatever work her parents did must have been very important and possibly dangerous but some faction wants it and must think she has it, or knows it."

Ciara nodded and said, "If I know something, I don't know that I know it, but that's what Curry thinks too."

"What in the world just happened and what are you guys talking about?" Jared questioned, staring at the destroyed room he shared with Tyler.

"Better tell them," Lex said consolingly, stroking her friend's short hair and adding, "Their lives have now been pulled into this too."

Ciara nodded and stared at the gathering of her first real group of friends since she was fourteen, and hoped that in telling them, they wouldn't abandon her. "It's kind of a long story, why don't we find someplace a bit more comfortable to talk. Plus, I need a drink, my nerves are in total chaos right now."

Without a word, they all filed out of the room and headed downstairs, waiting for her story. By the time she was finished, Ciara wanted her bed and filled with calm at her new friends embracing her, rather than abandoning her or condemning her for putting their lives in danger. Instead, they said it all made more sense: the way she seemed to look deeply into shadows, how she always hedged when asked questions about her past. With the enigma of her past sorted, the wall she had hidden behind seemed to crash, and Ciara finally believed she could be welcomed into the group instead of standing on the outskirts.

{ 13 }

Taste of Curry

Ciara fell asleep in Lex's lap almost immediately as the last rush of adrenaline left her system. At three in the morning, they stumbled past the Chucks guarding the entrance and up to Ciara's apartment, their minds in a fog and ready to fall into their beds.

Lex and Ciara went to bed immediately, not bothering to take their makeup off, only pausing to change into pajamas before crumpling onto Ciara's double bed.

The next morning, as the two girls sat ravenously eating omelets, Lex brought up The Shadow. "You know you should tell Curry; he needs to know about this and will be pissed you didn't call him last night."

Ciara sipped her tea as she stood to unlock the door before Ash could knock. With a tired smile, he lumbered in with his own breakfast of a toasted bagel and a generous amount of cream cheese in hand. She plopped back down onto her chair, a knee tucked up against her small chest as she grumbled, "I know I should, but what can he really do?"

"What are you talking about?" Ash questioned, rubbing blearily at an eye and pulling out one of the dark wooden chairs. He still appeared half asleep, and his brown hair stuck up on one side of his head like a disgruntled hedgehog. Ciara bit her lip to stop her smile at the sight of his misbuttoned shirt and disheveled state, unwilling to acknowledge that she found the sight of him endearing.

Lex swallowed her overly large bite with effort and sold out her best friend, "I think she should call this Curry fellow, but she said he won't be any help. If anything, he might tell you why The Shadow is after you."

"What choice do you have other than telling him?" The young man asked as he attempted to flatten his hair. "I mean, it's his job to protecting you, and he can't do that if you keep things from him."

"I'm being teamed up on, this isn't fair," Ciara huffed while staring at her whitewashed walls. The passing desire to hang something on them for decoration tried to draw her attention away from the current crisis. "The only other choice I have is leaving again and running, but my money would run out eventually and I don't want that kind of life again. I want a life where I can put pictures on my walls and not worry they will eventually be left behind." She frowned at her omelet and stabbed at a mushroom before glaring at the fungus as if it had caused her great offense. "Do you guys want to help me decorate my walls with something today?"

Ash stumbled for a moment, trying to keep up with her random thoughts. Through a mouthful of food he bargained, "Call Curry and tell him what happened and when he gets here, then maybe we can talk about a way to end all of this."

"I want to be here for this as well; I haven't yet met this *Sergeant* Fredrick Curry," she mused. With a raised eyebrow, Lex pursed her lips as she commented, "It makes him sound like a puffed-up ass, but I still want to meet him." She whipped her head around to face Ash as she complimented, "And solid bargaining, you pass."

Ash blinked in bewilderment at Lex, while Ciara snorted before admitting, "He can be sometimes, but, once he gets deflated, he is a pretty decent person. I won't call him though until someone helps me decorate my walls," she said, countering Ash's bargain with one of her own.

"I thought it was obvious that I would help you with that," Lex stated, picking a spinach leaf out of her eggs and popping it into her mouth with a satisfied smile. "Still wasn't the deal Ash was trying to make, but good job spinning it to better serve yourself. You have been learning from me after all!"

"What does decorating your walls have to do with calling Curry?" Ash asked as he pushed around a piece of leftover bagel on his white plate.

Lex patted his hand as if she felt sorry for his lack of understanding as she explained, "Everything, it means a lot to her to have a place. Decorations on the walls makes a place more homey, which is something Ciara hasn't had since she was fourteen."

His eyebrows sprang up, and he looked between the two girls and then down at himself. He brushed at the crumbs on his baggy t-shirt as embarrassment at not having put those pieces together on his own colored his cheeks, and mumbled, "I should probably get dressed."

"Why? We're still in PJ's too," she stated, and at a glare from Lex and a flaring of her nostrils, she held up her hands in defeat. Then pulled her cell phone out, accepting defeat. "Okay, fine, I'm calling him." Within a few minutes of dialing the number and a few holds and transfers, she was speaking with the man assigned to her case.

Calmly, she explained what happened and was promptly reprimanded for not having called him immediately afterward. Ciara rolled her eyes toward the ceiling, silently begging for patience, before countering, "What good would that have done, other than taken away a night's sleep from you?"

The line fell silent for a minute before Curry reluctantly agreed, "Good point, but I will be there in an hour or so."

"Thank you, see you soon," Ciara said and hung up, turning back to the two waiting to hear the full conversation.

Once they had completed breakfast, they lazed around her living room waiting for the man assigned to her. Lex pointed at the empty space above Ciara's medium-sized television as The Doors played in the background. "Look at all that untapped potential, that blank canvas just waiting to flourish!"

"I know, that's what I was thinking, except I can't decide on what I want to do with it," she pouted, willing the spot to tell her what it wished to become. Ciara tapped her chin with a long finger as she viewed it, wondering if she wanted watercolor or charcoal, a sketch in a frame, a colored drawing, or a painted canvas. There were so many options to choose from, Ciara felt excited by the challenge her wall presented, but overwhelmed at needing to make a decision.

"Do either of you *do* art?" Ash inquired, not comprehending the dilemma, but wanting to help as he watched the serious contemplation the two girls were giving to the wall.

Lex's jaw dropped open, and she slowly turned towards him with raised eyebrows as she sputtered, "Do you know this girl at all?"

Ciara blushed and glared at Lex, softly undermining her talents, "I paint a little bit and draw."

"A little!" Lex blurted in exasperation before immediately sprinting into Ciara's bedroom, diving under her bed for a clear container.

"Lex, don't!" She exclaimed, running after her, but Lex was too nimble and had already grabbed the container. She tugged out the sketchbook and wiggled away from her best friend to dive back into the living room. Ciara tried to grab the large spiral-bound sketchpad from her, but Lex twisted around Ciara. Ash caught the book as Lex tossed it in his direction while watching the two women with shock in his yellow-gold eyes. Ciara growled at her friend, cheeks red from both embarrassment and frustration at the smaller girl getting the better of her.

"I can't believe you!" Ciara crossed her arms over her chest and glared, but her friends ignored her.

"Take a look, and those are just the sketches. The actual paintings are much better, but those are mostly at my mom's or KT's." She stuck her tongue out at Ciara, who attempted to snatch it back, but Lex wrapped her arms and legs around Ciara. After being knocked to the ground, Ciara could only worm a few inches further before finally giving up.

Ash gently flipped through to see beautiful portraits of people from all walks of life. There were sporting events such as football, diving, dance, and martial arts; landscapes of fields, lakes, rivers, forests; and scenes of different highways, cities, and rustic old barns. Ash was shocked that he had never known about this talent of hers.

"Do you realize you could sell these?" He shook his head in disbelief before flipping to the last page and saw an incredible rendition of Lex with a handsome man beside her.

Lex smiled fondly at the sketch as she said, "That's KT and I. We've met a couple of times, but never with Ciara unfortunately. He's a funny guy, you two would probably really get along. He is basically like a giant teddy bear."

"Have you been to all these places?" Ash asked, flipping through the sketchbook to take a slower walk through the pages as Lex let Ciara go. Sean dominated many of the drawings in renditions in pencil, charcoal, and ink, with each mark depicting the love she had for her brother.

Ciara brushed her fingers over an image of him swinging on a tire swing behind a barn, with a horse tossing its head in the background. "These are mostly places we lived at one point or another, but I have a few different sketch pads. I'd mail them back to Lex or KT whenever they got filled up and then buy a new one."

"If you think these are good then you should see the colored copies," Lex bragged, enjoying showing off her friend's hidden talent. "You should do something with music and put it up there, like a violin because you always wanted to learn how to play."

"That would be cool," Ash agreed, nodding his approval, before offering, "I could teach you how to play if you wanted."

As she contemplated the wall, Ciara tapped her foot and began to create a design in her head. "I like it, that's what I will do." She turned and beamed at Ash before hesitantly accepting his offer, "I would love to learn, if you have the time to teach me."

"I have the time," he declared, noticing a devilish look from Lex, but decided not to tell Ciara about it. He imagined she might be able to interpret it and become upset.

"Cia," Lex began, but was interrupted by a knock on the door.

Quickly, Ciara jumped up to answer and let Curry in with his dark hair tousled by the wind and a carefully trimmed goatee covered in crumbs. It appeared he had been in a haste to get there.

Ciara waved him over to the living room, and he looked her up and down as if reassuring himself his charge was alright. "I will need to bump up security around you and I can get the complex to hire on some guards so they will blend in better. Same will be done at the university and we might want to consider posting some on your balcony too, but I don't want to encroach on your personal privacy either." His voice trailed off in quiet contemplation as he stroked the crumbs out of his facial hair, having eaten breakfast in his car on the way over. It seemed like it was shaping up to be one of those days again.

"I have a better idea," Ciara ventured with uncertainty because they wouldn't like what she was about to offer, but she wanted all of this to be over. Flicking her blue bangs out of her eyes, she determinedly gave voice to her idea, "What is the point of incessantly hiding me? The way I see it, until The Shadow is dead or behind bars, I will never be safe anywhere, can't we use me as bait to get to that end?"

"Absolutely not," Ash fervently demanded in an uncharacteristically stern voice. He blushed, knowing he had no right to say that, to tell her what she could and couldn't do, but the words were out before he could stop himself. Sheepishly, he apologized for his outburst, "Sorry, but that is a terrible idea, you would be the one ending up dead."

"I agree with the giant, terrible idea," Lex agreed, tossing her head and causing her blonde waves to toss like the ocean. She did not apologize; she felt she had every right to tell Ciara no. "Come up with something else."

"Right now guarding you is the best option," Curry said dismissing her plan, seemingly without any consideration. Then he frowned and sighed as he declared, "We will never leave you completely unguarded."

"Start thinking of a plan to trap this guy then," Ciara demanded, her nostrils flaring. And then crossed her arms in frustration as she added, "Because I am getting sick of him popping into my life and I don't want to have to move again, until I choose to. I want him brought to justice and if you don't do it, I will."

Curry nodded his acceptance but seemed lost in thought as he moved through all the possibilities he could imagine. He had been through them all a thousand times, but without more knowledge about who The Shadow worked for, many of the options were out of the question. Right now, he seemed to be operating alone, but if they went for him and he called in rein-forcements, a plan to pull him into the open or trap him could seriously backfire. It was a risk Curry wasn't ready to take.

"Why does this guy want her so badly?" Lex asked, leveling her cornflower blue eyes at him.

Curry frowned again, and Lex noticed he must do that of-ten from the lines surrounding his goatee. "Well, to be honest we can only guess at this, but we think whomever he works for believes Sean and Ciara had information about what their parents were doing." He stopped, staring at a spot on her wall and added, "Or that they could fill in the gaps left behind in the research. I don't know much more about it than that and some of it is well above my pay grade."

Lex and the other two looked from one to the other and back at Curry and Ciara sighed in annoyance, "In other words, what we guessed all along. You said everything without saying anything because you are not allowed to tell me. Typi-cal politician."

"I'm not a politician," Curry groaned and rubbed his tem-ples. "I just can't completely answer your question and I apol-ogize for that. I know it's frustrating for you, not understanding. Feeling like you are being kept in the dark. We can't inform you because it would be more dangerous if we did, but like I said, and Ciara, I am telling you the truth, even though I don't know everything. I am still trying to get clear-ance for me and for you. You deserve to know the whole truth, not just part of it."

"I understand," Ciara muttered and tried to give him a reassuring smile as she acknowledged his effort. "It isn't your fault and I appreciate that you're trying."

Curry stared around her apartment and checked, once more, for all possible entrances and exits before departing.

Once he left, the three pretended as if he had never come. He hadn't given them any hope for a better situation, and Ciara didn't like the idea of never being left alone. Instead, Ciara began to sketch ideas for her new wall and would show the small renditions of her ideas to her friends. They would vote on the ones they liked, and then she would enhance them. This continued until just before lunch, when they decided on the sketch they all liked the most, and then her real work began.

{ 14 }

Conspiring

Lex left the following night with a tearful goodbye, surrounded by Ciara's guards. Ciara needed to convince her arms to release Lex at the security checkpoint, and everything seemed to shift after that. The people she had hesitantly considered her friends quickly proved themselves to be something more when they embraced her into their midst. But soon, the shock at the homecoming party wore off, and the realization of what she had revealed sank in. Although Ciara sought to explain to the group that she didn't require help and didn't want them to get hurt, their group ignored her.

Fall began to set in a few days after the last visit from The Shadow, and with warm beverages clutched in students' hands, they shuffled faster from class to class. Hats and scarves hid the students and kept the chill from sinking in as the students wandered hastened down the concrete paths to the parking lots. The wardrobe choices put Ciara more on edge as it grew more challenging to investigate profiles of the surrounding people, but she coached herself not to be paranoid.

The coffee shop neighboring Ash and Ciara's apartment complex became their group's favorite hang-out and study

{ 123 }

space with its quiet atmosphere, decently priced beverages, and study rooms.

Thus, Ash was unsurprised several weeks after the incident when Leah set her matcha down hard against the painted table and declared to their friends, "We need to do something about Ciara."

"Finally, someone said it," Jared sighed his agreement and closed his bio-chem textbook with a resounding thud as he added, "I've been thinking that for a while now."

"You were thinking?" Tyler asked with open astonishment.

"Shut-up Tyler," Jared retorted with a playful shove, letting his hand linger on his upper arm. "But seriously, she needs help even if she says she doesn't."

Ash closed his music composition book with his mind spinning because he had thought of so many options but visualized Ciara's rejection of every single one. He needed to do something, though, or he was going to lose his mind from constantly worrying about his independent and strong-willed friend. Ash cleared his throat as he viewed their group and inquired, "She already has guards posted everywhere, what do you honestly think we could do?"

"Don't you want to try and protect her?" Jez and Nate exclaimed eyeing Ash in shock.

"Of course I do, but we know nothing about this stupid Shadow of hers other than he is a trained assassin who has been following her for eight years." Ash drummed his fingers against the table in frustration at the conversation he had held with himself many times before. "This guy broke into her apartment back in the summer and threw as many of her be-longings as possible on the floor just to scare her."

Jez frowned in thought, her dark eyes boring into Ash's yel-low-gold. Unlike the others, Jez kept her calm, and Ash real-ized she was picking apart the problem with her analytical mind piece by piece, separating what they knew into different categories. While the others fretted, she plotted and planned, and Ash was grateful she was on their side.

Finally, Jez shrugged and simpered, "So, this Shadow likes to play games? I do too and now that we can do something about it."

"He likes to try and scare her, but he has probably done it so many times that it works for only an instant before Ciara recovers," Jared mused. "She's tough, I mean, at the party, she just looked pissed."

Nate nodded and elaborated, "We also know The Shadow probably could have killed Ciara during the party, but he waited till she was alone to try."

Ash shook his head and explained, "He doesn't want to kill her. He wants Ciara alive for some reason, and I think his murder of her brother, Sean, was an accident, or because he felt like he didn't have another option. Ciara has never really talked to me about it and it only happened a year ago."

"Okay, he wants Ciara alive," Tyler restated and tapped out a rhythm as he considered. "He could have taken her at any time then." His voice trailed off as he realized how they could keep her safe, and he expelled an excited gasp at the same moment as Leah. Then blurted in a rush, "Lex was with her the whole night, except when Leah met Ciara on the stairs and she was alone; it was his only opportunity."

"Before that night, before he slipped up, only Lex and Ash knew about her Shadow and this Sergeant Curry," Leah continued in a rush as Tyler grinned. "We wouldn't have known that she shouldn't be going off with some guy or that if she didn't come back for a while there might be something wrong."

Jared frowned and shook his head as he glanced between Tyler and Leah and admitted, "I don't understand, how is that going to help us now?"

"We know to be cautious about her disappearing and that he is dangerous and what he looks like, sort of," Tyler said, laying out all the facts for everyone. He watched Jez's smile turn into a grin, her slightly crooked teeth gleaming white against the caramel of her skin. Nate was bobbing his head rhythmically, and Ash drummed his fingers on the table as Tyler continued, "We can also guess that he won't try anything when she is with others."

Jez twirled a piece of her pressed hair as she reiterated and embellished, "So now we never leave her alone. Leah and I can sleep over at her place now and then and Ash lives across from her, along with that Mr. Durand guy. He is trustworthy right?" She queried and then added, "I'll do a search on him and anyone else we have any suspicions of, like this Frederick Curry person. I should have thought of that sooner," she mused.

"Mr. Durand is like a grandfather to her and knows about all of this. He's lived next door to Ciara since she moved there a year ago," Ash explained and began to feel a sense of relief that they were getting somewhere. He couldn't help but smile at the way his friends had folded around her, but he also understood Ciara wasn't likely to be fooled for long. Ash held back his sigh as he wondered what her reaction would be – frustrated, annoyed, relieved? It was always difficult to tell how she would react. "I can check up on her and we can probably drive together to school most days," he said and glanced at his phone to check the time. "Ciara should be here in a few minutes and I'm not sure how she is going to take our attempt to protect her."

"Then we just do it," Nate grunted with a shrug before letting out a brief chuckle. "No one said we have to tell her, she'll probably figure it out eventually anyway."

It took them the last few minutes before Ciara got there to figure out the best way to get her to and from classes and her work schedule safely. While they waited for Ciara to arrive, Leah and Jez decided it would be best to just randomly invite her to sleepovers so a pattern couldn't be recognized by the Shadow. And by the time they saw her Jeep pull up to the curb, their plan was set, and the group of friends felt very pleased with themselves.

>>>

Ciara strode into the coffee shop with the warm brown tones reflecting the caramel and coffee scents and sighed. She smiled, feeling suspicious when Jared and Leah glanced up at her simultaneously with guilty expressions when she walked to the counter to order a cup of hazelnut coffee. Her backpack weighed her down with its multitude of research books, and her messenger bag held two binders and her laptop. She almost spilled her mug as the strap slipped on her shoulder when she pulled open the door to their private study room and asked, "Hey guys, how's it going?"

They responded with a burst of noise and then laughed, the sound devoid of its normal harmony. Ciara raised an eyebrow but said nothing as she dropped her bag with a resounding thud next to Ash and the only empty chair. It was way too obvious that the group had been discussing something they didn't want her to overhear, but she wasn't surprised after their discovery of The Shadow. She decided not to let it bother her.

"What's in the bag?" Ash questioned, undoubtedly trying to cover up the awkward greeting they had given her.

Ciara rolled her shoulders, trying to get her muscles to relax after hauling the heavy bag all over Pine Harbor. "Books I just got my term paper guidelines from Professor Norcross. I need to pick a topic, but when I went into the medieval section all these books jumped out at me and I couldn't decide." She laughed awkwardly, understanding that it made her look like a complete nerd. But she accepted that she was in good company with her gathered friends and their books and study materials spread across the table.

Jared raised an eyebrow at her in what she could tell was feigned judgment as he inquired, "So, you took them all?"

"I understand," the law student said, patting her hand in a sympathetic gesture. "That always happens to me too, it's what finally made me decide to go into law." Jez sighed and gestured at her overflowing second bag as she explained, "I realized I would make a terrible professor, because I would just spend my time reading one book. And then wanting to learn more about another topic I came across in that book. At least this way I can do that in my spare time. Otherwise, I am sure I would have gotten myself fired in the first year, that's if I could have committed to a research topic for my doctoral program."

"Once I find a focus, I'm fine, but I need to find one first," Ciara explained as she nodded in understanding. "I'm glad you get it though."

"I do that with English books too," Leah admitted from her seat further down the table, her sheet of blonde hair obscuring her face. "Thankfully, I'm a fast reader. And I know Jared also nerds out about micro-organisms and other science things, so don't act like you aren't the dork we know you are."

Tyler snorted and raised his hand to high-five Leah as he said, "She got you." Jared's cheeks reddened slightly. "Oh don't give me that look. it isn't a bad thing, I love it about you."

"Awww," the girls all chimed along with Nate, who batted his eyelashes dramatically, before Leah added quietly, "You two are so adorable."

Never Left Alone

Within a week, Ciara discovered her friends' plan, but she was far from being angry as Ash had worried she would be. In fact, she had never felt so loved in her entire life and, instead of informing the group she had caught on, allowed her friends to take pride in their success. Internally, however, she couldn't stop her laughter over what excuse they would come up with next to spend time with her.

While a few were very great at creating reasons to spend time with her, others were not as adept. And, as expected, among those less proficient were Jared and Tyler. Tyler was extremely transparent in his motives from the beginning, and when she asked him why he was waiting outside of her classroom, he said he saw her sitting inside. She glanced back at the solid door and brick wall of the classroom with no windows and had to bite her lip to contain her mirth. After a moment of silence, she thanked him and asked him about his latest project, understanding his motives were completely altruistic.

Jared was more practical than Tyler, but his scattered and down-to-earth manner made it challenging for him to lie about his reasons. She understood he genuinely wanted to spend time with her, but also saw him watching every single person walking by as if they were a potential threat. But then, he also offered to help her with her science homework, which she gratefully accepted, as it was the only class she was struggling in. Thus, every Tuesday morning, Jared and Ciara could be found drinking warm beverages in a study room, going over Biology 111 at the university library.

The quiet and reserved Leah was a bit more subtle, and since they were in the same creative writing class with an upcoming deadline, she proposed a sleepover. Said sleepover would entail lots of writing, but also movies, crafting, and baking, Leah claimed.

Ciara was ecstatic at the invitation and could not recall the last time she had spent the night at a friend's house. "I've only had a sleepover at Lex and KT's and not since high school," she exclaimed, grinning from ear to ear, her backpack bouncing as she skipped a step. "This is going to be so much fun, thank you! Oh, and Ash's a few months ago, but that barely counts."

Leah smiled back and softly said, "I'm glad you like the idea, do you want to come over before dinner? We can get carry out Chinese and my mom sent me a box of baklava."

"Sounds perfect!" Ciara almost shouted in excitement, then covered her mouth at the widening of Leah's eyes. "Sorry," she whispered, with color growing in.

"By the way," Leah said, eyeing the taller woman with a twinkling question in her eyes, "Why did you stay the night at Ash's?"

Ciara blushed and was instantly annoyed at the ridiculous reaction, because it made no sense. There had been nothing romantic about it, nor did she feel that way about him, or the other way around. Ash had simply done a thoughtful thing for her when she had been frightened, something any good friend would have done. She shook her head to clear her wayward thoughts, especially the ones lingering on his misbuttoned shirt, and cleared her throat to explain why she ended up on his couch. "It was the night my apartment was broken into, so he let me crash on his couch and I left first thing in the morning, that's all."

"That's all?" The strawberry blonde asked with a raised eyebrow.

"That's *all*," Ciara reiterated and tossed her head as they walked down the sidewalk. The trees covering the lawn were all gold and flaming red as the dusty smell of fall permeated the air. "We're just friends," she stated, but Ciara ignored that it was more for her benefit than for Leah's and didn't understand why she had believed she needed to clarify that. She watched as Leah hid a smile, turning her head to watch a squirrel try to bury a nut in the well-tended flower bed.

The following Friday, Jez and Nate cornered Ciara in the library while she shelved books in the music section. Inwardly, she wondered what their reason would be for finding her there, but unlike some others, their reason possessed some semblance of logic. Nate held up a slip of paper with the call numbers for a book, and when he wandered off to find it, Jez looked Ciara up and down with a critical eye. "I think you need a new wardrobe, or at least new shoes, but heels would never do, unless the only people you hung around were Ash's height."

Ciara wiggled her toes and pouted, "But they're so comfy."

Jez raised an eyebrow before commenting, "I can see that you are wearing one blue and one green sock today and what are you doing next Wednesday for your presentation? I need some shopping detox, and I want you to come with."

"I'm not much of a shopper," Ciara warned as she pushed a book onto the shelf and glanced at Jez in her silky purple top and skintight black jeans. She didn't want to hurt Jez's feelings and admit she didn't believe their styles could ever mix in the fashion industry. Jez constantly looked like she had just glided out of a magazine, while Ciara dressed from thrift store discount racks.

"Probably because you have never been shopping with someone like me," she reassured with a smile, showing her slightly crooked teeth. "I see of it more as hunting and I can find clothes that look good on anyone and fit their style choices." She winked one dark brown eye at Ciara before clarifying, "Believe it or not, the only things I ever buy full price are shoes and bra's, and I save up for those." Jez narrowed her eyes at Ciara's chest, hidden by her loose t-shirt. "That's also something we should get you. That and some matching socks."

Ciara blushed, but only at Jez's brazen, nonchalant manner of sizing her up, and then sighed in defeat, "My last class ends at 5:30."

"Excellent, that's just before I get off work, so meet me at the administration building. We can go out for dinner, and I expect you to sleep over, because I don't know how long this will take," she ordered and clapped her perfectly manicured hands in delight.

Nate strode back down the colorful aisle of books as if he'd been waiting for some hidden signal from Jez and asked, "Did you just find yourself another project, love?" Jez nodded in delight and he gave Ciara a hard look as he counseled, "Wear comfortable walking shoes because she can shop for hours to by only two things."

"Yet, you're still dating her," Ciara pointed out.

The young man scratched at a dark cheek and admitted, "I only shop with her when I have to. I normally make sure she has someone else to go with and, thankfully, I was saved this time."

"Wednesday 5:30, don't forget or I will find you," Jez warned as she linked her arm with Nate's and threw over her shoulder, "We'll see you later."

>>>

The next time she ran into Tyler and Jared, the two young men slyly asked if she liked soccer, and she was unable to stop the wide grin that spread across her face.

"Ash told you I used to play, didn't he?" Ciara questioned the boys, while wrapping her sweatshirt tighter around her long frame.

"Well, yes," Tyler admitted, before pointing at a flyer taped to the wall of the academic building and hinting, "But I don't know if you heard or saw the signs posted."

"Each department tries to get a team together and over the semester we play each other, and we came in second last year," Jared rattled on, staring her down.

"I haven't really played in a few years," Ciara mumbled and scratched her head. Contemplating the idea of getting back out on the field after so long seemed daunting, but her mind was already in motion as it imagined every possible opponent. So, she straightened to her full, imposing height and inquired, "When are the practices?"

"Every Monday night at 7:30 in the dome," Jared said, tugging down the flyer and handing it over to her as Ciara tapped her side.

"We can go together after dinner, then go on to the coffee shop," Tyler cajoled with a wide grin.

"Alright, you have me," she said in defeat and took a glance back over the flyer with a keener eye.

That night, Ash and Ciara sat in his apartment while he practiced through a new song and she continued to work on the design for her new painting. They had both been silent for almost an hour before Ash finally broke it with a soft voice, "I was serious about teaching you how to play violin right?"

Ciara twirled a pencil in her long fingers as she played with art gum in the other. It took her a moment to come out of her own mind and hold on to the words he spoke to her, "Were you?"

He bowed his head and scratched his scruff, not meeting her ocean eyes as he turned a page in the song. "When do you want to start learning?"

"This Sunday?" She asked with excitement.

He chuckled lightly at her enthusiasm and said, "Dinner is at 6 with Mr. Durand, so, how about we start at five pm?"

She smiled slyly at him and thoughtfully tapped her pencil to her chin as she mused, "It seems like everyone wants me to hang out with me all the time."

He blushed and fidgeted with the sheet music in front of him, murmuring, "Were we that obvious?"

"From the start," Ciara informed him, patting his arm from where she sat before peering up at his white cupboards where a picture of him and his siblings was taped. She really liked that picture of him; he looked very different from the Ash she recognized, but it intrigued her. After a pause, she finished, "It's nice though to know you all care about me enough to do all that, thank you."

Ash nodded and sighed. "Next time, maybe we should not try to be secretive and just tell you and it probably would have been easier."

"Less fun though," Ciara observed with a laugh and explained, "It was a surprise every time, trying to guess what story everyone would come up with."

>>>

Ciara stumbled around her room, throwing items into her bag: a pair of baggy sweatpants, a hoodie, an old t-shirt; then she tossed everything back out onto her bed. A pair of shorts and a tank top replaced the other clothes, before she growled and upended the entire bag onto her bed again. A knock sounded on her door as she grumbled to herself. She walked to the door and saw Ash through the peephole.

She pulled the door open to let Ash step into her quaint apartment. With one sweep of his eyes, he took in the disaster of her kitchen and her disheveled state and hesitantly asked, "Uh... what's going on?"

"I'm not going, I don't know what's okay to bring, or what I'm supposed to wear. The closest I have gotten to a sleepover is watching *Grease* and I'm pretty sure that's not what they are really like," Ciara confessed. She pulled a blue tortilla chip out of the bag and stuck it in the guacamole in an attempt to eat through her stress.

Ash set his phone down on the counter and leaned against the sink, unsure what to do with her obvious anxiety and said, "Lex spent the night a few weeks ago."

"That's different; That's Lex, but I know I'm being stupid. I just don't want to seem like an inexperienced idiot," Ciara admitted before shoving another chip into her mouth, almost spilling the dip down the front of her shirt.

"You won't look like an idiot," Ash said and reached out a hand towards the chips. Ciara handed him the bag as he confessed, "Jez was just texting me and wondered if you were still coming. Said you hadn't texted her back and wanted to know your favorite snacks and drinks. I think her and Leah are plotting over at Leah's place and they wanted me to tell you they changed the menu to tacos."

"Really?" Ciara asked in bafflement. She liked Jez but was surprised that the other woman was taking such an interest in her, especially since they hadn't yet taken their shopping trip together. It was postponed until the following week after a delay caused by Jez's project partner turning out to be extremely incompetent.

"Jez is nothing, if not thorough," Ash acknowledged and stepped next to her to dunk a chip into the green dip. "It's just Leah and Jez; I know you aren't a huge fan of the others."

Ciara's face flushed slightly as she confessed, "That obvious?"

"You aren't the greatest at keeping a poker face." Ash chuckled at that while her cheeks grew rosier and tried to assuage her discomfort, "They are a lot, especially when they all get together."

She sighed and strode back into her room to pack and quickly respond to Jez's stream of text messages. This time, as she packed her bag, she tried not to think too much about it.

It wasn't long before she was seated on Leah's hand-me-down couch and tossing popcorn back and forth with Leah as they tried to beat their record of popcorn catching. Jez shuffled through the movies she had brought and finally chose one.

"This one's great for background," she declared and popped the DVD into the player. As she waited for the start-up screen, Lex explained, "Because we have margaritas and tacos to make and this is seriously the best guac I have ever tasted."

"Lex's mom's recipe," Ciara admitted. As the girls cooked and watched movies, Ciara relaxed even more, scolding herself for almost having canceled because it turned out to be one of the most perfect nights.

In some ways, she felt cheated that her younger self had been denied this experience, but she wondered if it would have been the same. Leah and Jez just seemed to fit with her, and they weren't dolled up or trying too hard. Leah was in an old high school soccer t-shirt and flannel bottoms, while Jez had her hair piled into a bun and wore a pair of sweats clearly stolen from Nate. The pictures she had seen on social media of kids from the various high schools she attended were in too much make-up, booty shorts, and push-up bras with tank tops. As if they were forcing themselves to have fun so they could get the perfect picture to post. Instead, this was easy friendship and relaxed, the kind of friendship that rang true.

They clinked their margaritas together and leaned over the counter as they bit into their tacos, making the insides squish onto the plates. Ciara snorted as a dollop of sour cream splattered onto Leah's plate, spraying onto her t-shirt and became grateful she wasn't the only one making a giant mess.

{ 16 }

Halloween

Time marched on, faster than Ciara had ever believed possible between soccer practice, work, and classes. Her papers kept her running to her study room in the library between her classes, referencing one book and then tripping among the stacks searching for another. Most Mondays and Wednesdays she would find Ash either in her study room or outside her classroom waiting to walk her there. Having grown comfortable in the routine and each other's presence, she no longer questioned why he was there or worried that one day he just wouldn't be there.

On a long late fall afternoon, Ciara discovered that Ash's sister attended their rival school and was only a year apart in age from Ash. "I thought she was a few years younger," Ciara commented, turning a page in the latest history book she was reading on a park bench.

Ash shook his head, "Rival is a bit of a stretch, at least where we are concerned. It's more of a joke, because Jenny's in music education, so when the bands play each other, we always made a big deal out of it, mostly to be dramatic."

"She's a lot like you then?" She probed, tapping a pencil against her chin and looked up at Ash and saw him studying her. She quickly corrected herself, "I mean not that your dramatic, I meant the music part."

Ash chuckled and flushed his sister out. "She plays different instruments, but she does love music and is also a swimmer. Jenny got a scholarship for swimming and set a bunch of records in her senior year of high school. She managed to stay on the team in college until last year, but things got a bit too busy this past year. I didn't even try to stay on the swim team though, but next time I video chat with her, you should come over to meet her." Ash rubbed a hand against his stubbled chin.

Ciara felt her stomach flip at the offer, and her fingers tingled with nervous energy. *Why am I so nervous suddenly?* She shook off her thoughts and stated, "Sure, I would love to meet her."

"Did you ever do sports other than soccer?" He asked after a few minutes of scratching at a music sheet with a dull pencil.

"I was a dancer," she admitted, recognizing how out of character it always seemed, and with a smirk elaborated, "Ballerina to be exact and I was really good. Julliard had been recruiting me and when I was sixteen and Sean and I were living in San Franscisco he would play guitar and I would dance. We made enough money, that we could stay in a hotel and buy groceries for two weeks, so we started doing that in all the major cities we lived in." She counted off some cities on her fingers as she spoke, "New York, Boston, Denver, New Orleans, D.C., Chicago, a few others." Ciara smiled at the incredulous look on his face and confessed, "It was a lot of fun, the freedom of the movement and immediate gratification of knowing people enjoyed watching."

Ash shook his head in awe and marveled, "It may have been fun, but it couldn't have been easy."

"It was hard, yes, but I wasn't alone, my brother was always there. He loved me and took good care of me," she paused, recognizing how much she had depended on him and, in many ways, taken advantage of that. "We had some pretty epic arguments but he never abandoned me. It would have been so much easier for him if he had. But, no matter what, I knew he was always there if I needed him," her voice trailed off as heat pricked at the back of her eyes.

Ash drummed on the bench and frowned, unsure how to respond. And was saved when Ciara added, "I also had KT and Lex and they more than make up for everything."

>>>

Over the few weeks he had spent teaching her violin, Ciara had already progressed to playing a few easy songs, and her fingers were becoming quicker as they learned the patterns. Ciara began to learn to alter notes and riff on her own, but she hadn't quite gotten the hang of it. And then, a few nights a week, the group would meet up at the coffee shop or at the boy's house, where they would collectively make dinner. To Ciara, they made up for the family she had missed for so long.

Despite their similar age, Jez became the older, wiser sister, where Lex had always been like her crazy twin. Jez gave her advice about boys, how to dress for all occasions, how to wear makeup, and how to talk to adults. And best of all, to Ciara, how to shop for anything without spending too much money. Ciara never had a reason to shop before, nor did she have the money, time, or means, but now she did. She needed clothes for presentations and concerts, but her old clothes didn't fit well or were falling apart. Since her mother had been taken from her before she fully matured, Ciara relied on her own ideas for bra's and clearly that hadn't gone too well. Jez helped her pick out new ones which fit better and succeeded in finding ones on sale.

"My theory is always purchase undergarments that make *you* feel good and never buy them with a boy in mind." Jez winked at her as they strolled through a store completely dedicated to underwear, as she elaborated, "Because then, you only wear them for him. And, if something goes wrong, you're out of a nice bra and pretty panties."

Ciara laughed and cemented the advice in her mind, as with help from Jez, who proved her talents in finding clothes that fit other personalities. Their second outing was dedicated purely to finding Ciara three new outfits, along with some new socks and a business dress outfit for her midterm presentation. Jez made sure all the outfits could be combined into at least nine; she was a master with clothing, and Ciara fully appreciated the help. The only other thing she added to the list was a Halloween costume, her first in seven years.

As a young child, Halloween was one of her favorite holidays, but once on the run, the idea of a room bursting with people hiding behind masks was intimidating. The result of this was that Sean and Ciara stayed far away from any Halloween festivities, except for carving pumpkins. This year, though, the boys were throwing a huge Halloween bash, and Ciara was dead set on participating. Although Curry frowned at the idea, he finally agreed so long as five guards were at the party as well.

>>>

Sprawled on her living room floor with books and papers strewn about and her laptop playing Tchaikovsky to kick-start her brain into writing her paper, Ciara groaned. It was Sunday, and she wanted it to be Friday already. A light tapping sounded on her door, and she quickly jumped up, gracefully avoiding her laptop, before staring through the peephole to see Mr. Durand with two pumpkins cradled in his arms. Excitedly clapping her hands, Ciara threw the door open, exclaiming, "You are the greatest!"

Mr. Durand chuckled and motioned to his door, "Come on over, I already brought up another and *The Great Pumpkin* will be on in ten minutes."

A grin exploded across her face, and she hurriedly said, "That's my favorite, let me grab my keys. Did you ask Ash?"

"This one is for him," Mr. Durand explained, holding up one pumpkin and answering her question, "He said he had something to finish up and would be right over."

Ciara locked her door and headed over, and Ash entered not far behind with his laptop playing *The Monster Mash* and a bowl of candy corn balanced in a large hand. "Saw them in the store and couldn't resist."

Ciara snagged one of the tri-colored pieces as he set it down and admitted, "The pumpkins are the best though."

"They taste exactly the same," Ash countered with an eye roll at their weeklong argument. Then reached into his back pocket and tossed a bag of the candy pumpkins at her and said, "Happy Halloween."

Ciara squeaked gleefully and impulsively threw her arms around his neck as she squeaked, "Thank you, you're the best!"

Ash blushed and grinned as he awkwardly patted her back. "Course, I guess Lex was right when she said all a guy has to do is buy you food. Better make sure your Shadow doesn't find that out."

She slapped his arm playfully and opened the bag with her teeth as she stated, "You're horrible."

Mr. Durand set down two bowls, knives, and a few permanent markers on the table. "This bowl is for pumpkin seeds, this one for the guts." He eyed the two of them with a twinkle in his eye and announced, "Let the carving begin!"

>>>

Ciara twirled around in Jez's room at her tiny house as Leah and Jez clapped their hands. "You look wonderful, but I still say wear the black heeled boots though," Jez mused, tapping her cheek with a tube of bright red lipstick and ordered, "Come here."

Ciara sat on the edge of her bed in Jez's room so Jez could swipe the lipstick on her, before bouncing back up to peer are her reflection. She played with the hem of her bright red and black lace miniskirt and tightened the knot of her red and black corset.

Leah handed her a pair of demon horns, which she placed on her head before pulling the boots on and zipping them up. "You have spanks on, right?"

"Those really tight shorts?" Ciara asked her friend, who had turned into an angel with sparkly feathered wings and a blue dress tightened at the middle with a silver rope, as Leah nodded. "Of course, I never wear skirts or dresses without them; men can be heathens and females even worse sometimes."

"Hear that," Jez agreed and grinned at them as she proudly stated, "Those are my girls, smart and safe. Leah, come here, can I fix your mascara and I want to add a hint of blue to your eye shadow."

Leah walked over to the peacock, elaborate feathers framing a collar around its neck and a tight blue-green dress. Ciara and Leah both knew it was really a conversation starter for people who didn't know she was dressed up as the male.

Once the finishing touches were in place, the girls walked the block to Nate's home. Ciara frowned as she saw something flash behind a bush, but it was hard to say if it was her Shadow with so many people milling about. But she still whispered, "I think I just saw something."

"You too?" Jez glanced over at her.

Leah gave a brief inclination of her head and murmured back, "I wasn't going to say anything, but I saw it too. Watch your drinks tonight and keep a hand on it and make sure to only eat food if you know who made it."

While there were fewer people there tonight than at the Homecoming party, somehow with all the costumes it seemed even more crowded. Ash showed up a few minutes after the girls and, with a little convincing, Ciara got him to dance with her, a few girls giving her glares as they twirled.

"Fire's started!" Tyler called through the screen door a few hours later.

Ash put a hand between her shoulder blades and leaned down to speak into her ear, "Want to grab some food and head out there for a bit?"

"It might be a bit chilly, and I didn't bring a coat, which in hindsight was not very smart, but I thought it would ruin the costume. "

"It's a great costume and well, I would say you look nice, but as a demon, I guess that may not be complementary." Ciara snorted at his comment and raised an eyebrow as he unbuttoned his pirate coat. "You can wear my coat, it's black, so kinda matches," he blathered.

"Thanks," Ciara said, and let him wrap it around her shoulders before she pulled him into the kitchen, feeling like the night was just getting started.

The Call

Ciara lay with her feet on the back of her futon, her head nearly touching her soft blue carpet. For once, she had nothing to do other than laze about and read her favorite play; her cell phone buzzed from the table like an angry bee. She wiggled and flipped over before pushing herself to her feet. As the blood rushed back to her head, Ciara saw a strange number and quickly exclaimed, "KT!"

"Hey you, got some free time?" He asked, the laughter filtering through the connection, making her smile grow.

"I am completely alone and have nothing to do," she said, reveling in the freedom of it. "It feels so wonderful *to not have something to do*," Ciara emphasized while pushing herself up, excited to talk to one of her oldest friends.

Three years had passed since Ciara had last seen KT in person, which had been the result of an argument with his family. KT had driven for two days to stay with Ciara and Sean for a weekend, but he didn't mind the drive, and it had meant the world to Ciara. And their friendship had saved her in more ways than one, because KT, like Lex, had given her an anchor. They had stuck with her, believed in her, and sent her things like clothes, food, hygiene products, anything at all that she needed when they knew the siblings were struggling. KT's family, though, had never quite understood what Ciara had gone through or even attempted to understand. It wasn't that they were bad people, but KT was a child born late in life and hadn't been planned for. They loved him but didn't understand him or have the energy to keep up with him, but they were strict and had high expectations that KT almost constantly failed to meet. His only out had been joining the military, and after four and a half years of deployments to the Middle East, Ciara was ready for him to come home.

His six years were almost up, and his final deployment should be over soon, and she already had a list of different things she wanted to do over the summer. She had hope that Curry would let her travel to visit him and that KT would come and visit her. She wanted to go to the beach and go hiking, to go to a drive-in movie and eat milkshakes with fries, have bonfires, and simply exist in the same space.

"Been really busy then? Lots of homework and practice?" He questioned her with genuine curiosity, painting his voice.

Ciara stood and walked into the kitchen to pour herself a glass of juice, then pushed herself up onto her counter, swinging her legs back and forth as she answered, "*So* busy. I have two papers due before Thanksgiving, one is my term paper for history class and the other is a paper on western music influences. It has been sucking up all my free time, but I, finally, got ahead and it opened up my Sunday until five. It feels so good and I even took a bath this morning!"

She heard KT's deep laughter crackle over the connection as he joked, "I'm surprised you can fit in a bath tub."

"I'm not *that* tall, jerk," she huffed in response, not bothering to hide the glimpse of a smile on her face.

"No, I guess you're not," he amended, tapping on something as he talked, and Ciara could sense he was thinking as the sound of people moving past him faded in and out. He pressed her for more details, "How are your other classes going? What songs are you singing for your Christmas concert, didn't you say it was going to be a pretty big one?"

Ciara nodded her head vigorously despite the knowledge he couldn't see her as she said, "It's a two-hour long concert, but there is another group singing as well. It's going to be a lot of fun though and I made a couple of friends in choir and I get to sing a solo for the song *Holly and the Ivy*. My other classes are going pretty good too, especially since Jared is still helping me with Biology, I really am not a fan of science, but I'm still doing alright. And Leah and I have writing workshops once a week on whatever night I have time to sleep over or she does because the class is so time consuming. And Ash helps me out with music as do a few of the other guys."

"Wow Pea Pod, that was a lot to take in; you have a very full schedule. How are you staying afloat?" He questioned with a hint of worry in his deep voice.

Ciara laughed lightly and shrugged as she explained, "It is, but if I want to graduate in two years then I need to take them all. Plus, I didn't want to be too far behind the people my age."

"You mean like I am going to be," KT stated, but there was no self-pity in his tone; it was just a statement of fact. "I don't mind so much though and at least it will all be paid for. That was the goal either way, make it so the folks couldn't dictate what I did or how I did it."

She jumped off the counter and began gathering her lunch together. "Yes, but you have good reason. Plus, you knew that would be the case when you signed on."

She imagined the smile in his voice again as he responded, "At least I have that." He began tapping again as more people walked by. With the mouthpiece covered, KT responded to someone and then yelled to someone else, but she couldn't decipher his words.

"So, what can you tell me about things over there?" Ciara asked him hesitantly. She didn't want to press, because it sometimes became uncomfortable when the conversations with KT were so one-sided. Although he never seemed to mind, Ciara didn't like that she couldn't help him share the load when he had always done that for her.

"What can I tell you?" More tapping as he sifted through his thoughts and changed ears for the phone as he hummed in thought before describing his current housing. "Well, we have a really nice gym and work out room and we all need to stay in condition, so I spend every morning there. Then an awesome breakfast-"

"Is it awesome?" She interrupted in disbelief.

"No, not really." He snorted and explained, "All food is on a three-week rotation and after about three months it gets really dull. I've been here for much longer than that, so it's really, *really* dull." KT made a gagging noise. "Anyway, we do drill every day and get to shower about twice a week, and then free time in the evening and early mornings if you get up early enough. I did and that's why I can talk to you more often now."

"And I appreciate that so much! I know how much you enjoy your sleep." Ciara grinned as she spread butter on the back of her bread to make grilled cheese and inquired, "So, do you need anything?"

"Oh, I got your package a couple of weeks ago. Since I got it, I've been using that pillowcase you sent and the guys laughed at first, but then realized I was more comfortable than they were, then they stopped laughing." She heard tapping again as he seemed to contemplate her question. "I'm not certain about you sending anything though, because I'm not sure I would get it on time."

Ciara paused in her sandwich making, with anxiety rising as she pressed, "On time for what, are they sending you guys out again? I know you probably can't answer that." Her eyes narrowed, and she felt fear and frustration rising within her. It felt like he had just gotten back to base after being gone on a mission for several months. She hated when he was out of touch and the fear that he wouldn't ever call her back.

"I have some travels coming up," he hedged, and this time she heard the mischievous tone in his voice.

She decided to play along, hearing the teasing tone in his voice, and lamented, "I see and will these travels take you to far off places?"

"Well, there is a time where I will be gone for a few weeks. But then I will be traveling to a far-off place," he said, leading her on and deciding not to say more than that, as he hoped she would catch his drift. Before she could cover the sound, Ciara squeaked loudly into her phone.

"Are you allowed to tell me where this far off place is?" She questioned, crossing her fingers as she placed cheese on her bread.

"Yes, I can tell you."

Ciara waited for him to continue, but it seemed that he wasn't going to without her continuing to press him. "Well?"

"Well, what?"

KT's laughter echoed down the line and Ciara rolled her deep blue eyes as she pleaded, "Tell me... please?"

"Oh, fine, if you really want to know," he joked, still laughing at her impatience.

"I do, please tell me KT."

He laughed even harder as she jumped up and down and he clarified, "One month and I am coming home, for sure this time Pea Pod. It may be more or less as they tell all of us different things for security, but I will be seeing you soon after I get back in the states."

The tall woman let out a scream of joy and began dancing around the living room and kitchen. "Seriously? Oh my gosh, I can't believe it."

"You better believe it, because it's happening and I want to see you and meet this Ash who is taking up almost all your time and Jez and Leah. All these new friends who are taking such good care of you," KT declared and sighed. "They are still taking good care of you right?"

"Of course they are," Ciara insisted and then blurted, "I can't wait for you to meet them and they will be thrilled to meet you and I've told them all about you. I am so glad you are coming home."

"Me too," he paused as he listened to someone on his end yelling and groaned. "Ahhh man, I got to go, but I will call you when I get more time, sound alright?"

"Sounds perfect," she said and sighed in contentment. "Thanks for calling me and stay safe."

"I will if you are," he said and quickly asked, "No shadow encounters lately?"

"None for a few weeks now," she confirmed as more shouts came from his side of the phone. "You better go, don't want you getting into trouble."

KT chuckled in his easy-going manner as he signed off, "See you soon."

The phone clicked and she danced around until she smelled her grilled cheese burning.

{ 18 }

Invitation

For the next week, the group was on edge with the upcoming finals, recitals, and labs all closing in around them, begging for attention. Until the following semester, all intramurals involving music students were suspended because of the concerts and extra rehearsals that would continue until the break. Ciara was more than okay with that, even though their soccer team was in third place and gunning for second.

Ash had recently begun practicing until the wee hours of the night every single day for his own composition concert the Friday before Thanksgiving. And the boys had their percussion concert directly following, while Jared was busy monitoring his experiment at all hours of the day and night. The music students were nervous and anxious because the selection was harder than in previous years, and a few of the boys had solos.

Ciara's semester, meanwhile, seemed like it was slowly beginning to wind down, even though she realized it was truly the calm before the storm. She had completed her term papers and her short stories for her history and creative writing classes, and a solid part of her presentations was finished or prepped. Then, Ciara was informed that she didn't need to attend classes two days before their break for Thanksgiving began, which gave her even more unexpected time to prepare. All she worried about was finishing up her projects, practicing her vocal pieces, and studying for exams. Instead of fretting about them, she devised a schedule of what to study when and continued joining her friends for their study sessions at the coffee shop when their schedules permitted.

Jez and Leah invited her to come with them to the boys' concert and out for the traditional dessert once it was finished. Linked arm in arm, the girls gathered up their tickets and headed off to watch Ash's songs performed live for the first time with eager anticipation. Ciara had helped him pick out his dress shirt and tie, and she smiled at the effect it had against the whitewashing lights from the stage.

The nervous giant stepped up to the box and began conducting the selected students from the wind ensemble with precise movements. All three girls had listened to bits and pieces of it performed before, but never the entire thing together, and it was mesmerizing. Ciara closed her eyes and let the music carry her away to a place that reminded her of bees buzzing through cherry blossoms and wind rushing through long grass.

Directly following his performance, the stagehands began setting up more chairs and stands for the band while Ash joined the girls with the appearance of a newborn fawn just finding its feet. He sat down with a heavy, relieved sigh as the band began entering the stage to tune their instruments. This performance was rougher than Ash's, but it was still a spectacular performance and, once again, Ciara was impressed with the amount of talent in their group.

When the last song ended and the lights came back on, Leah and Ash stood with a few friends from other classes chatting, while Jez waited eagerly for Nate. With plenty of congratulations and delays from other friends, the group finally congregated in the parking lot to head out for dessert.

In their freshman year, the group began the tradition because no one ever got dessert when they went out to eat, but the desserts always looked so good. After the concert seemed the perfect opportunity because everyone was hungry, but it was too late for dinner. Ciara readily agreed with this wonderful theory and dug into her giant ice cream sundae with a huge brownie at the bottom.

She moaned in exultation as the sugar hit her taste buds and listened to her friends' interpretations of the concert. The parts they believed were done well, the parts they messed up on, and what they heard from others. Ciara commented here and there, but otherwise attempted to devour her sundae before all the ice cream melted. Ash tried to steal a bite, and Ciara fended off the attack before suddenly lunging and spooning up a scoop of his rice pudding. Ash laughed and shoveled out some of her ice cream and brownie.

After a time, the conversation turned to the upcoming holiday and what their plans were. Most of them seemed to be going home to see old friends and their families. Ash glanced at Ciara, who sat across the table, shoving loaded spoons full of ice cream into her mouth. "Are you sticking around here or going to visit Lex?"

"She's visiting family in the south," she explained, licking whipped cream from her spoon. "I was thinking about trying to pick up a shift or two at the bar I worked at last year."

Jez raised a perfectly plucked eyebrow at her and noted, "That doesn't sound like fun to me."

Ash rubbed the stubble turning to beard on his chin before hesitantly stating, "You should come out to my house."

"Go to your house for Thanksgiving?" Ciara asked with shock and surprise at the invitation, her loaded spoon hovering before her mouth.

"Why not, everyone else has somewhere to go," he commented, tapping out a rhythm on the table as he thought it all the way through. "It would possibly become chaotic if my parents want to get in the way, but they usually stick to themselves and leave the rest of us alone."

Ciara ruffled her hair, transitioning through the strange process of going from short to long. "I'm not sure, I mean, it's a great idea and I would love to, but it would be terribly expensive to get a plane ticket on such short notice. And I need to get clothes for my presentations, I just don't know." Ciara grew increasingly nervous at the prospect, something she had never been with KT or Lex.

Ash frowned and cajoled, "I'm sure if I explained it all to my parents they would pay for your ticket. Don't feel bad about it either."

Overwhelmed, Ciara realized there was no reason to continue objecting, and the prospect of spending the holiday alone didn't seem appealing, especially with how everyone else talked about their own plans. "If you're sure, then okay," Ciara said, conceding defeat, before taking a giant bite of brownie. Ash grinned at her, and Jez bumped into Nate with a sly smirk shining brilliantly against his dark complexion and squeezed her leg under the table.

Leah tapped Ciara's hand and said, "Try to find a jewel-colored blue top that goes good as a dress shirt, but also snazzes up jeans and will make your eyes pop."

"Make sure to send me pictures and I can give you advice," Jez requested with a wink.

Ciara laughed at their comments as warmth soaking into her veins. It was still taking her some getting used to having fashionable friends, but she appreciated their advice and felt like she would be lost without them. "I will do my best, but I'm not making any promises."

"Everyone else has a place to be, right?" Tyler questioned, and they all nodded. "Good, no one should be left out on the holidays."

"Don't forget to call Curry," Jez reminded Ciara, who nodded as she dropped a cherry into her mouth and dramatically pulled the stem off with a snap.

>>>

That weekend, Ciara felt scattered and, once again, didn't know what to pack as it had been such a long time since she had gone anywhere on anything resembling a vacation. Plus, she knew enough, from the little Ash said about his family, that they were on the more ostentatious side of wealthy. Ciara didn't quite know what that meant and didn't want to embarrass Ash in front of his family. She packed and repacked a couple of times, worrying about how to dress, and was grateful for the help Jez had given her in updating her wardrobe. Even though he didn't really seem to like his parents all that much, Ciara nevertheless wanted them to respect her. Therefore, she packed her least faded shirts, and only packed one band shirt for sleeping in. Then, she put on her new pair of dark jeans with no rips, along with one of the new tops she had purchased with Jez a few weeks ago.

As she packed for the final time, she dialed Curry's number and greeted him, "Hi Curry, it's Ciara."

"Is everything alright?" He immediately asked, and she heard him set a heavy cup down.

"Yes, everything is fine," she said dismissively at his concern. "I was invited to go out to Ash's for the week, is that alright."

"Let me check that over with my boss and look through a few things, but that should be just fine. I can draw up your flight schedule without a problem and post people throughout the airports and I'll get a squad to take you to and from the airport in town." She waited while he typed something into the computer. "I will make it work, but promise me, you will not go anywhere alone. What are your plans when you are there? Will you be leaving his house at all?"

Ciara frowned and admitted, "I'm not really sure what to expect, but I know I plan on going shopping with his sister one of the days. And I think we might go out to eat, but otherwise I think just sticking around his house." She shrugged and realized how little she had really thought this through. For a moment, she second-guessed her decision to go, but then realized how ridiculous that really was. She of all people understood it didn't really matter where she was; her Shadow could get to her anywhere.

"Do me a favor and don't go anywhere alone," he said for the second time. "And I mean not to a public bathroom, not into a changing room, not even over to a different section of his house alone. Do you understand me? That is my deal, you can go, if you follow those rules." He sounded so serious, but she understood. He wanted her to have a good time and be able to have a real life. But because she was leaving his close jurisdiction on such short notice, he couldn't post guards or keep as much of a watch over her.

"I will," Ciara promised with a nod and said it again, to make sure he understood she was serious, "I promise and thank you."

"Stay safe and watch over yourself."

"I will Curry, have a wonderful holiday," Ciara added.

They hung up, and Ciara looked at the sparse clothes selection in her giant suitcase. She was bringing her big one on the off chance she found a good deal on new clothing, something not from a thrift store. Although she didn't really think there was anything wrong with that, she wanted clothes that were not already preshrunk and that truly fit her well. *Hopefully, we don't go anywhere very nice right away. I have never owned anything that would fit in those places, and my parents didn't really like those restaurants.* She closed her suitcase, still half empty, and left for Ash's room. It was time for her violin lesson and, their Sunday dinner with Mr. Durand was just after, but the aromas were already tantalizing her tastebuds with their mix of sweet and savory.

Ciara's fingers stumbled over the middle stanza time after time, and she stamped her foot impatiently. "I'm sorry, I just can't seem to get it right and I swear I practiced it possibly a hundred times."

"I know you have, I've heard you a few times and I know you had it on Wednesday." Ash smiled at her kindly and said, "I think you just have other things on your mind today, like the smell of that turkey." He licked his lips as he dramatically sniffed the air.

Ciara laughed and took a deep breath of its fragrance. "It smells heavenly and I didn't eat much for lunch, because I wanted to save room for dinner. Do you know I haven't had a real Thanksgiving in years? Last year, Mr. Durand left for the entire week, and I had to work at the bar."

The broad-shouldered young man carefully took the violin from her hands and set it into the case. "Well, this year you get two Thanksgivings!" he enthusiastically stated, and she smiled at him with gratitude written all over her delicately boned face. "We can be done for today and I just expect to hear you playing at my house over break. Let's go over to Mr. Durand's early and see if he needs any help."

Loosening the bow, Ciara agreed, knowing he just wanted to start snitching pieces of the meal. "I just want to know what all he's making. He told me to just bring some salad."

"He only asked me to bring some pumpkin pie," Ash scratched his head and shrugged, not too concerned. "Guess we will find out, let's go."

Quickly, she finished packing up the violin and snatched up the bowl of salad. Ash locked up behind them, and after a quick knock on the older man's door, Mr. Durand admitted them with a big smile spread across his wrinkled face.

"I didn't think it would take me calling you two for dinner. In fact, I'm surprised it took that long for you both to get over here. My turkey and stuffing is why my girls always ask me to come back home for the holiday, of that I'm certain," the old man chuckled in pleasure at his own jest.

Ash and Ciara sniffed the air while putting down their own contributions. "I can imagine they want you home for other reasons as well, but... with these smells, I don't think I would ever let you *leave*." Ciara laughed and placed her salad bowl on the table amidst the other cold dishes and trays of food. She helped herself to a cheese cube and stuck her finger into the hole of an olive before popping it into her mouth.

"Do you need help with anything?" Ash questioned, taking Ciara's lead and snatching up a piece of broccoli and swiping it through the small dish of dressing.

"Oh no," Mr. Durand said, waving them away before opening the oven and basting the turkey, turning it a delicious golden brown. "Sit and play cards, pull out a board game, or just talk."

"How about some Thanksgiving poker?" Ciara suggested, waggling her eyebrows and prompting, "Or Euchre, have either of you ever played that?"

Ash looked up at her with a confused look on his face and a mouth full of crackers and asked, "What?"

Ciara explained, "KT taught it to me, so it may be a Michigan thing, I'll teach it to you."

Ash and Ciara plopped down on the carpet in the middle of Mr. Durand's living room, and he watched her begin to shuffle the cards and explain the rules. Mr. Durand asked a few pointed questions from the kitchen, and as she began to deal the cards, he came in, warm mugs of tea in hand. Their elderly neighbor then sat down and picked up cards in his wrinkled hands, a strategy for the new game already formulating in his mind. They played until the timer went off with a new understanding of the card game as their bellies rumbled.

{ **19** }

The Mansion

Ash and Ciara made it to the airport and through a private gate by noon, and before she knew it, they were boarded and ready for takeoff to New Hampshire. Several hours later, as they exited the airport, Ciara saw a man who, from a distance, looked just like Ash, waving at them with exaggerated enthusiasm. As they got closer, Ciara noted that the two men had both inherited the same broad shoulders and dark brown hair. But the older brother's hair waved slightly, and he kept it longer, and Ash's brother's eyes were a blue-green, instead of the golden-yellow of Ash's.

"You must be Ciara, Ash's told me all about you, but he forgot to mention just how beautiful you are." The man, almost as tall as Ash, took her hand and kissed it; Ciara raised an eyebrow at him, her eyes narrowing dangerously as she pulled her hand away.

Ash placed a protective arm around her shoulders, admonishing. "Calm down the theatrics Brody and I did tell you she was pretty *and* to leave her alone, if I recall."

Ciara noticed the slight blush tinging his cheeks as he said this and wondered how often in the past he had stood up to his older brother. "It's nice to meet you Brody and thank you for picking us up."

"It's not a problem, I know Ash doesn't like it when Mom and Dad send a chauffeur, none of us do. There is nothing like a family greeting anyway. Jenny would have come," Brody added, looking at Ash as he explained, "But she just got in about an hour ago and smelled like she just climbed out of the pool. She wanted a shower and said she would see you when you got in."

Ash nodded in understanding as he said, "Let's not keep Jenny waiting then. She likes to go to bed early sometimes." With his arm still around Ciara's shoulders, he led her to Brody's parked car.

An hour later, they drove slowly up a dirt road, which Ciara belatedly registered was Ash's driveway. The house sat back behind woods and opened onto a well-tended field, complete with an ornate garden and a Victorian-style mansion on the side of a hill.

Ciara's eyes widened as she gasped, "I feel like I was just transported to nineteenth century Victorian England, you grew up here?"

"If by grew up, you mean I tried to escape, then yes," Ash grumbled with a frown at his childhood monstrosity before adding, "It's a bit overdone in my opinion."

"In *all* our opinions," Brody said, laughing good-naturedly. "We hated it here growing up," Brody explained while parking his car on the lawn.

"Mom's gonna be pissed," Ash stated.

"It's why I did it," Brody confessed with a shrug as he opened his door.

The inside of the house was spacious and decorative. To Ciara, it looked more like a museum than a house. Ash looked uncomfortable the moment they stepped out of Brody's car, but from the balcony came a girlish squeak of enthusiasm. By the time the three made it into the entryway, a tall, sandy-haired girl with the same eye color as Brody launched herself into Ash's waiting arms.

"What took you so long; I've been waiting for *hours*," Jenny lamented as Ash set her back on her feet.

Brody chuckled his response, "You've only been here for three hours, Jenny."

"*Hours*, that's still hours," she refuted and laughed in a way that sounded like wind chimes. Then turned to look at Ciara with a sincere smile lighting up her entire face as she said, "Nice to finally meet you in person." She reached out a hand to Ciara, instead of trying to hug her, and Ciara took her hand and squeezed her long, graceful fingers with affection.

"It is," Ciara honestly responded in return before warmly smiling back. "You are much bigger in real life, a girl my size is quite refreshing."

Jenny laughed again in her chiming way. "I like you, you're a keeper," she proclaimed with a wink at Ciara. "Do you guys want food? I just ordered a couple of pizzas."

Ash vigorously nodded, and Brody mimicked him as he patted his stomach, while Ciara said, "I feel half starved."

"Good thing I got more than one then," Jenny chortled and waved her hand beckoningly. "Come on up to our floor, the maid will get your bag. You're going to be staying in my room; it's much more comfortable than the guest room, I promise."

"Thank you," Ciara said, while attempting to look around and take in her new environment. "What I really need is a bathroom, it was a long trip."

"This way," Ash said, tilting his head in the direction of another side hall. As Jenny and Brody walked towards the stairs, Ciara mouthed to Ash, *whole floor?* Ash nodded with a slight blush.

Ciara followed him with an overfilled bladder, gratefully saying, "Thank you so much."

"You should have told me you needed to go so badly," he admonished, steering her gently down a hallway. "Right in there."

Ciara scampered in and froze when she saw the gold-embroidered hand towels, ornately carved burnished bronze sink, gold-framed and silver-backed mirror with an intricate design, and the marble flooring. Looking at the displayed wealth, she carefully sat on the toilet to relieve herself, feeling almost as if she were desecrating the place. After coming out of the bathroom, she asked Ash the question that had been bothering her, "Where are your parents?"

"No idea," Ash murmured and shrugged in an uncaring gesture, but she saw through the hidden pain at their absence. "Probably in their own studies on their floor and you probably won't see them until dinner tomorrow."

Ciara frowned with a deep sense of sympathy the lonely childhood he obviously had lived. Her parents could get wrapped up in their research and they always had conferences to attend, but they made sure to spend time with her and Sean. They went on wonderful vacations together, and during every summer they would spend a week over on the west coast of Ireland visiting their grandmother. It was Ciara's favorite place on earth, and her soul seemed to crave it after being absent for so long from her ancestral home. Ciara pulled herself back to the present and questioned, "Can you show me around?"

"Sure," Ash said and glanced around as if he weren't quite certain what to show her. "Alright, there isn't much down here. An overdone living room only used for parties, a large study with books that never get read, the kitchen, and the dining room that only my siblings and I use. The second floor is ours and the third floor is my parents," Ash explained and took her on a little tour of his parent's giant house. Ciara was astounded at the magnanimity of it and how useless it all appeared.

"Do they have parties often?" Ciara asked as he opened the door to the ballroom, and she stared at the giant chandeliers, stage, and beautiful wood floor.

"Three or four times a year. New Year and the 4th of July are the big ones. Then usually Memorial Day or Labor Day, sometimes both. Cheers to high society," Ash said with dripping sarcasm as he closed the door more forcefully than required. "Over here is the study, looks more like a miniature library, but don't get too excited."

Ciara froze with a half-excited expression on her face as she inquired, "Why not?"

"These books are never read and are all for show." He pushed the door open to reveal a large living area surrounded by floor to ceiling bookshelves and two bay windows. As he read, "Insect encyclopedias or the whole *Encyclopedia Britannica* or *The Readers Digest*. None of these have any real use and my parents each have four bookshelves in their private studies and then we each have our own in our rooms too."

She looked disappointedly around her at the wasted space and mused, "We had a little library in my house growing up and I would hide in their whenever I was upset."

"This house doesn't really have a place like that," he trailed off as he walked to the door and waited for her to exit before softly closing it behind them. "Down that way is the formal living room and dining room and the kitchen and through there is the game room and pool. Can I show those to you later?"

"We can go upstairs, if you want," Ciara said and impulsively rubbed his arm, receiving a small smile in response. He reached over and gave her hand a light squeeze before quickly letting go.

They climbed the grand staircase, and Ash opened a few more doors on the way to his bedroom to show her a second game room, a theater, and a large study. "The rest down that way are guest rooms, but Jenny volunteered her room though. I think she is really excited about it."

Ciara nodded and admitted, "I'm looking forward to it."

"My room is here," he explained, pushing open his door and leading her inside. It was covered in music posters and other instruments that he hadn't brought with him to school sat on the dresser. There were pictures of some of his old friends and a few swimming medals from high school, but his green walls were plain other than that. And she guessed it was to help furnish his apartment, but his personal living room had a bookshelf full of science fiction novels, music biographies, and old schoolbooks. A few gaming systems sat hooked up to his flatscreen television and a shelf full of different kinds of movies. Linked to his room was a personal bathroom with a large bathtub and shower. Ciara wondered if she had stepped into some alternate reality, as the vastness of it all was so out of sync with whom she knew Ash to be.

Ciara found out that each sibling's room was set up in a similar fashion. Brody invited them into his typical male room with a grin. Posters of his favorite basketball team lined almost every inch of his walls, making it impossible to tell the color underneath. A giant bookshelf filled with medical books and video games, movies, and basketball trophies stood in a corner.

Ash pulled her out of his older brother's room to take her to Jenny's so she could unpack and get settled. In complete contrast to the boys, Jenny's walls were a deep lavender, with framed photographs of high school friends and paintings of different places she had visited in high school. Her walls were lined with books from all genres, and musical instruments sat in every spare nook, and her room also had more comfortable places to sit. Now Ciara understood why Jenny insisted on Ciara staying in her room, instead of one of the guest rooms.

Brody and Jenny seemed to genuinely like Ciara, and she was amazed at how much she enjoyed being in their company. It seemed like Ciara had known them her whole life, and they stayed up laughing and talking until late in the evening, eating pizza and popcorn with movies playing in the background. She scooted closer to Ash without thinking much about it and snuggled under the blanket spread across his long legs on the couch.

Surprised by her action, Ash smiled down at her. "Cold?" Ciara nodded, blinking heavily, and stuck her cold toes on his ankle. Ash yelped and, carefully, so she could see his action, he wrapped his arm around her shoulders. With her ocean-blue eyes, Ciara looked up at him and smiled. His arm felt good around her. Within minutes, Ciara was sound asleep.

>>>

Jenny sat grinning at Ash once she was confident the older girl was unconscious and stated, "I like her, can we keep her?"

"The better question is: Ash, will *you* keep her?" Brody asked with a smile at his younger brother.

"She isn't a toy," Ash protested as a blush coloring his cheeks at the turn the conversation had taken.

Brody rolled his eyes and probed, "I will be more direct: are you going to date her?"

Ash's face was a deep red now, and his throat constricted as he tried to find a way out of the conversation. He had only dated a girl before and it had ended very badly. Girls had always been a mystery to him, and that experience only cemented that for him. He spluttered, "What? N-Ye-I don't know, maybe."

"I think he's speechless," Jenny crowed, her smile widening into a Cheshire grin. "I will make it even easier for you: do you like her?"

Sighing, Ash knew they would keep at this until he admitted it to them. When Brody and Jenny teamed up, there was no end in sight. Ash let out another sound of frustration. "Yes, I do, but it isn't that simple."

"But, my dear little brother, it *is* that simple. You like her, so do something about it."

He squeezed Ciara's shoulder slightly and mumbled, "It really isn't though. First, I think she might like another guy, someone she has known for a lot longer. Second, she has been through hell and is still trying to crawl back out and she has too much on her plate already and I don't want to complicate things."

Jenny thought about that for a moment and then shook her head and asked, "Who is this other guy? I mean has she talked about him tonight at all?"

Ash nodded with a slight frown and said, "KT."

"Oh, him," Jenny murmured and laughed quietly as she explained, "She doesn't like him. She talks like he's a brother." Jenny shrugged and then said matter-of-factly.

Ash narrowed his eyes at her with confusion plain in the golden irises as he pressed, "How do you know that?"

"Because of the way she talked about him. She didn't hover over his name or insert it randomly into sentences, there was no love or adoration in her eyes when she talked about him." Jenny grinned and tried not to laugh at the look on both her brothers' faces. "You two keep looking at each other though and find reasons to be near. She likes you; you shouldn't complicate things by not saying something."

"You don't really get the situation though," Ash stated with a heavy frown.

Brody rolled his eyes and groaned, "Then explain it to us so we *can* understand."

Sighing, Ash looked between the two and then down at Ciara and murmured, "I wish I could, but I can't. It's not my story to tell and I won't break her confidence; she would never forgive me."

{ 20 }

Siblings

The following night was extremely awkward, and Ciara had experienced a lot of awkward in her life. Such as new friend's parents asking what her parents did, explaining where she lived, or why she asked her brother for permission, the list went on, but this made the top.

Jenny and Ciara were almost late for dinner after an afternoon of riding horses around the extensive property, while the two brothers played a few rounds of basketball. It resulted in all four needing to shower before dinner, and Ciara and Jenny ran in right as food was being served. Their parents sat with looks of refined annoyance on their faces.

It all just seemed too grand to Ciara as she wore borrowed finery from Jenny. Finery that she couldn't wear quite right as it was just a bit too snug around her chest and her pants were a bit too loose in the waist. Ash's parents greeted her with firm, unwelcoming handshakes, and their eyes seemed to coldly appraise her net worth. They didn't ask why she was with them or where her own family was, nor did they seem to notice she wore their daughters' clothing. They didn't question about the trip, her major in school, how Ash and knew her, or where she was from.

Instead, they calmly, with barely a hint of emotion, questioned their children about what their semester held academically and what they were learning. The parents seemed most interested in what Brody was pursuing because of his career choice, unlike their other children's career choices of music education and music composition.

In her imposter clothes, Ciara let her attention drift from the conversation and looked at the paintings on the wall, which all seemed to match each other. Framed in the finest oak, the mock artists tried to replicate the greats, but Ciara noticed in some areas they hadn't done a great job, but she doubted Ash's parents knew that. Ciara locked eyes with Ash sitting across the table from her. He shrugged, and Ciara frowned at him. He stuck his tongue out, and she squeezed one eye shut and made a fish face. In return, he pretended to pick his nose and eat it. The meal continued in that fashion, and time started passing faster. Finally, it ended when the parents stood and said good night in the most un-empathetic voices Ciara had ever heard from parental figures.

Jenny flicked a pea at Brody the moment they left the room, and once out of hearing distance, she slammed her feet up onto the table and lamented, "Thank God that's over."

Ash sighed in relief and stared at Ciara and explained, "We won't see them again until possibly Thursday and then probably not until Saturday for our 'farewell' dinner. I apologize for that awkwardness."

"So," Brody said, dragging out the word as he sent a pea sailing across the table at Jenny and asked, "Who's up for a night hot tub and swim?"

Immediately, Jenny threw up her hand, and Ash raised an inquiring eyebrow at Ciara, who wondered, "I can just wear my clothes, if I can borrow a pair of shorts."

"I have bathing suits." Jenny grinned at her. "I have the perfect one too." When Ciara looked back at Ash, Jenny winked at him dramatically.

He ignored his sister and nodded to Ciara. "Let's go then."

Ciara was not prepared for what Jenny called 'the perfect one.' Ciara had never worn a bikini, but none of Jenny's one-pieces fit without giving her a wedgie as she stood about two inches taller than the younger girl. That gave her no option but to wear the bikini Jenny had originally presented her with. To make matters worse, the suit Jenny claimed would fit her perfectly was a extremely snug on top.

"I can't go out in this," fretted Ciara as she wrapped her long arms over her chest and flat stomach. "I'm falling out and naked."

Jenny laughed and ordered, "Come over here and let me see... here's the problem." She reached over and pulled the scrunchie to give her chest more space and then went around back and retied the strings to hold her up better. "See? It fits just fine and think about it this way, guys can wander around in boxers and rearrange themselves and it's forgiven by society most of the time. They can pee in public and stroll around shirtless, but girls always have to be completely clothed and if we tell someone we enjoy peeing outside it's like we're an alien.

However, some genius invented a bikini, basically underwear for swimming, and it became acceptable. Embrace it, because it's the only true clothing freedom you will ever get and not be called a slut or skank for it, at least not all the time."

Thinking about Jenny's words, Ciara began to think about what she was wearing differently. Before, she always thought about it as basically wearing underwear and believed it to be inappropriate. In the light Jenny explained it, so was what guys wore. Especially competitive male swimmers, where they might as well be wearing whitie tighties in the pool. Swim jammers were like tight boxers, and board shorts were like loose boxers. Ciara set her head straighter on her shoulders and stopped trying to hide herself as she declared, "You're right, let's go."

With a grin, Jenny gave her approval, "That's more like it. We have towels down there so you might want to bring a cover up for the walk down because it's on the other side of the house." Ciara snatched up a hoodie and pulled it over herself.

The pool room had steam hovering over the hot tub, where a waterfall crashed down from rocks set to replicate a hot spring with a stone slide on one side. Ciara glanced up and realized the pool could be opened to the backyard in the summer, and among the rafters hung beautiful tropical plants with colorful blossoms dotting the greenery. Ash and Brody waved at them from the hot tub, appearing as if they had been waiting for ages. But Ciara knew they had left only minutes before them and had heard their feet chasing each other down the stairs.

"It feels wonderful," Ash called over, "Hurry up."

Ciara and Jenny pulled their baggy hoodies off and scampered over, jumping in with a splash and popping back up with a sigh. Ciara swam over and ran her hand through the waterfall as she said in wonder, "It does feel wonderful and this is so pretty."

Ash's eyes were wide as he looked at her in amazement before forcing himself to choke out, "Uh-huh."

Coughing to loosen his constricted throat, Ash shook his head and said to Ciara, "I'm surprised you agreed to that."

With a smile at Jenny, Ciara stated, "If guys can walk around barely clothed, then so can I."

The boys laughed, and Brody began a water fight as Ciara ran over to the stone slide with Jenny following. Then, Jenny wrapped her arms around the other girl's waist, before careening down it, gathering speed with the double weight, and screamed as they entered the colder water. Pulling herself out of the water, Ciara ran back around. This time, Ash was also running for the stairs, but he waved her ahead. Laughing, Ciara took his hand and pulled him up behind her before shoving off back down the slide. The wind threw Ciara's wet hair back as they rocketed into the water, and with a splutter, rose back up to the surface. Ash easily picked her up and tossed her into the water, further from the edge.

A few hours later, the four lounged in the hot tub, and Brody peered over at Ciara and, without preamble, asked, "Where's your family?"

Ciara looked over at him and then at Ash with slight surprise and questioned, "You didn't tell them?"

"Of course not," Ash said, shocked that she thought he would. "You never said I could."

"Well, you could have at least told them they died," her voice trailed off, and she looked back at Brody and Jenny. With a heavy sigh, she explained, "My parents died when I was fourteen. My only other family lives in Ireland, but I have no way of getting into contact with them or getting there and my brother passed away a year and a half ago."

"I'm sorry, I had no idea," Brody said with embarrassment that he had asked so callously.

"It's alright," Ciara murmured with a shrug before adding to Ash, "I do appreciate you not saying anything without asking me first Ash."

He gave her a soft smile and reminded, "Didn't you say wanted to go shopping at some point."

She spewed water out of her mouth like a fountain and nodded as she elaborated, "It has to be a slightly cheap place, but I need dressy clothes for my presentations."

"I can get you something nicer for your birthday," he offered, realizing it was the only way he would get her to agree to him spending money on her.

Ciara blushed, and Jenny cut her off before she could say anything and gleefully exclaimed, "I heard birthday and shopping." She tossed her hair, darkened from the water over her head in a sheet of sparkling water as she asked, "When is it your birthday?"

"December ninth and I need clothes for a presentation," Ciara explained.

Jenny shook her head and demurred, "Oh no honey, we can do way better than that."

Raising an eyebrow, Ciara felt as though the hand of God was about to rearrange her life with the ecstatic and determined look covering Jenny's face. Nervously, Ciara inquired, "We can?"

"For your birthday, sweetie, I'm going to give you an entire wardrobe makeover." Jenny proclaimed before glancing over at Ash. "And I guess he can help, Ash, can I borrow some money?"

Ash snorted at his little sister's question and shook his head at her ridiculous question, but played along as he said, "Of course."

Ciara chuckled, enjoying the resemblance she was picking up between Jez and Jenny, and verbally admitted, "This will be interesting. When did you want to go?"

"Black Friday is the best time," Jenny said and saw her face blanch. Hurriedly, she insisted, "It isn't that bad, I swear. There may be a lot of people, but I know how to get around."

Ciara and Ash traded a look because he understood the deal Curry had made with her and bit his lip. Ciara swallowed hard, debating what exactly to tell them and how. "So, that's not the problem." She glanced at Ash and asked, "Should I tell them?"

"It's up to you," he said, deferring to her wishes as he moved to stand under the waterfall.

"I can't go out and about in public very easily, you see I made this deal with my guardian? He kind of is anyway, his name is Curry and, for my safety, I was allowed to come here for the week with the understanding that I wouldn't go anywhere alone."

Jenny frowned in confusion, and Brody's eyebrows were knit together as he tried to understand. She said haltingly, "Well, we would be in the store with you."

"If you are going to tell them, then do it right," Ash said and added, "Otherwise, it makes no sense, and they should know why you will be jumping at shadows."

Ciara snorted at the pun and clarified, "One shadow, my Shadow. When I said my parents died, I mean they were murdered and the same person then murdered my brother. That's when the government, finally, caught on and they have this guy Curry as my personal protector now. Normally, I have guards all around me and what not, but obviously this isn't where I normally am, but they couldn't come with me without alerting the man following me."

Jenny and Brody didn't speak for a moment, and Ciara gave them the time to process her information. Finally, Jenny spoke, "We will all stay right by you the entire time. It may take longer, but it will be okay."

Ciara blushed as she murmured, "It extends to changing rooms, bathrooms, and dark hallways."

"We will be right there," Jenny promised, nodded, and then laughed. "Well, I will be there for the changing rooms, the boys can stay outside for that."

Brody punched the water and huffed, "Damn, we were this close Ash." He pinched his fingers together.

Ash rolled his eyes at his brother, knowing he meant getting out of Black Friday shopping *and* being a voyeur to Ciara's wardrobe changes.

Black Friday

Over the next few days, the college students amused themselves by playing on the jungle gym in the backyard, which was really like a giant challenge course. Then horseback riding through their private forest, and hanging out by the bonfire until the smoke sank into their skin and hair. To cap off the night, they would play in the heated pool and steaming hot tub before falling asleep, usually all together, in Jenny's room on the various chairs and sofas.

Thanksgiving passed with another tiring meal in the company of the parents. The meal was laid out like a giant feast across the long table meant to hold upwards of twenty people and not their modest group of six. Ciara had smelled the cooking and had heard the chef making it since early in the morning, but to see all that they had concocted was incredible. There were turkey and ham, four different types of potato dishes, and two types of salad. Every type of cooked vegetable she could think of, several baskets of bread, three types of butter, and every kind of dressing were spread out along the table. After dinner came the desserts, brought out on two trolleys and served with coffee and a nightcap. Ciara was impressed with the chefs and their staff, but couldn't help but wonder what became of all the leftovers.

After Ash's parents left, Ciara asked about the remaining food and was reassured that the staff would wrap up some leftovers for them to eat, but the rest would go to their families. Grateful that it wouldn't all go to waste, Ciara tucked herself into the covers of her pull-out bed in Jenny's room early, understanding she would be awakened in a few hours.

Jenny woke them up at four AM, and they tumbled out of bed and off the futon and sofa, dressing quickly at Jenny's urging. A few minutes later, the four skipped down the steps to the kitchen, speedily inhaling cereal and pouring coffee into thermoses with the promise of a meal later that morning. Ciara narrowed her eyes at Jenny, promising herself that she would get that promised meal no matter what.

Brody drove them to the mall, half an hour away, and Ciara was amazed to see the parking lot already had hundreds of cars in it. She checked her phone for the time and groaned, wanting no part of interacting with the rest of humanity yet. But the way Jenny looked like she was preparing for battle, it didn't seem like she was going to have much choice in the matter.

"People actually shop this early?" Ciara asked in surprise, interrupting herself with a yawn. "Why would they do such a thing?"

Jenny chuckled and explained, "Just on Black Friday because of the sales. Almost everything is on sale today and the deals change depending on the hour." They piled out of the car as Jenny dragged them off to the first store on her list.

In no time at all, they were fighting their way through the crowds to get one thing or another and then standing in line to try things on. Ciara and Jenny dressed the boys up in a multitude of winter apparel. And then, with Jenny's help, Ciara was outfitted in a whole new wardrobe of dresses, blouses, blazers, jeans, socks, underwear, bras, tights, skirts, sweaters, and shirts. The only thing they let Ciara buy was a winter coat and matching scarf, while the rest, the three claimed, were her birthday presents. Overwhelmed by their generosity, she took them out to breakfast before they headed back into the war zone of Black Friday shoppers.

They elbowed and pushed through the people from all walks of life: mothers, grandmothers, teenagers, and college students, along with dads, middle-aged men, and a few businessmen. As the morning wore on, the crowds began to disperse a little, but now it was people looking for specific deals fighting like vultures squawking over their prized find.

Loaded with packages and parcels, they finally gave up, having found gifts for almost all their friends. Ash's stomach growled, and Brody was yawning again. Jenny sent them to the back seat and took Brody's keys as she said, "Let's stop at Guild for food and take it back to the house. We can eat and then relax in the hot tub before we try everything on again to make sure it looks alright in normal lighting."

Ciara blinked heavily and admitted, "I'll feel much better once I have food in my stomach. I never knew shopping could be so dangerous."

"Every year it's like that, but some of those deals are completely worth it," Jenny explained. Proudly, she held up the bag containing almost five hundred dollars' worth of undergarments that she only spent one hundred and fifty dollars on. "My parents might be willing to spend four hundred dollars on one outfit or a pair of shoes, but I'm not. Never in a million years will I make that much on a teacher's salary." She laughed and ran her fingers through her sandy hair and said, "That's why I took a personal finance my first year in college."

Ciara leaned her head back. "Very smart and Thank you, Jenny. I appreciate your help and Brody and Ash too."

"It's not a problem, it fun and I don't get the chance to do things like this very often." Jenny patted Ciara's knee as she sped out of town and grumbled, "I do have two brothers after all."

>>>

"I really like that one," Jenny commented on Ciara's presentation outfit. She wore a cotton wine red knee length dress with knee-high black leather boots, and the dress had a black belt around her middle to accentuate her waist.

Ciara put her hands in the pockets and smiled as she said in wonder, "It's very comfy; I didn't know dress up clothes could be so *comfy.*"

Jenny laughed at that and ordered, "Go try on those jeans and that teal blousy-shirt."

The other girl obeyed and came back out with the one request Leah had given her for shopping. While she loved her band T-shirts and her baggy jeans, there was something about dressing to impress that gave her a confidence boost she hadn't expected. It also didn't hurt that Ash's eyes had widened, and he had issued a tiny gasp of shock when she came out in one of her new outfits. She definitely enjoyed that and looked forward to getting to do that several more times to him. Ciara felt like she finally understood what Lex and Jez had been talking about when they said clothes had power.

The rest of their time over vacation was spent in movie marathons and studying, that all four had put it off for far too long. Ciara practiced her music and her solo with Ash and Jenny's help. Brody listened as he studied for his own medical exams. Jenny shifted through her lesson plans and drew up new ones while practicing her flute and her scales, while Ash practiced by conducting Jenny's lesson pieces and Ciara's songs for them. When they all became to brain-dead from studying, they would relax in the hot tub or go for walks in the woods by horseback or on foot. It was nice and relaxing, and despite the cold atmosphere of the mansion, Ciara felt comfortable and at ease.

By Saturday night, after another awkward meal with Ash's parents, she was feeling ready to go back to her own apartment. They crashed in Jenny's room for one final movie after dinner and said goodbye to Jenny at breakfast the next morning, promising to stay in touch.

Ciara and Ash climbed upstairs to tackle the chore of trying to fit all her shopping and friends' presents into her suitcases. Then, with Brody, they strolled down to lunch, and a maid brought their luggage and placed it in Brody's car. Once finished eating, he drove them the hour to the airport. Again, Ciara and Brody exchanged numbers, and she gave him a hug.

A few hours later, they landed during a rainstorm, and Ciara donned her new coat before rushing through the puddles to the car waiting for them with her guards. They drove the two back to the apartment and with a wave at the Chucks who had picked them up, Ash and Ciara climbed up the stairs to their rooms.

"Thank you for taking me," Ciara said as she unlocked her blue door and added, "I had a really great time Ash."

Ash smiled at her, admitting, "I'm glad you decided to come; you made it a lot better."

Ciara dragged her bag inside and asked, "We're still going to Mr. Durand's, right?" She questioned, hovering just inside her doorway. "I'm up for a game of Bridge and there's a hockey game on tonight."

Laughing, Ash got his door opened and pushed his bag inside and emphatically stated, "Of course, I wouldn't miss a dinner with him."

Her apartment was just as she had left it the week before, except for one small thing. A slip of paper sat on her table, covered with a scratchy scrawl she didn't recognize. With shaking hands, Ciara picked it up and read:

> *You think you're safe with all these guards?*
> *You're not. I am the shadow*
> *of the night – always hunting. I am the*
> *Eyes of the Dark – always watching.*
> *Anytime I want, I will catch you. I*
> *know your name for me, just as I know*
> *your little friends are trying so hard*
> *to keep you safe. I have evaded*
> *Curry for years, your friends are like*
> *cobwebs compared with that. I can*

> *brush them aside anytime I choose.*
>
> *Try harder —*
>
> *Shadow*

Ciara sank to the floor, unable to think or move for a moment, unsure what to do, but she did realize one thing: her Shadow left the note when she wasn't home. When the security had been less because of her absence. *Maybe he is bluffing and just wants me to be scared,* Ciara thought and forced herself to stand up. *I'll send the note to Curry and not tell my friends. It would only worry them, and there is no sense in doing that.*

Quickly she wrote a letter to Curry and dropped the Shadow's note in. She sealed it up and handed it to the guard on her balcony before she began to unpack and carefully cut the tags on all her new clothes. She was unwilling to let the note bother her and ruin what had been an almost perfect vacation. For years, she let The Shadow rule her life with fear, but no longer. As she continued putting her things away, Ciara began to devise a plan in her head and determined she would carry it out, with or without the help of the others.

No longer will he control my life, because it is my life and I want it back, she fumed as she shoved her now empty bag under her bed.

{ 22 }

First Snowfall

December brought a hectic schedule for everyone, and there wasn't much time for Ciara to discuss the plan she had been creating with anyone, nor was she ready to. She wanted her life back, but not at the expense of it, and she knew that it would take a while to work everyone else around to her way of thinking. When she brought it up, she knew that it would need to be done under the right circumstances.

Everyone observed a change in her besides her wardrobe, and when the group asked Ash, he said he thought something had happened, but he didn't know what it was. When her friends asked her, Ciara would find ways to change the subject to something else, and eventually, they gave up asking. The rest of December was spent in hard study and, for Ciara and the other music students, in long rehearsals for the choir concert and private music lessons.

Ciara trudged with Ash up the stairs, bleary-eyed from the four-hour long choir rehearsal. Her foot caught the ledge, and Ash caught her with a muscular arm around her waist, prompting her, "Keep your eyes open just a few minutes longer, Cia."

She rubbed her eyes and groaned, "But I'm so tired, why did you agree to wait for me?" She couldn't quite understand how the choir was supposed to sound good when the director seemed hell-bent on making them all brain-dead and mute. Not only did they have the extra practice from nine to midnight every day this week, but he also had kept them an additional hour of their normal practice time.

Tucking her arm into his, he started walking again, enjoying the sensation of her leaning against him. He reminded, "I don't have to be up early tomorrow."

"You suck," Ciara murmured as they finally made it to their landing and Ash opened the door.

"I know, I'm the worst," he conceded with a smile down at her as he released her arm move to her apartment door.

Ciara turned and hugged him impulsively and murmured, "Thanks Ash, get some good sleep and I'll see you tomorrow for lunch at the cafeteria?"

He hugged her back and said, "I'll be there, the week from hell is almost over."

Ciara stumbled through the rest of the week in a fog, but as she stood with her choir and Ciara sang her mezzo-soprano solo beautifully. It was then that she realized the torture of the previous week was worth it. When she left to meet her friends in the entrance hall, Jez greeted her with a stunning bouquet signed by her and Leah, while Ash handed her a thermos of Throat Coat tea. Sighing, she gripped the thermos and took a long drink before croaking out a grateful, "Thank you." She smelled the fragrant flowers and hugged her friends, beside herself at how it felt to have them all there for her. She blinked a few times to keep the tears firmly in her head.

"You did an absolutely beautiful job," Leah praised, gripping her hand. "I wish I could sing like that; it took my breath away."

"You soared right over that part you were having trouble hitting," Ash commented as he helped her into her coat without even thinking.

"Hey, nice job," Nate called as he came into view. "You're coming back to our place for gingerbread cookies, right? Then Ash can take you home because you look like you could use some sleep."

Ciara looked at Ash, and he shrugged as she agreed, "Sounds like a good idea. I'm exhausted, but I still have three presentations this week and then all my exams the following week." She frowned and shook her head, trying to figure out how she had gone from being so on top of things to slowly sinking into a peat bog. "And now I have a frog in my throat."

Nate laughed at the croaking young woman and promised, "I have something that can fix that, homemade recipe."

"Not by you I hope," Ash said with a snort.

"Of course not," Nate clarified and chuckled good-naturedly as he led them to their cars and dodged the people filing out of the music department. "It's my mom's recipe, you know she's an herbalist."

Ash pondered that for a moment and murmured, "I think you made that for me a few years ago." Ash's voice trailed off as he tried to remember and finally just shrugged and joined the group walking out to their cars.

Even though Ciara desperately needed sleep, just like all her friends, she was up early the next morning, wistfully remembering how, just before Thanksgiving, she had been ahead of the curve. Now she felt miles behind everyone else, and the night of sleep only made her more panicked than the night before.

Ciara spent every spare hour reviewing her notes and flipping through flashcards, and studied while sorting through stacks of books being returned by students finished for the semester. Ash, who was almost done, would bring her coffee, tea, and snacks every chance he got, feeling terrible she still had so much to do, along with losing her voice right after the concert.

By the end of the week, her voice came back, and with her presentations done, Ciara could finally breathe. That weekend the group sat in the warm study room of the library with a window looking out on the school's biggest courtyard. The snow had begun in little tufts a few hours ago, but their attention had all been reserved for their final papers and exams left. Ciara was almost done going through the last section of her notes when Jared looked up from his overly highlighted notes and the view outside was obscured by the heavy snow.

"Look!" the scientist exclaimed, pointing at the view with a pen.

With a squeak of glee, Leah clapped her hands and began shuffling her papers together as Ciara watched her with confusion. It was a very out of character response for her quiet friend.

"I knew there was a reason I dressed in jeans and boots today," Jez squealed as she also began stacking her books up and pushed her braided hair over a shoulder. She tugged a large hair tie from her wrist and wrapped it around her braids, excitement flooding her face.

Nate beamed and ordered, "Give it another hour, no one will be out there just yet." He tapped the page in front of him impatiently.

"I've been carrying around extra gloves and hats since December 1st," Jared admitted with a laugh as he leaned back in his chair. "If anyone needs some just let me know."

Tyler chuckled at his boyfriend and closed his book, declaring, "That's the reason we keep you around, the only reason, I might add." Jared rolled his eyes at him and let his chair slam to the ground.

"What is everyone talking about?" Ciara questioned, looking slowly over to Ash as she set her book down.

He looked up from a packet of papers and explained in a slightly backwards way, "Campus tradition, it's incredibly dangerous and there are usually a few students who end up with concussions. Last year, someone broke a leg, but it's a ton of fun. Campus wide snowball fight every year on the first true snow fall, I sometimes forget this is your first year."

"Even alumni in the area come back for it sometimes, it's that epic," Tyler pronounced as he gazed out of the window dreamily. "I can't study anymore, come on, let's pack up and get ready."

"I see people out there," Jared commented with his eyes trained on the window as his hands packed up his belongings.

As quickly as they could, the group packed up and headed for the courtyard, leaving their bags locked in Ciara's study.

Snow powdered the ground in a wet coating. Already it was about three inches in depth, and other students tossed the sodden balls into the melee forming out of the flurries. Jared ran in with a war cry, flinging a ball of hard-packed snow as he went.

Scooping some up in a gloved hand, Ciara packed the snow and tossed it at a boy charging her. With a gleeful laugh, her group swarmed in. Ciara had been part of snowball fights before, but nothing like this.

Hundreds of exam-weary students flooded the courtyard, rejuvenated by the excitement and cold air. Their excitement and energy was primal as they created minute truces, only to be broken when their original group became reunited. White balls flew out of soaked hands to smack into faces, and Ciara ducked and dodged as she flung them back at her attackers. Now and then she recognized people from her classes and waved, but no one was safe; even Ash tackled her into a fluffy patch of snow, and she gave him a whitewash in return. Leah and Jez teamed up against her, but then turned on each other with wicked grins.

It wasn't long before she lost sight of everyone in her group. Unconcerned, she stuck it out in the middle of the crowd and watched as a girl lost her footing, hitting her head against the cement. About to run and help the girl, she saw a couple of others come running in, and they picked her up and helped her limp away into a building.

The fury of the snowfall began to subside and vision became clearer as the snow war dragged on. Ciara threw ball after ball, ducked behind frozen bushes and snow piles, lobbing and successfully hitting someone on the shoulder. Ciara glanced around for some of her friends but couldn't see them anywhere amidst the chaos. And when she stopped to think about it, could remember how long it had been since she had actually seen any of them.

Careful not to slip, the tall woman made her way back out of the center of the fray to look for them. As Ciara balled more snow, she was pegged in the head, and it dripped in cold rivulets down between her shoulder blades. She screeched and turned, ready to fight off the person aiming at her. She was greeted by a face covered in a black mask, eyes glowing with a triumphant glint.

"Time to come with me," he growled and hit her hard at the base of her skull, and Ciara fell into darkness.

{ 23 }

Taken

Ash lost sight of Ciara about half an hour into the fight, and in the process of dodging and ducking all the whirling snowballs, it wasn't quite a surprise. As minutes passed with him still searching for her and not seeing head nor tail of Ciara though, Ash began to grow worried. His other friends were still in the vicinity, but they weren't in danger of being kidnapped or killed almost every second of their lives.

Stepping out of the way of a hard-packed ball of wet fluff, Ash tossed one back at the assailant. Ash craned his neck, trying to catch sight of her, but there were too many people milling about. A snowball splattered into his face for the second time that night, and he wiped the cold liquid off with a frown this time, instead of laughing and launching back into the fight. He splattered one back into the person's face and dodged another. Unfortunately, Ash was a big target, and he got hit one more time before making it to Nate and Jared.

"I can't find Ciara," he yelled over the screaming and yelling of the hundreds of students.

Immediately, the two young men stopped their war with three others. "You can't find her?" Jared questioned loudly.

"Where could she have gone?" Nate asked at the same moment.

Ash shook his brown head with worry painted clearly across his face as he fretted, "I saw her go that way and then she disappeared. I don't like this, will you help me find her?"

"Of course," they both said immediately.

"We should have been watching her closer," Nate added.

Soon the rest of the group spread out to search for her, checking their cell phones constantly, hoping for a message from her or one of the others saying they had found her.

It was Jared who finally did, but his message wasn't good:

"S.O.S. Science Building, Shadow."

The moment they received his text, the boys flooded into the science building, with Jez and Leah close behind. Ash was the first one there, and they saw him waving them down a dimly lit hallway and saw Jared further down the hall, pointing the way.

Nate turned to Jez and demanded, "Stay here."

"Hell no!" she argued and stomped a booted foot. "She is my friend too."

"Please, stay here," Tyler tried again, looking more to Leah than Jez, because Jez was made of a bit firmer stuff than Leah, who he always thought of as a fragile doll.

Leah smiled sweetly at him, kissed his cheek, and ran after Ash and Jared. The boys groaned in frustration and followed after her. After a few minutes of following freshly melted snow down the twisting corridors of the science building, they heard a strangled scream.

Ciara fought like an angry wildcat despite her tied hands, picking up a textbook and flinging it at The Shadow before rolling off the table. She screamed in fury, hoping someone would hear, "You vile cretin! Leave me alone! I'll kill you!"

Furious with himself for not hitting her harder the first time, The Shadow ran at her, but she stumbled out of his grasp and continued screaming at him, "Be quiet, you useless girl!"

"Be quiet? Useless?" Ciara kicked at his face, screaming, "If I'm useless then *leave me ALONE!*"

The Shadow finally gripped her wrist and wrenched her toward him, but it was easier than he had expected. Then he saw the smirk on her face as she slammed her heel against his instep and gripped his family jewels before giving them a hard twist. The Shadow bellowed, and Ciara pulled free, launching herself under the nearest lab table.

He recovered in seconds and took off after her just as a door slammed open and Ash came angrier than a swollen thundercloud. Behind Ash came Nate and Jared, and a few seconds later Jez, Tyler, and Leah sprinted in. Ash gripped his arm and pulled him to the ground, but the man rolled to his feet like an acrobat. The Shadow kicked Ash in the stomach, knocking the wind from him. Meanwhile, Jared punched him from behind in the kidney, causing him to stumble and Nate ran at him, tackling the man into a table, and they fell with a clatter.

Jared pulled Nate to his feet as Ash grappled with the assassin again, then silver glinted in the dim light. "Knife, Ash! Knife!" Jared called in warning.

The tall martial artist gripped the hand holding the knife and twisted, forcing him to let go with a gasp of unexpected pain. The other fist swung up at Ash's jaw and collided with a crack, and he dropped, kicking his legs and sweeping The Shadow's legs from under him. Once more, Jared threw himself into the fight, trying to pin him to the ground. Ash pulled another knife from the man's belt, followed by a gun that he slid to Nate.

"Call Curry!" Ash called to Nate and mentally scolded himself for not thinking of it earlier.

The Shadow threw Jared off for a second time, and the young man's head cracked as it hit the slate of the laboratory table. Jared saw stars and for a moment couldn't focus.

Nate dialed the number in a rush, his fingers shaking as he did. The other line clicked as Curry answered while he watched Ash receive a knee to his stomach. A foot swung up hitting The Shadow in the face, giving Ash enough time to snatch The Shadow's wrist and twist, forcing him onto his stomach on the cold tile.

"Hello?" came Curry's voice, and Nate realized he had been saying that for a few seconds.

"This is Nate, one of Ciara's friends, we're in trouble," Nate said quickly, too quick to be understood.

"Slow down," Curry said through the phone, "I can't understand you."

"Ciara is in trouble," Nate said at a normal speed. "At the science department, room 235. The Shadow is here."

"On my way," he rushed and clicked off.

Nate looked back and saw Ciara punching wildly at the masked man with tears streaming down her face. Tyler finally got his arms around the girl, yelling for someone to barricade the doorway.

The other man nodded and pointed toward one door, and someone moved to block it. But The Shadow figured out that he couldn't fight against all of them, and with a giant heave, he threw Jared off him one more time. With a gush of crimson, he elbowed Ash in the nose and swung at Ciara, who ducked before running forward and slamming her head into his stomach. She kept running, and he stumbled backward and took Ciara with him.

Wildly, she began hitting him again, but he fought her off and ran out of the only open door to come almost face to face with the guards dressed as different school aides. He turned quickly and headed in the opposite direction.

Ciara collapsed in a heap, angry and scared. She began shaking the moment he was out of sight. Jez and Leah were both beside themselves and tried to help, but they too were frightened and didn't know what to do. Ash quickly came over, ignoring his bloody nose, and wrapped his long arms around her and pulled her into his chest, holding her tightly.

"Ciara, deep breaths. Deep, long breaths. Tell me your full name," Ash ordered in a calm tone as he held her against him.

For a moment, she tried to scramble out of his arms, not realizing who he was, but then his voice registered. She began to listen to what he said to her, and Ciara took a few breaths and stuttered out, "Ciara Niamh Fitzpatrick."

Ash chuckled slightly, realizing she had one of the most Irish names he had ever heard. Niamh (Nee-of) was a common name in parts of Ireland, but rare in the United States. He felt her shaking and prompted, "Deep breaths and tell me about your favorite place on earth."

"My grandmother's cottage in Glen Colm Cille, on the coast. The hills are so green there and the water is all different shades of blue," she said haltingly at first, but as she spoke, her shaking began to subside and her voice grew stronger. "From the watch tower, you can see the different levels of the ocean and the beach, the beach has some of the softest sand in Ireland. Her cottage smells like the ocean and lavender." Her voice trailed off as she looked up at Ash with tears in her eyes. "He got away, again. I wanted to kill him."

"Do you still?" Ash asked her as he wiped her tears away. Ciara shook her head and stood up as he questioned, "Then what do you want to happen to him?"

"Justice, I want him locked up forever, but I shouldn't deal out death. I don't think I would ever forgive myself, even though he killed my whole family," Ciara admitted with a sniff and wrapped her arms tightly around Ash and began to sob uncontrollably.

He held her until she let go, and by that time, Curry appeared with paramedics right behind him. The paramedics looked at all of them, as their group collectively explained to Curry what had happened.

Curry nodded as the explanation ended and grunted, "I'm glad you all were here, thank you, I am in your debt. Ciara, I

don't want you to sleep alone tonight as you have had a serious scare."

Jez looked up at the goateed man and stated, "I can stay
with her. I think I've had a serious scare too."

"Me three," Leah admitted from where she stood with
Tyler's arm around her shoulders and asked, "Can I stay over
as well?"

"The more the merrier," Ciara said with a sigh, and her legs
shook slightly. "Thank you, all of you, you saved my life." She
laughed a bit hysterically before glancing up at Ash and begging, "Can you take me home now?"

Her eyes looked so wide and blue in her pale face that he
wanted nothing more than to hold her and nodded.

She took a shaking step and clung to Ash before her legs
gave out. Ash looked down at her with a raised eyebrow and
questioned, "You alright their?"

"I'm good, just need another moment," she stated, taking in
a slow, long breath. She told her legs to move, but they refused
to listen.

Ash squeezed her shoulder before turning slightly and
bending down and offered, "Climb up, I've got you."

Ciara sighed and wrapped her arms around his neck as Ash
slid his arms under her legs. Ciara clung to his back, and a
slow smile spread across his face. And he got his wish when she
set her chin on her arms, face right next to him, and let out a
sigh of relief.

With a broad grin, Nate followed Ash and Ciara out and
explained, "I'll follow you back to the apartment with your

things and Jez, we all left our stuff in your study room. Leah, did you drive yourself today?"

"No, I walked this morning," she mumbled as her heart slowed its rapid beating.

Tyler turned to Leah and asked, "Would you like a ride with the two of us? I can stop by your place so you can pick up anything you need and drop you off at Ciara's."

"That would be great, thanks," Leah said with another jaw-cracking yawn.

Jared wrapped an arm around Tyler's shoulder and declared, "You are sleeping in my room tonight, because I'm going to be shaking in my bunny slippers when we get home."

Raising an eyebrow in question, Tyler shook his head and questioned, "And how is that different than every other night of the week?"

"You have a pair of bunny slippers?" Ash asked as he looked over his shoulder at the couple.

"Got a problem with that?" Jared inquired defiantly, pulling his shoulders back and puffing out his chest slightly.

"Not at all, think it's pretty manly actually," Ash said with a snort and admitted, "Takes a lot of confidence for a guy to wear something like that."

Curry walked on the other side of Ash, ignoring the young men and their choice of footwear. "Stay with her until they get there, make sure she gets a warm shower before getting into pajamas, and she should also eat something."

Ash nodded at the advice as he responded, "I will don't worry."

"Thank you," Curry mumbled, rubbing his temples before adding, "I wish there was more I could do at the moment. I can't understand how this happened, I need to make some calls." He walked off, already dialing a number as he mumbled to himself.

Ash saw Jared with his arms wrapped around Tyler as he glanced back over to his friends. The smaller man had his face pressed into Jared's chest, with one arm holding onto Leah and the other clutching Jared. Their relationship confused Ash but just then he didn't envy the different varieties of love rolling off the three.

{ 24 }

Surprise

They slept late the next day, grateful it was Sunday, and that they had the chance for their nerves to rest and give their exhausted brains a chance to recover from all the studying. No one brought up the events of the previous night, fearful of what it might do to Ciara. The tall woman already seemed to be brushing off the encounter, despite the fact that The Shadow had never gotten so close to capturing her before. Ciara acted unfazed in the morning, putzing around and humming to herself, but after several hours of pretending that everything was alright, Ciara couldn't hold it in any longer.

"I thought I could handle it, but when everything went dark and I woke up on a table, I panicked," Ciara admonished herself. In frustration, she gripped her hair as she plopped down heavily on the futon, coffee trickling into the pot in the kitchen. "I can't believe I acted like such a child."

Jez knelt down in front of her and took her hands, giving them a squeeze, as Leah wrapped her arms around Ciara's shoulders comfortingly.

Leah pulled her in tightly to her side as she spoke, "Not many people can easily face down an assassin, don't beat yourself up because of it."

"It's not just that, it's more," Ciara paused, trying to think of how best to explain as she let herself sink deeper into the cushion of the futon. "It's more that I just can't believe I thought I could kill him, I wanted to. I believed I could defend myself better and I swore to myself that the next time we met, I would end it, but I didn't."

"You're only human," Jez reminded with a kind smile. "We can't always get or do what we want, no matter how determined we are."

"That is some sound advice," Leah said, acknowledging Jez, and added, "I don't know about you two, but I believe I'm in need of more coffee and it sounds almost done. My head feels packed full of fluffy bunnies."

"You both are right," Ciara said, before elaborating, "He is an assassin and I am only somewhat trained in martial arts, he was bound to get me at some point." Ciara sighed ruefully and murmured, "Coffee sounds wonderful, hopefully there is enough. I'm surprised the smell hasn't lured Ash over here yet; he's a total coffee mooch."

The following week was filled with tension and acute anxiety, and all her friends sat listening in the audience, but to her they just looked like a dark blob. They all finished their exams that morning, and Ciara was the last one. The group filed out after her last song and waited while the professors talked to her about her performance, touching on parts she did well and on what could use improvement.

Sighing with pleasure at their comments, Ciara left, smoothing out her jewel-colored top and black skirt as she went to meet her friends in the main part of the music building. As she turned the corner into the main hallway, she froze, eyes wide in surprise. Standing next to Ash was one of her oldest friends, and across their face was the smuggest smile she had ever seen. For a moment, Ciara could only stare, her heart leaping into her throat and her mind baffled in absolute amazement.

"You just gonna stand there with your mouth open or are you gonna come give me a hug?" KT asked with a smile lighting up his face. His arms opened wide as she threw herself into him with a screech of pure elation.

He spun her around in a circle, his thick muscled arms encasing her like steel bars, and she felt his hard chest and stomach against her body with surprise. KT hadn't been like that the last time she saw him. When he set her back on her feet, Ciara kissed his broad cheek and fluffed the little red hair left on the top of his head as the rest gradually shaved to nothing. His brown eyes sparkled at her from his deeply tanned and freckled face.

"I missed you so much, I thought you said you were going to call first?" Ciara hugged him again.

KT squeezed her back and hedged, "I did call, just not you."

Ciara looked back and forth between KT and Ash, almost not believing her eyes. It seemed like a dream that he was in front of her just then. It had been years since she had stood face to face with KT. "But really, how did you make this happen?"

KT rubbed at his day-old shave, explaining, "There's this girl we both know, bit crazy in a loveable way, and she gave me the big guy over here's number." He waved over to Ash, who shrugged as he said, "I gave him a call and asked if he wanted to be in on the surprise."

>>>

It wasn't exactly how it had gone down, maybe the easy version, but Ash remembered feeling distinctly uncomfortable at first. He shifted at the memory and hoped KT hadn't been able to notice or read too far into it, and Ash still berated himself over the awkward conversation.

Ash had almost not answered the phone when he had seen the strange number, but then reasoned that it could have been Curry. But it wasn't, and Ash had been extremely shocked to discover it was KT who sounded way too calm, and easy-going to be speaking to someone he had never met before. It was a skill set that Ash had always envied.

"Hey, this is KT, Ciara's friend. This Ash Callaghan?"

"Yeah," Ash had answered, sounding way too uptight in his own head; he only hoped he didn't sound that way in real life.

Then, to his horror, KT had laughed and apologized, "Sorry for catching you off-guard like this, if I could have texted you a warning I would have."

Ash had jumped to reassure him, "It's all good, I wasn't, I was just expecting it to be Curry or one of his people."

"I don't have a lot of time, but I wanted to do something for Ciara and I needed an inside person," KT had explained.

"Okay," Ash had said, knowing he sounded a bit wary, but he couldn't help it. He hated that he was already feeling slightly jealous

of their friendship, but he had reminded himself that they were just friends.

"I wanted to surprise her, and I get leave earlier than expected and it would mean a lot to her if I made it to her recital. I know it's a lot to ask, but do you mind picking me up from the airport and letting me tag-a-long to it with you?"

There was no good way to say no, and Ash wouldn't have either, because he had known KT was right; it would mean a lot to Ciara to have him there. "Sure, her recital is early though, will you be able to make it in time?"

"It's gonna suck, but yeah, I found a flight that leaves at 5:15 a.m. Can I get your email and then I can send you the details?" KT's side had suddenly grown loud, and Ash had the impression that he was covering up the phone to shout something back. Then suddenly he responded back into the mouthpiece, "Email?"

Ash had given him his email, both happy for Ciara and frustrated that he would have to share her before going back home to his parents' mostly empty home.

When they had finally met in person, it was better. He had seen one picture of KT, but it was of a much younger version. This version had corded arm muscles and a tight fade instead of dark red hair falling into his eyes, and he was darkly tanned and seemed to be the same height as Ciara. Ash had taken his proffered hand and shaken it, stating, "You look beat."

KT had snorted his reply, "The things we do for women." Ash felt his jealousy rising, but then KT laughed as he admitted, "I can't even take myself seriously with that." He had clapped Ash's shoulder and began moving towards the exit as he corrected himself, "Family, the things we do for family."

Feeling more at ease after that comment, Ash glanced over at the medium-sized backpack, asking, "That all you got?"

"Military dude, I don't need much." KT rolled his head on his neck before he questioned, "What I do need is a coffee, do we have time?"

After that, things had become easier with KT, and he was almost as easy to talk to as Nate and Ash could see why Ciara had kept in touch with him. Ash could picture this young man running out of class after her, a girl he had never even talked to before, and all the other adventures they had been on together since.

Ash pulled himself back to the present to watch their reunion and felt happy that he had helped bring them back together. He hoped she would feel that comfortable with him one day.

>>>

Ciara looked between the two in shock and admitted, "I had no idea."

"Clearly," KT stated with a laugh and added, "I wouldn't miss your singing, no way, your voice is too angelic."

She blushed and beamed at him, sincerely stating, "Thank you, thank you so much for being here." Then Ciara turned to Ash and gave him a tight hug and kissed his cheek in gratitude, "And thank you for bringing him here."

It was Ash's turn to blush, although the winter beard he was growing somewhat covered it up. "Not a problem, this is just the second part of your birthday present," he declared with a grin. "Plus, we can't have you by yourself for any length of time and I have to go home in a few days. Mr. Durand is already gone and everyone else is leaving and tomorrow we are celebrating your birthday that was last week."

"You are the most thoughtful person ever," she stated and gave him another hug. "I think I am on a freedom high: good things and no exams. Oh, it feels wonderful."

KT rolled his eyes and said soberly, "You're always like this once you finish exams."

"This is normal behavior then?" Nate asked with a laugh.

KT nodded and questioned, "So, Pea Pod, your voice might be the food of the soul, but it is *not* the food of the stomach."

Jez tapped her cheek with a manicured finger, inquiring, "Do you like pita's?"

"I like *food*, anything, as long as I can eat it and digest it." He put his arm around Ciara's shoulders with the simple comfort of old friends, admitting, "Good thing you aren't wearing heels."

She looked at the man who stood eye level with her and stuck her tongue out, rebutting, "Good thing you didn't shrink. You'll like this place, they let you build your own pita. So, you can make it as strange of a combination of foods as you want."

"Sounds awesome, let's go."

{ **25** }

KT

"Could you take a longer shower?" Ciara asked sarcastically, hand on her hip and eyebrow raised as KT finally came out of the bathroom in a cloud of steam.

"Oh, come on, you know what it feels like to only bathe here and there, in very short increments," he admonished with a grin, digging into his duffel bag to search for a shirt.

Ciara sat down on a chair in her kitchen to tie her calf-high boots, with a two-inch heel, as she eyed the new ink on KT's shoulder. Nestled into his map of the world in the Robinson style was the Marine's symbol. "I like what you did with your tattoo, is it finished?"

He pulled a blue shirt on over his head before he answered, "Has a bit more shading to be done when I get back to Jackson." KT shoved his feet into a pair of tennis shoes and asked, "Ready to go?"

"How do I look?" She asked and did a slow twirl in her holly green dress with red trim, which hugged her body to perfection, that she had recently purchased for their Christmas party. Jez had helped her pick it out on one of their brief studying reprieves over the past few weeks.

KT whistled before stating in a serious tone. "Girl you look gorgeous; I think there is a certain someone who may not take their eyes off you."

Ciara blushed and waved him off, spluttering, "It's not like that."

"Don't try and deny it and he's a good guy, *and* how many guys can you wear heels around without towering over them, freaking giantess."

Ciara ignored the comment and led him out of her apartment and to her Jeep. On the way over, Ciara could barely contain her excitement as she drove a little too quickly over to the boy's house. KT held on to the 'Oh-shit' handle as he laughed while she croaked out Christmas carols. Her mood was considerably uplifted compared to last year's holiday season.

"I'm not quite sure how to handle you right now," he admitted with a laugh and shook his head at her. "I thought you despised Christmas."

"Well, when you are stuck celebrating by yourself, it's a bit hard to love. I know that's not really the point of Christmas, but it's hard to feel in the giving mood when you are watching the joy of the holiday through other peoples' windows." Ciara's smile turned slightly sour., but refused to give into it, so turned the music up and obnoxiously belted out, "'I wanna hippopotamus for Christmas!'"

"And to think, I flew halfway around the world to hear *this* voice."

She playfully shoved his shoulder as she pulled the Jeep up to the curb and boasted, "Of course you did, voice of an angel over here."

They joked and laughed as they walked up to the door, and Ciara barely made contact with the surface before it was opened, and she was greeted by a wave of warm air and Ash. "Great door service," she complimented as Ash awkwardly waved the two in, making Ciara raise a brow before she moved past him. Her jaw dropped, and she croaked, "You didn't, oh my gosh."

"Happy birthday!" Chorused her friends.

"And merry Christmas, ho, ho, ho," Jared added through a fake white beard. Tyler hit his stomach, and he folded in half, choking.

Ciara snorted with a hand covering her still gaping mouth as Tyler rolled his eyes at his boyfriend, admonishing him, "That didn't hurt, stop being a baby."

"I'm not a, oh hi Ciara," Jared coughed, wrapping his arms around the tall girl as she pushed him into Tyler and the rest of their group.

"Thanks man," she heard KT say behind her, followed by Ash rumbling in response, "Not a problem, I should have thought of it. I'm glad you mentioned it."

Ciara looked over at KT and Ash standing off to the side of the group hug and demanded with a snap of her fingers, "Get over here you two."

"Nah, I'm good," KT said, and gave her his best shit-eating grin as he crossed his arms over his barrel chest.

She promptly ignored the grin that had made many a woman weak at the knees and raised a threatening eyebrow. "Not an option, if this is now my birthday too, then my current wish is for both of you to come over here and get in on this hug."

"Wow, kinda bossy Pea Pod," KT retorted and scratched at his non-regulation dark red scruff.

"You're one to talk," Ciara volleyed back and rolled her eyes.

"Come on big guy," KT droned, letting out a dramatic sigh and gestured for Ash to join him and added, "She won't stop until we give in."

A while later, Ciara dug into her fudge brownie baked by Leah and frosted with care, her name in elegant script in blue-green across the top. It had been years since she had anything resembling a cake, which she guessed KT had passed along, that she didn't like cake, and was going to savor every morsel of the brownie.

Ciara had never been big on presents, and the years living with almost nothing and limited space had made presents scarce. It wasn't something that she was used to anymore, nor the action of opening them in front of people. Most people liked getting things, but she couldn't stop making strange faces the entire time. At least others had opened presents before she had, and that made it a bit better, at least.

As she tore into the first package, she found a set of wireless headphones from Tyler and Jared, ones she had been looking at online, and they hit the mark. She knew she would love them, and they were even the color she had wanted. From

Leah, she received a new journal and her favorite type of pens, which she was aware made her seem like a nerd, but she was okay with that. However, if that made her a nerd, then Jez and Nate nailed down her coffin. In the bag they handed her sat the complete works of Agatha Christie and her biography.

KT then pulled out his own present from his pocket and handed her a small box. Ciara didn't notice Ash's face pale as she took the box, but when Nate bumped Ash's shoulder and she glanced at him, she noticed the odd look on his face. Ash fixed his face, then held back his sigh of relief as Ciara opened the small box and squealed.

"Oh my gosh, they're beautiful!" She wiggled around in her seat.

KT chuckled and teased, "You're such a dork." But everyone saw his blush of pleasure at her excitement as he said, "Glad you like them."

"What is it?" Jez asked and moved to peer over Ciara's shoulder. "Oh cool, are those real, sorry, rude."

"Nah, it's fine and I think so, I *hope* so. It's always hard to tell," KT admitted with a shrug as he explained to everyone else what they were, "Old Persian coins. They make a lot of jewelry out of them, but finding just plain coins was a bit of a challenge."

"These are so cool, thank you." She leaned over and kissed his scruffy cheek.

He squeezed her knee and said again, "Glad you like it, but now the bigger question is if Lex will like her scarf."

Ciara narrowed her eyes at the worry in his tone and told him for the second time, "She will. But that conversation is bigger than that single statement and will need to wait until later." Her eyes twinkled mischievously, and KT groaned, making Ciara laugh as she picked up her last item. It was her name on a light blue envelope in Ash's handwriting.

Ciara opened the card, and surprise crossed her face as she met Ash's eyes with her wide, ocean-blue depths. "Really?" She let out a disbelieving breath of air.

She watched Ash's face turn a ruddy red, and he refused to meet her eyes as she continued to stare at him in shock. He murmured apologetically, "It's stupid, I'm sorry."

Cutting him off, Ciara stated, "It's awesome, I've been trying to talk myself into getting a subscription for months. You are going to regret getting me a music streaming service because I am going to annoy the hell out of you and Mr. Durand now." She jumped up and wrapped her arms around Ash as he leaned over the couch and murmured, "Thank you," into his ear.

Ash gave her a squeeze as he grumbled, "I wanted to get you art supplies too, so you would actually have a present to open, but I know nothing about that so, gift card."

"It's perfect," Ciara reassured and added, "I'm super picky about art brands. Thank you everyone, this was, wow, can we go make gingerbread houses now?"

Jez snorted and asked, "Want out of the spotlight?" Ciara vigorously nodded, glad that she understood the desire. "Then to the kitchen, Tyler you're on my team!"

"Ouch, really?" Nate put a hand to his heart and said dramatically, "That hurts."

"Get real, you wouldn't even be on your own team if you had the choice," she pointed out and patted his shoulder sympathetically.

"True, I destroy everything I touch," Nate laughed good-naturedly and questioned the group, "So, who wants to be on my team?"

"I'm game, mostly just because I want to eat it," KT confided and stepped over to Nate. "Don't care about building."

"What is your stance on gumdrops?" Nate questioned seriously.

KT raised a brow in silent inquiry, "How do you feel about red hots?"

At the same time, they both answered the others question, "Hate them." Followed up by a quick "Awesome," as they high-fived.

Jez and Ciara laughed before Ciara stared up at Ash and asked half desperately, "Need a teammate?"

"Sure, but I am a competitive gingerbread builder," Ash cautioned.

"That's alright, I can handle it," she acknowledged and tossed her hair back, and then wound it up with a black hair tie. She rolled her shoulders as if she were gearing up for a fight.

"Can you?" Leah asked as she tied her hair back too, and Jared pushed up his sleeves.

"We've been practicing," Jared said as he pulled out a blueprint.

"Are you serious?" Tyler snorted before questioning, "You made a blueprint of your gingerbread house?"

"You're going down Ty, this year we're winning," Jared challenged as he rubbed his hands together, then heard the crack of gingerbread breaking.

They all looked over to see KT and Nate shoving pieces of the spice-laden cookies into their mouths.

Through a mouthful, KT said, "I think you're all nuts."

Nate nodded his agreement and swallowed down his bite before adding, "Yeah, food is for eating, not playing with."

An hour later, a timer signaled the end of the building competition, and with steaming mugs of cocoa with a dash of peppermint schnapps, Jared and Leah toasted their win. Their magnificently decorated building sat in the center of the coffee table, glistening, and the group applauded the new victors.

Ciara tucked herself between Ash and KT and lightly kicked Ash's ankle and said sympathetically, "Don't worry, we'll get them next year." She didn't need to drink the hot beverage to feel a warm sensation soaking in, because she already detected it at the words she had thought she would never be able to say again.

{ 26 }

Christmas

The next morning, KT and Ciara said an early goodbye to Ash, who appeared to be heading towards his doom with his broad shoulders slumped and his face drawn. Although she knew he would enjoy the time with his brother and sister, she couldn't imagine what Christmas looked like at his parents' mansion. It was probably beautiful, but sterile, and Ciara could tell he wasn't looking forward to the time away.

The rest of the day, they spent relaxing in her apartment, making gingerbread cookies to pass out to her guard Chuck's and drinking hot chocolate with candy canes. With KT no longer on mission or communicating over a device, he could share more about what he had been through, and Ciara finally felt their friendship round out again. He showed her some goofy videos they had made and practical jokes they played on one another, while Ciara took him around town to show him her new city of Pine Harbor. "So, tell me more about this Ash character," KT said as a flurry of snow came down and sprinkled onto their hats.

Ciara wiped at her eye, dislodging a flake from her full eyelashes and responded after a thoughtful pause, "He is a really nice guy. I don't know what you want me to tell you that I haven't already. He's a double black belt, plays the violin and viola beautifully, a decent percussionist, has an older brother and younger sister, his parents suck. Ash can make me laugh no matter what and he just always seems to be there when I need him. I'm not sure why he spends so much time with me."

KT tried to hold back the grin threatening to creep out. He hinted, "You aren't?"

She eyed him with suspicion and coaxed, "You seem to know something."

"I will let you figure it out for yourself," he chortled and turned to lead her up the driveway to the church glowing in the dark before inquiring, "When is Lex coming out next?"

"The day after you leave, but that's twice in one year I get to see her. It seems like some kind of miracle," Ciara crowed, pulling off her coat, hat, and gloves before hanging them up and heading into the narthex.

The following morning, they drank hot cocoa with a mountain of mini-marshmallows on top while watching Christmas movies. Through the glass patio door, they saw the snow falling softly, dusting the town in a quiet blanket. Later that day, Ciara drove them out to a park that afternoon to commandeer the giant hill that was perfect for sledding. The two friends sledded until night came and their fingers turned purple.

She was sad the day KT had to be taken to the airport, but it was Christmas Eve and he needed to be home with his family. He hugged her tightly, and they kissed each other's cheeks before he disappeared into the line heading for the security checkpoint. Ciara moped all the way home but forced herself to get dressed to go to Mr. Durand's church for the Christmas Eve service despite the older man's absence.

Although she was sad at having to say farewell to KT, as the night passed, she grew excited once more because this time, Lex was coming to visit. The next day, Ciara, once more, went to the airport with two of her guards, but this time to pick up her other best friend who dragged a massive suitcase behind her.

She waved and tossed her sea of golden waves over her shoulder and looking like a disgruntled delivery elf. "Blame my mom," Lex declared as she landed in front of them with half the people in the lobby staring at her. "I think she packed up the world for you in a box that she refused to mail. It takes up half my suitcase."

Ciara smiled, "That's alright. I was just surprised you came with so many clothes. Let's get food on the way home, Chuck's do you mind? It's on me."

One guard nodded with a stony face, and Lex raised an eyebrow at him and said quietly in Ciara's ear, "They seem to have gotten *more* dull." Ciara sighed and shrugged, and in her normal volume, she stated, "I could eat a herd of cows, where are we going?"

"It's just down the street," Ciara said with a laugh and took her bag.

Over the next few days, Lex attempted the impossible, having tried when they were in middle school and failed miserably, but she was determined as she ordered, "And turn!"

Ciara threw her leg out and spun uncontrollably before her remaining foot came out from under her and dumped her onto the ice. "This is impossible, I am never going to do this on ice. Give me a wood floor and pointe shoe's any day."

Lex laughed and performed a perfect double axel, her blonde hair waving out from under her black hat. "Nothing to it."

"Show off," Ciara teased from her seat on the ice. "I'm throwing in the towel for the night, let's go sledding. There is a perfect hill over there and a saucer and sled in the back of the Jeep, interested?"

Lex easily came to a stop in front of her and began skating backwards until they came to the edge of the frozen makeshift ice rink in the park, and exclaimed. "Let's do it!"

They quickly removed their skates and put their boots back on before Ciara trudged to the Jeep and pulled out the sleds. Lex took the handle of one and, with Ciara by her side, ran up the hill to their left and belly-slid down the other side. The downside of their plan was not bringing snow pants, so in soaking clothes, they made their way back to Ciara's apartment. But waiting for them was one of their favorite activities: turning the bathtub into a hot tub. They poured large glasses of wine, pulled on bathing suits and climbed in, sighing at the heat of the water on their frozen limbs.

"What was KT up to?" Lex asked as she created a mountain out of bubbles.

"He was going back for his own family Christmas and apparently, they were quite livid with him for almost missing it."

Ciara bit her lip and pulled bubbles onto her face, giving herself a beard. "How do I look?" She questioned in a deep voice.

"So sexy," she snickered and reached over for her glass of wine, as she said sadly, "I don't think KT likes family holidays very much."

"He doesn't," Ciara responded and added, "They get really tense and argue a lot from what he told me. I feel bad for him, but I'm glad he came out here. With Mr. Durand and Ash gone, it would have been a very lonely Christmas."

"I can imagine," Lex murmured and dunked her head under the water and came up with her hair looking like liquid gold. "Oh, I meant to tell you, good choice on all your new clothes. They make you look so much more confident; I mean, band shirts are always a must, but every now and then it's good to strut your stuff and look like a woman. One must play their better hand every now and then and speaking of," she paused to let a grin spread across her face before completing her thought, "Didn't you say Mr. Durand gets back tonight?"

"I did, why?" Ciara inquired at Lex's sporadic and off-kilter train of thought.

"He owes me a rematch in Texas Hold-em," Lex stated and asked, "Is it okay to go and crash his evening?"

"I'm sure he won't mind if we bring him some dinner," Ciara said, standing up and shaking the water from her nearly black hair.

>>>

Lex and Ciara were just sitting down to a bowl of popcorn and wine when a knock sounded on her door. Ciara raised an eyebrow and set the glass on her coffee table as she stood to answer, and with a glance through the peephole, she spotted Ash and threw open the door. "You're back early... Ash are you alright?"

"Not really, I'm sorry to," he began as Ciara opened the door further to allow Ash entrance, and he paused as he saw Lex. "I'm sorry, I forgot Lex was still here. I don't want,"

Ciara interrupted him with a hug and stated, "It's fine, come in, relax, and have a glass of wine."

Ash hugged her close and whispered, "Thank you."

After pouring him a glass of wine and sitting back down, Ciara prompted, "What happened?"

"My parents, they are what always happens," Ash confessed and took a long drink before elaborating, "Believe it or not, they were pleasant when you were there. This time around, they said, well, said a lot of pretty mean things."

Ciara leaned over and squeezed his leg as she stated softly, "You're here now, among friends."

"Feeling better already," he admitted as a natural smile touched his lips and he took a smaller sip from the glass this time. "Lex, how are you doing?"

"Good, glad to see you. Are you going to join us tomorrow then at Mr. Durand's?" Lex questioned. "New Year's Eve!"

The next night, Lex eyed the filled table in front of her with a frown. "More chip dip Cia," Lex called from the floor in front of the television. "Ash and his gargantuan appetite at it all!"

"She's lying, it was all her." Ash tossed a chip at her, and she exclaimed, "Stop that! For someone so tiny, she eats like a starving teenage boy. I was one, so I would know."

Mr. Durand chuckled at their banter as he dealt out the next round of cards for their game of poker. "There should be more in the fridge on the bottom shelf," he called.

Ciara opened the fridge and pulled out the bowl, announcing, "Got it." She peeled off the saran wrap and snatched the Chex Mix off the counter before stating, "Lex, I know it was you; Ash is right. I love this song!" She held her hands out to Lex, who popped up and began dancing around the living room with her.

"This song, really?" Ash questioned with surprise mingled with horror. "Did you hit your head last night?"

"How dare you," Ciara put a hand to her chest in shock. "Before I ran, Lex and I used to go to all their tours together."

Lex wrapped her arm around Ciara, dramatically lip-syncing the words. Ciara joined in before they both slowly encroached on Ash's personal space as they sang along.

He eyed them warily and muttered, "Okay, okay, sorry I insulted your taste in music."

Mr. Durand shook his head at them as the song ended and the camera swung quickly to show the ball in Times Square, New York. "And the count-down begins," he announced, snatching up the bottle of champagne sitting on ice as the centerpiece of his coffee table.

They stood together and began the countdown, "10, 9, 8, 7, 6, 5, 4," Lex entwined her fingers with Ciara, "3," Ciara took Ash's hand in hers as they ended, "2, 1, happy New Year!"

Lex stood on tiptoe and kissed Ciara on her cheek as Ciara did the same. Mr. Durand popped the bottle of champagne as Lex placed her lips on his wrinkled cheek and bubbled, "Happy New Year Mr. Durand."

"And Happy New Year to you, my dear," he responded before pouring her a glass.

Ciara set her hands-on Ash's shoulders as he leaned down. She gently touched her lips to his now stubbled cheek as he mimicked the gesture on her smooth one. She inhaled mint and rosemary, and his hands automatically wound around her waist. As she leaned back and stared into his yellow-gold eyes, Ciara felt a warmth blossom in her stomach and travel into her chest. "Happy New Year Cia," he said in a quiet voice before letting go.

{ 27 }

The Truth

Arms embraced her in warmth and the smell of flowery perfume as he friend breathed into her ear, "I missed you." Jez ran a proprietary hand over Ciara's silky hair with a sense of friendship and familiarity and declared, "You look wonderful."

"As do you, like you finally got some sleep," Ciara teased.

"I needed to because this semester won't be giving me any, I have that internship with Trescott, remember?"

Nate stepped in behind her and stated, "Don't let her fool you, she is ecstatic about it, just dreading the workload." He hugged Ciara, then clapped hands with Ash, pulling him in for a bro-hug as he added, "As for me, I have my senior recital to look forward to."

"I'll trade you, I have my med school exams. You do my exams and I can bang sticks on hollow objects," Jared offered from where he sat lounging against Tyler's knees.

"You would fail, miserably," Nate grimaced and rolled his eyes, knowing the previous comment wasn't meant as an insult, but couldn't help adding, "He makes music sound so simple."

Ciara sat back down on the couch between Leah and Ash, musing aloud, "It sounds like we all have pretty intense schedules this semester. Leah was just saying how she has an independent study to work on her short story collection and Tyler has his senior recital too."

"It's going to be a rough one," Jared agreed, taking a long pull on the beer in his hand as he reached back to weave his fingers into Tyler's.

Ash frowned and tossed in his workload, "I have three movements to compose and orchestrate."

"I have that and one of my seminars this semester," Ciara grumbled. "Curry also wanted to meet up this week, not sure what about, he wouldn't say over the phone."

The group all looked at her in silence for a moment before Jez broke it by asking what everyone had down over the long break. The chatter resumed in earnest, and Ciara felt their warmth envelope her in a sense of peace, but Curry stayed hovering in the back of her mind. She wanted to understand what information he had, and still hadn't shared her idea with her friends, but she didn't want to infringe on their first night back together.

The stories of their various breaks wrapped around her as Jez laughed while telling them about her older brother and his family's visit. Her youngest nephew had been determined not to wear his diaper and somehow wiggled out of it in the middle of the church service on Christmas Eve.

"It was a nightmare, for them at least but, for the rest of us, comic relief," she chuckled. "You should have seen it, Bryce had climbed off the pew and was outta that thing in a second and then tearing off under the pews. He decided it was the best game ever and have you ever tried to catch a two-year-old crawling under benches?"

Nate shook his head, and so did everyone else as Jez continued, "Let me tell you, it's much harder than it looks. Course, I wasn't really trying, I thought the whole thing was way too funny. My brother and his wife did not appreciate my humor in the entire thing, but it made for a much more entertaining hour."

"Nothing like that happened at my house, but we did have a really good time building a snow fort, just like our old snow days," Leah shared.

"And we built an epic one this year," Tyler added, momentarily reminiscing, before clarifying, "When we say snow fort, we mean like full on live-able igloo."

"Where do you live again, Alaska?" Nate asked with a snort.

Tyler deadpanned as he stated in a monotone, "No, the north part of the state."

"We played cards and ate in there, even had a little electric heater. It was really cool, no pun intended," Leah giggled.

"It was," Jared's smile was a bit forced, and Tyler put his arm around his shoulders and gave him a light squeeze.

Nate looked at Jared quizzically as he inquired, "I thought you were staying home the whole break."

"That was the plan," Jared mumbled, then added on a sigh, "My parents were being a bit, harsh and then my grandparents came into town. And they started in on the questions of if I had met anyone yet and all that. I started to answer and it blew up into this whole thing," he said in a rush and swallowed hard, and Ciara could see him holding back tears. Tyler pulled him in tighter. "Anyway, I was...I was told to leave," Jared admitted and took a long drink of his beer. "It's fine, it's happened before and by summer, I'll be welcomed back. Would be nice if I could introduce them to my boyfriend and not worry that the peanut gallery will go up in arms."

"That sucks Jared," Ciara said with a frown. He had alluded to his family not being completely accepting of him, but he had never explained it before.

"It really was an awesome fort," he said, forcefully changing the topic. "We should try and build one in our backyard the next time we get a good snow!"

>>>

"We have a story to tell you," Curry said as Ciara and Ash sat at a table across from Curry and another man.

Ciara eyed the new man, trying to figure out where his place was in everything as he seemed too soft to be like Curry, and his eyes were beady with a slight squint. She could tell he wore contacts with the wrong prescription as he ran his hand through his thinning hair. She looked around her and noticed the students already taking lunches-to-go even though it was still in the first week of the semester, and repeated, "A story?"

"Yes," Curry stated and glanced at the thin man sitting next to him before introducing him, "This is Quinten Marsh."

At the introduction, the man met Ciara's eyes for the first time, and he forced a smile; he appeared uncomfortable in this meeting. "You look just like your father; it's an incredible resemblance," Quinten softly said and glanced at Curry, and the goateed man nodded. "I work for a certain part of the government that is, not typically acknowledged publicly. That is the same department your parents worked for and we met each other in meetings that happened bi-annually and, primarily, through untraceable video conferences. It was dangerous for us to be in the same place for too long. Our job, you see, was to create a certain type of weapon."

Ciara and Ash looked at each other and saw surprise mirrored on the other's face; this was not what they expected to hear. Ciara had never known exactly what her parents did, but she was disappointed to learn it had been weapons.

"These weapons though, you must understand," Quinten blurted as he raised his hand, trying to hold off how upset Ciara suddenly seemed. "They were, or are going to be different, because the chemical compounds involved won't kill. They are meant to just put to sleep entire cities the size of Hong Kong, New York City, LA, Tokyo, giant cities. Our purpose is to create a weapon that does that so we can *disarm* them if there is a threat, even a threat from within." At the relief on her face, Quinten smiled as he added, "Your parents were in charge of the project; they were the most brilliant people I have ever met. We started the research when you were only five, I don't believe you remember, but I met you that first year. Your parents had already made their fortune by creating a medicine to help arthritis, which gave them the means to dedicate the rest of their lives to this."

"The project," Quinten continued, "did the opposite effect for a time. It killed and destroyed everything; the vegetation for miles around the area of the city became decimated. They grew strange diseases and decayed, but after a few years we found the compound doing this and altered it. Except then the sleeping agents were too powerful and the victims never woke up and they died of dehydration."

"Who did you test these on?" Ciara demanded, horrified, as an army of people chained together marched across her vision before shriveling up like raisins.

Quinten's eyes widened, and he exclaimed, "Oh no, we didn't test these on people. It was on simulations and if they passed those then on vegetation, then we progressed to animals, but we hadn't yet made it to humans. We would never test on people right away and then we would test on ourselves first."

"Good, that's alright then," Ash approved and took a sip of his tea, drinking in the story.

"We all worked on different parts of the project, and we didn't ever keep all of the information, only parts." He sighed and ran his hand through his thinning hair, as Ciara suspected he did quite often. "We were worried others may get the information before it was perfected, or the wrong people may get it and use it for ill. Perhaps change the effects back to what they were in the beginning."

"But someone did have that information, didn't they?" Ciara asked, fiddling with her scone, and declared, "Someone had all of it."

Quinten nodded and murmured, "Yes, your parents did but none of us were informed of where they kept the files and that is what got them killed. Whoever ordered their murder must have believed they knew where the information was stored, but they were wrong."

At that point Curry stepped in, "Now you understand the background, this is why The Shadow is after you. The Shadow must assume you and your brother had information, or that your parents told you about their research or where the flash drive and papers were kept hidden."

"But I don't," Ciara protested and added, "They never told us anything." But in her head, she realized that wasn't necessarily true, because they did discuss their research with Sean and her a bit at dinner sometimes, but it was always over Ciara's head. She didn't understand any of it because it was all scientific. Sean had been the one interested in it, not Ciara. The Shadow had killed the wrong sibling if information was what he wanted.

Curry held up a hand to acknowledge her words and silently request her to pause. "I realize that, but you probably know more than you think, everyone always knows more than they think they do. You recognize surroundings and places that are imprinted on your mind because they are so common place to you. This is what your Shadow is counting on. He wants to draw up these memories to find their research, but his purposes are not good."

Ciara buried her head in her hands and moaned, "why are you telling me all of this now?"

"To prepare you in case something like what happened back in December happens again. I also want you to know that your Shadow goes by the name of Joseph Grendale. He is a bounty hunter who works for the highest bidder and is being paid a lot of money to take you alive and get the information and the drive."

Her face looked bewildered, and she chewed her lip in anxiety. "But I don't know anything. I just want to be left alone. I want a life." Unbidden tears welled up in her eyes and threatened to spill over.

Ash automatically put his arms around her protectively. He glared at Curry and Quinten as if it were all their fault. "Isn't there anything you can do about this?"

The young woman clung to Ash like a lifeline as Curry stroked his goatee, appearing to have a difficult time getting the words out. "I really don't like this, just so you both are aware but I talked this through with my supervisor and he agreed that this is the last thing we could think of. Before we even could contemplate bringing this up to you, Ciara, we spoke with Quinten who, would know the most about your parents work and the consequences." Curry paused and took a long drink of his coffee. "We believe the only way to get rid of Joseph Grendale is to trap him. Ciara, with your permission, we would like to use you as bait, I mean, we wouldn't *like* to, but it may be the only way to stop him."

"Absolutely not," Ash spluttered, almost knocking over his mug of tea in his shock at the request.

"I've said of that too, but everyone rejected the idea. I'll be your bait, I want this over," Ciara said, still clinging to Ash.

"Ciara you can't," his voice shook, and she saw the fear in his golden as when he stared into her face and asked, "What if something happened to you?"

"I need this to end, Ash," she murmured sadly, before continuing in a louder voice, "What kind of life is it always watching over your shoulder for danger? I want a life where I can go somewhere by myself and not worry about my apartment getting broken into or getting kidnapped."

Ash closed his eyes in acceptance, "You do what you think is best and I will do everything to protect you and help you."

"Ciara, do you agree to our plan?" Curry questioned seriously.

Ciara nodded and declared, "I do. When do you plan to put it into action?"

"I am in charge of determining all of the safety precautions," Quinten piped in with a smiled and added, "I was supposed to be your guardian in the United States. Obviously things didn't turn out that way," Quinten said, his smile dropping as he explained, "With help from Curry, of course, we will think of ways to protect you and track you. The first thing is we want to get a chip, a tracking chip, put in. Once this is all over, we will have it removed and we have ways to do it that won't scar."

Ash sighed and grumbled, "As long as it's all safe."

"We will do everything in our power to keep her safe," Curry said. "I have been trying to catch this guy for years, which is why I was there the night your brother died, I'm only sorry I wasn't there on time."

"Me too," Ciara mumbled, staring into the swamp-like swirl of brown in her mug.

{ 28 }

Planning

Ciara didn't bother knocking; truthfully, the thought hadn't crossed her mind as she stepped into Ash's apartment with her arms full of popcorn and books.

"Here for the long haul?" Ash asked, taking the bowl from her hands and trying to read a few of the covers of the books to see what she was about to do. He guessed the history from a glance at the titles and wear on the bindings.

"I totally forgot about a paper, I'm gonna need some caffeine, pronto," she said and unceremoniously plopped down on the floor by his coffee table.

Ash felt her disheveled panic and scooped fresh coffee grounds into the coffeemaker and stated, "Give it five." He walked over and sat down on his couch, where he was combing through sheet music. "Anything I can do to help?"

Ciara rubbed her forehead with the heel of her hands and grumbled, "Not really, I have the research done and I started it a few weeks ago, but then just totally forgot. I can't believe I did that but I had that other paper in my music theory come up and then I was studying for that biology test with Jared. Then Jez and Leah wanted me to hang out last weekend, I should have said no so I could work on this. But I didn't write it in my planner, which is so unlike me; I can't believe I let this happen."

Ash bit back a chuckle and looked at her with sympathy in his eyes., "We all do it at some point, but you're an excellent writer though and can probably whip out an A paper in one night. I mean, you have pulled all-nighters before, right? I feel like that is a college right of passage to have to do that every now and again."

"I have, but I just don't *like* to do it," she mumbled and frowned at the books she was stacking into categories. "Eight pages with footnotes *and* an annotated bibliography; I *hate* annotated bibliographies," Ciara grumbled to herself, as if the professor had assigned it just to annoy her.

"Okay, so, write up your historiography first and then see where you're at with the rest. That way you can start building steam and it will help you figure out what you have to work with. Once you get something down on paper I'm sure it won't seem like such a big task," Ash advised and gave her shoulder a light squeeze.

She reached up her hand and returned the grip to his long fingers before sighing out, "You're right. It may not be a perfect paper, and you know I am a recovering perfectionist, but it will be a paper." She let go, cracked her knuckles, and opened her laptop and said, "Just tell me when you need me to leave."

Ash pushed back up from the couch to go and make her a cup of coffee, just the way she liked it and chuckled, "I don't remember ever telling you to come over." At her wide eyes, he snorted and amended, "You're fine; you know you're always welcome and stay as long as you want."

After her second and then third cup of coffee, Ciara had a working outline, quotes, and paraphrases lined up. Ash refilled her cup and peered over her shoulder around one in the morning, commenting, "Looks like you're almost done."

"Bibliography," she moaned, sounding haunted, while her fingers flew across the keys and added, "And I still need to edit."

"I can look it over," he offered and squeezed her shoulders, making Ciara lean back into the pressure. He dug his fingers deeper as he massaged her tense muscles, and she sensed her eyelids fluttering and groaned.

She pulled away with a grumble, "Gotta focus, almost done."

She woke up with a blanket wrapped around her and Ash's arm around her waist, wondering, *When did we end up spooning?* Carefully, she untangled herself from the blanket and his arms before walking over to restart the overworked coffee pot. *At least I remembered to plug in my laptop.* Ciara checked her phone and was happy to see there was just enough time to run a final edit.

>>>

Ciara hurriedly changed out of her athletic clothes and back into her normal attire, not liking when the boys had to wait for her. As she exited the girls' locker room, she strode around the corner to where Tyler and Jared typically stood waiting for her and saw that the hallway was dark and empty.

Her heart began to pick up the pace of its beating and tried to remind herself, *It doesn't mean anything, calm down.* She strained her eyes to see to the end of the hallway and tried to focus her hearing to catch any small sound and slowly stepped towards the darkened area. The shadows moved, and a paper fluttered towards her.

The young woman felt her stomach flip as the shape of a man began racing towards her and dropping her bag, she braced herself for the attack. But then he was gone as the locker room door banged open and voices filtered out to her, harsh against the previous quiet, and Ciara sank to the ground.

"Ciara?" Tyler raced over to her and asked with worry in his voice, "Are you okay, what happened?"

Ciara reached out to her friend, and he wrapped his arms around her. In a wobbly voice, she answered, "I'm okay, I'm good, just thought for a minute The Shadow," she leaned into his arms, letting her voice trail off. His hand rubbed up and down her back, and Ciara let his familiar scent calm her.

"Look at this," Jared directed and bent down next to her to pick up the piece of paper, then held it up to her. Trepidation rose in Ciara like a tidal wave as she took it in her shaking hand and read the threatening words.

"Not the time Jared. Time and place, we've talked about this," Tyler admonished and moved his hand up to her hair, to run his fingers through it in a soothing gesture.

Jared blushed and glanced at his feet, murmuring, "Sorry Ciara." He sat next to her against the wall and rubbed her back as his boyfriend held her. When her breathing calmed, Jared said, "I think you need some food."

Tyler snorted as he released Ciara and chuckled, "I think *you* need food, I just heard your stomach growl." He shook his head as Ciara joined the chorus and admitted, "Okay, you both do, come on." He pulled them both to their feet and led the way to a diner down the street.

On the way, Jared texted their group to let them know about The Shadow encounter, and within minutes of them sitting down and ordering, they were all there. Ciara felt Ash's arm wrap around her shoulders in a comforting gesture, and she leaned into him.

"I'm sorry, I feel ridiculous because I shouldn't be so surprised, but it just caught me off guard. I mean I know how to fight and everything, well, sort of," she chastised herself and stared into Ash's stubbled face and firm jaw. "I'm nothing compared to you, but," her voice trailed off as her burger arrived with its plate of cheese fries.

Leah shook her head at the amount of food in front of the skinny girl, knowing she was going to eat all of it. She pulled her Greek salad closer and then snatched up one of the cheese-drenched fries from Ciara's plate. "After hearing that story from Curry though, it's not surprising that your reaction might change slightly. I wouldn't be so hard on yourself, even though things aren't truly different, your perception has probably shifted slightly."

"What she said," Jared said as he shoved a chili dog into his mouth.

Tyler shook his head at the man inhaling his food and snorted, "So eloquent, it's a wonder I chose you out of all my many suitors."

Leah piped in, "I do recall many a conversation we had on this topic, would you like me to reiterate some of the key points on the pro's list of reasons you chose Jared?"

Jared perked up and looked between them and asked in excitement, "I have a pro's list? Wait, you made a pro's and con's list about me? How is this the first I am hearing about this?"

"Can we re-focus?" Jez laughed lightly as she sipped at her mug of hot tea and added, "Leah did make a good point, but has anyone called Curry yet?"

Ciara nodded and said, "I called him as we were walking over here. I know The Shadow, this was just another one of his stunts to put me off balance. It's his favorite thing to do: show up when you least expect it, just enough that he is seen, but he won't do anything. Then once you get used to seeing his ugly mug and start unintentionally ignoring him, he goes in for his real move."

Jez tapped the counter with her perfectly manicured nails in thought and inquired, "Is Curry on his way?"

Tyler stabbed at a chili cheese fry and said, "He wanted to get a look at the message and see if they could do any tracing on it. Find out who The Shadow's employer is, but said it was doubtful they could get anything off it, but worth a shot regardless."

Ciara frowned down at her food, trying not to let her frustration show because there was only so much they could do and she knew that, but how could they not know who he was working for? They had the entire government backing them and after hearing more about what her parents had been working on, it seemed even more critical they discover who was behind Grendale. If her parents' research fell into the wrong hands, the results would be devastating for the entire world – entire countries could be leveled.

"Next question," Ash said and put down his gyro with a pointed look at Tyler and Jared, "Why was Ciara alone?"

"We talked about this Ash," Ciara said and raised an eyebrow.

Ash felt his cheeks heating and amended, "I know, you want to be bait, but *after* you get a bit more training."

Ciara groaned, "Fair point, I guess."

"We didn't mean for it to happen," Jared said as he went to work on his second chili dog. "She just got out of her locker room before we did, but there are more guys than girls and I had to wait for a shower."

"Another guy from the ensemble group also had some questions for me and that took up some time." Tyler frowned and added, "We really didn't mean to leave you alone for that long."

"You didn't," Ciara said, wanting to reassure her friends. "If he hadn't left the note for me then, he would have found another way, it's okay."

Ash grunted, letting her know he wasn't happy about it, but that he also recognized that it wasn't Jared's or Tyler's fault. She knew he wasn't happy with their plan, but it was her choice to make. If this latest encounter was any clue, Ciara was going to need to learn to control herself a little better. She couldn't let herself fall to pieces or lash out without thinking. She was going to have to teach herself to be cool and calm. She would not let The Shadow get the better of her.

Unbidden, a memory surfaced of her junior year of high school. She tried to ignore it, still ashamed of her reaction, but her brain refused to co-operate.

Ciara had laughed while walking arm in arm with her latest friends, who weren't even really that, but she had still been trying to pretend she could have what others had. Plus, they had been in that town for close to two months, and there had been no sighting of The Shadow. Comfortability and safety had slowly been soaking in until she was no longer peering into dark corners or double-checking before she walked around at night with her fellow teenagers.

She should have known better; she should have been prepared. But, her friends were taking her to her first teen club, and she hadn't told Sean where she was going. They had gotten into a fight when she'd begged him to let her stay the night at one of the girls houses and he had said no. She had been too immature to understand his reasoning and she had thought they were safe there. It was a small town, no cameras and no way for The Shadow to trace them, at least, that's what she had thought. She had not had any way of knowing one girl had posted a picture of her on her social media account.

As they had entered the club and paid their entrance fee, the noise had assailed her ears and the flashing had made her feel suddenly uneasy. Ciara had tried to convince herself it would get better, that she would grow used to the sound and the lights. But had quickly begun contemplating texting Sean on the burner phone to come and get her, but she was still mad at him. She had resisted the urge, and eventually had grown used to the noise and the flashing lights, and when they had left the club, she had felt vindicated that nothing bad had happened. Wrapped up in her triumph with her ears ringing, Ciara hadn't noticed the sounds of footsteps behind her until her friend had been grabbed.

Ciara had turned with a start, eyes wide, before narrowing angrily, her heart jumping to her throat, and she had seen the long blade in his hand. It was his weapon of choice; she had come to know and had understood it was because it was more difficult to trace and was soundless. Her friend had whimpered, and Ciara had wanted to scream in anger and frustration as her happy bubble was popped. She didn't know what to do, and the friend on her other side had screamed and had tossed her clutch at him, thinking they were being mugged.

"Let her go," she had said coldly, voice only slightly trembling.

"Only if you give me what I want Ciara," he had snarled as her friend's eyes had grown wide at his words.

"If I knew what you wanted maybe I would," Ciara had growled back. She had thought desperately that if she could keep him talking until someone else arrived, then maybe her friend could walk away with her life.

The knife had been aimed at her sternum, and he hadn't really been holding her all that tightly. Her Shadow coming to her there had possibly meant that he either knew her and Sean had gotten into a fight. And thus, was more vulnerable than normal, or it could have meant he had just tracked them down and hadn't known where they lived yet.

She had stumbled through every possible option of how to get them out of the situation, but she hadn't been able to rein in her thoughts. Her mind had continuously circled back to how stupid she had been, *that she didn't know anything, and that she was just a useless girl who couldn't protect herself.*

A brick had collided with the back of The Shadow's head, and then Sean had appeared over his shoulder as he had pulled him away. Sean had gripped the girl The Shadow had held and shoved them all forward with the command, "Move."

They had run down the dark alley and out under the streetlights, staying as silent as possible as they had run to her friend's house. Ciara hadn't even bothered trying to stay the night. She had quickly gathered her backpack and left without even a goodbye. The siblings hadn't spoken at all as they made their way out of town that same night.

Ciara had despised that feeling and vowed to never feel so helpless again, but she had failed that vow many times since then. It never seemed to matter how much effort she put into protecting herself, learning how to defend herself, or gathering information. Grendale always seemed to have the upper hand, no matter who was on her side or there to help her.

"Ciara, are you with us?" Ash asked, and she glanced up at him,

"Still here," she said and pushed her cold plate of cheese fries away from her; she had lost her appetite.

Training

Disgruntled about the way things were going, Ash struggled with the plan. He realized in his head it was the only way to end things between Ciara and the Shadow, but he still didn't like it.

"Ash get a grip," Nate said, patting his friend's shoulder as he reminded him, "It isn't your choice to make."

"I know," Ash huffed and glanced over at the dark-skinned man next to him. "Still doesn't mean I have to like it, but it makes me uneasy to think about what is going to happen."

Leah nodded as she nibbled on a carrot stick and turned the pages in her notebook and admitted, "Me too, I don't think any of us like it. For that matter, Ciara doesn't seem to love the idea either but I'm also fairly certain we all acknowledge it is the only actual option, because it will happen eventually."

"No, I don't like it either," Ciara agreed, twirling a pen in her fingers. "I never said I liked the plan, but it *will* happen eventually and I would have been taken by surprise without any training or warning. This is, realistically, the best plan we have and if I am less guarded, it will bring him closer. It really is the best idea. I get to pick the situation, even if it is up to him on the timing."

"I get it," Ash grumbled and fiddled with his sleeve cuff before adding, "but I still don't like it."

Ciara shrugged and retorted, "Get used to it, I don't like it either but it's the only way to end this."

Ash stared blankly at his music at the rolling a pencil back and forth over the paper. He realized he didn't have to like it and that it wasn't his life or his choice, but he struggled coming to terms with any of it.

>>>

A few weeks after Ash and Ciara learned the story, Ash drove Ciara to a facility where they were both picked up and transported to another building a few towns over. That's where Curry met them with a man wearing a lab coat and what appeared to be a permanent grin on his face.

"This won't hurt a bit," the man prompted, which Ciara understood to mean that it was most likely going to hurt as he took her forearm in one of his large hands. "We are just going to numb this up a bit," he explained as he rubbed a gel on her skin and then inserted the tracking device. "There we go, all done," he said and put a band-aid over the spot and left the room.

Ash frowned and complained, "Not even a cool design."

"I wanted Winnie the Pooh," Ciara said disappointedly, looking at her band-aid before asking, "Do I get a sticker before I leave at least?"

Curry rolled his eyes and mumbled, "I'll see what I can do. Quinten had to go back to his home, but he requested that we give you some extra self-defense training, is that agreeable to you?"

Ash experienced a sense of relief at that knowledge but didn't say anything, and Ciara fiddled with one of her braided pigtails before stating, "That is more than agreeable to me."

Her training began the next day and continued for a month, as she worked through different scenarios where she would hide bits of information someone gave her before the drill occurred. Other times, Ciara was trained in self-defense against different types of weapons, and she was taught how to stay calm in difficult and dangerous situations.

Although Ciara's training was more vigorous, Ash was also given similar training since they believed he might be taken with her, or at the very least, around when it happened. Since he would also potentially be at risk, they added him to the list to receive training. They offered the same to Mr. Durand, but he shook his head and said no one would get anything out of him.

The most difficult part of her training was building her tolerance to pain, because that, Curry and Quinten, were both adamant about. "Assassins understand torture and live by it, if it's information he wants, it is torture he will use."

Quinten, over video chat, nodded in agreement as he explained, "It is unfortunately true and I am so sorry you must go through all this Ciara. But by doing this it will be easier, or more tolerable, later on."

>>>

Her classes seemed as full of work as the semester before, but Ciara still found time to play intramural soccer for the music department. Ash, Leah, and Jez, with Nate, would all come watch the games, which happened every other week, and a lot of the time they would come to the practices as well. Ciara's talent for the game came back quickly over the past semester of practices, and their team made it to second.

Since she understood this semester what her professors expected, Ciara prepared for her papers and exams more easily. She studied on her breaks and used the library's work computer to find articles and research books that would aid her classes.

"What are you doing?" Jared asked, ringing the bell on the checkout counter.

Ciara jumped and apologized, "Sorry, I didn't hear you come up."

He laughed and shrugged his broad shoulders as he said, "You seemed very intent on the screen."

"I'm trying to find an article, but it isn't popping up and I can't figure out why." Ciara frowned at the lit-up screen and adjusted herself on the seat, before asking, "What's up?"

Jared leaned against the counter and hedged, "Not much, I'm just stopping by to say hello, actually, I was hoping we could go out tonight and talk." Ciara eyed him questioningly, and he laughed at her expression before clarifying, "It's just that last semester we hung out twice a week and it seems like I barely see you now. Are you busy tonight, say around nine?"

"I would love to do something and I'm free. How about we meet at the coffee shop?"

"See you there," he said and reached over to ruffle her hair affectionately.

A few hours later, Ciara walked into the coffee shop and saw Jared waiting at one of the tables, and waved before stepping in line to order before sitting down. He looked a bit uncomfortable, but talked normally about classes and professors, different projects, and research problems.

"My lab partner is totally incompetent though," Jared complained with a heavy frown. "He keeps spilling things and records numbers completely wrong and here I thought thermometers were straightforward, but apparently not." He fiddled with his cup and began pleating his napkin again.

Ciara realized he was hesitating to say something to her and smiled kindly at her friend as she prompted, "Jared, spit it out, I know there is something you want to say."

The young man smirked at her and groaned, "I'm horribly obvious." He took a long drink of his hot chocolate before finally explaining his main reason for asking to meet up. "Tyler and I have talked and Nate too, and it's probably strange to think of guys talking about something like this, but Ash means a lot to us. He's like a brother and it seems, well, it seems to us like you're playing him."

Ciara choked on her tea and blushed as she spluttered, "You think I'm *what*?"

"Not on purpose," he rushed to assure her before asking, "But you do like him, right? And it's obvious he likes you." Jared frowned, seeming suddenly uncertain, and shifted in his wooden chair and said, "We just want to understand what's going on."

"He doesn't though, and I... I don't... I guess I might..." a dawning light seemed to brighten in her mind, a light she had been trying to keep dim from force of habit. Before she had always closed off even the possibility of liking someone and built a wall around her feelings. The mortar of that wall seemed to be crumbling at an alarming rate now, causing those feelings to come at her like a flash flood.

Jared bit his lip and inquired, "You didn't know... did you?"

"I never really thought... I never had the chance before and the possibility never arose.... I was always the side show before. The interesting person to befriend for a time, but no guys ever paid me much interest. The thought never occurred to me that he liked me back and I just thought he liked me in the way KT does," Ciara puzzled, trying to make her pulse slow down.

Jared grinned and confessed, "Oh no, I've never seen Ash so head over heels like this. In fact, I'm not sure I have ever really seen him anything near being head over heels, just vague interest. I didn't think you were playing him on purpose and I'm glad I could enlighten you, but I think all of us would appreciate it if you made a move. Ash won't, he's too polite and doesn't think the time is right, what with your Shadow and all."

"Give me some time to come to terms with this first, alright?" Ciara asked as she took a shaky drink of her sweetened tea.

"That's fine by me," he grinned again at the slightly bewildered girl and reached across the table to give her hand a squeeze. He knew it was what Tyler would have done, as he added, "I'm glad we talked."

>>>

Please pick up, please pick up, please pick up, Ciara silently chanted while tapping the counter in her kitchen as she held her cell phone to her ear. She had never needed her best friend more in her entire life.

"Hey girl, what's up?" Lex's voice floated over to her with genuine cheer, and Ciara began to relax. Lex would know what to do; she was experienced in this kind of thing.

"Remember in seventh grade when Kyle used to give me his extra applesauce every day and I just thought he was being nice. And then two months later he asked me to go to the spring dance with him and I freaked out because I had no clue that he liked me and didn't understand what to do so I told him he was stupid and ran off?" Ciara blurted out in one long breath.

"Well, that was possibly the longest sentence I have ever heard, run on, for sure. Take a breath for me 'kay?" Lex was holding back a laugh, and Ciara was grateful for that. She took a deep breath and let it out, then Lex asked, "Feeling a bit more settled?"

"No, yes, what do I do?" Ciara started riffling through her cupboards for her favorite mug and tea.

"You haven't exactly told me what the problem is," Lex stated, and Ciara listened as Lex also pulling out a mug and tea.

"Are you really going to make me say it?"

"Of course I am really going to make you say it," Lex snorted and ran water into a kettle. "It's part of the process, you need to fully acknowledge all the emotions."

"You suck," Ciara huffed and after a moment said weakly, "I like Ash, like *really* like Ash and Jared thinks he likes me too."

This time Lex held back her laugh, but it came out sounding maniacal over the phone. "Course he does, what's not to like? So, what's the problem?"

"I've never had an actual boyfriend before," Ciara wailed. "I mean, sure, I met up with a few guys under the bleachers, if you know what I mean and you do, but nothing steady. It seems so real suddenly and I was doing so good at pretending I didn't feel like this about him, but... he's such a good guy and with everything going on."

"Okay, I'm gonna stop you right there," Lex said, cutting her off. "That isn't your choice to make and it's not a secret that some guy is coming after you. Ash has known the risks for months and has still stuck around. He gets to make that decision, not you."

Ciara let out a breath, letting her friend's words sink in, understanding that she was right; he could have turned tail a long time ago and yet had stayed by her side. That had to count for something, multiple something's, so she asked, "But what do I *do*?"

"I'm not sure I'm following, what do you mean?" Lex asked as her kettle began to whistle.

"I mean..." Ciara poured her own boiling water and moved to her futon while she explained, "Jared said there is no way that Ash is going to make the first move. He's too worried it would scare me off or be too much with everything going on."

Lex snorted and pointed out, "So the same dumb excuse *you* were just making."

"I guess," Ciara murmured, wrapping a blanket around her legs, and then pressed, "How do I make him realize that I actually like him, like that?"

"Flirt," Lex said, and this time there was no mistaking the evil laugh that danced across the phone line. "I know, tall order for one such as yourself."

"Yeah... not sure I will manage that one," Ciara grumbled and blew on her steaming beverage as she admitted, "I'm not you."

"I should hope not," Lex said and used her superpower and took a long sip of her steaming tea with a sigh. "But really, how about just being a bit more touchy-feely, that usually does the trick: lean into him, grab his hand, kiss his cheek, and compliment his hot bod. You can flirt without words, people do it all the time subconsciously."

"I guess," Ciara said, unsure if she could do that.

"I'm serious, you probably will start to notice that you had been doing it all along. So, when you do, just start doing it with more intention and I'm sure he is bound to notice. When the time is right, ask him out," Lex said, making it all sound so easy as she opened and closed what sounded like a sliding door.

"Ask *him* out?" Ciara shook her head.

"Twenty-first century, *yes*, ask him out," Lex asserted, and Ciara sensed Lex's shrug, before adding, "I've only been asked out twice by a guy. All the others, I asked them out. If they like me enough and know me like they should, then it shouldn't be so surprising."

"You are a force," Ciara marveled, as her tension easing. Lex was right; she could ask a guy out, and it was Ash after all. "Alright, I'll do it, but don't expect results right away."

"I can't wait to hear how it all plays out," Lex said as she landed on a chaise lounge on her balcony.

"You're in Italy, right?" Ciara questioned as the sound of violin music and singing drifted up to her.

"Yep, love it here and you would too. I really hope I can take you on one of my trips one day," Lex remarked with a sigh.

"Where exactly are you?" She questioned as she built an image of Lex on her balcony, gazing out into a sunset, not that she actually knew what time it was where Lex was. She had texted her a picture a few days ago, and it had been a gorgeous view of an old city with laundry blowing in the breeze between the apartments.

Lex dreamily said, "Florence and I've got about two more weeks here."

"And what exactly are you writing about?" Ciara inquired, amused by the types of things Lex's boss would send her to research because none of it made sense until she got the article from Lex months later.

"Art trade and how it has changed over time. How it affects modern day capital and blarney blah," Lex grumbled before bragging, "I get press passes into all the art museums and even had a private tour yesterday. I tried to convince my boss to let me tie in wine and how shipping that has also affected capital and tariffs, but she said no."

Ciara laughed in response and admitted, "I'm shocked, it sounds like you would have had a great article there. Meet any one worthy of your time there?"

"There were a few men who struck my fancy and you know I'm not a huge club goer though. I prefer to lounge with a nice glass of the local fair and strike a man's imagination," she said in an overly dramatic voice. Then snorted as she amended, "Actually, I did meet some really awesome people. One of the tour guides had me go for dinner last night and it was *to die for*; the food was so incredible and the wine was from her friend's vineyard. Really glad I took Italian in college, it was a bit rusty, but it came back quick."

Ciara mouth watered as Lex went into even more detail about the food and beverages. Then began to tell her about the city and the few other places she was going to get to visit as she took notes on her latest article. After a long conversation, Ciara finally hung up, feeling more settled than she had before. She may not be overly confident in her growing plan, but she at least had a plan, and that had to count for something.

{ 30 }

Waiting

With this new information settling in her mind, Ciara began to see things differently, and she now understood why KT and Lex always asked her about Ash. She noticed the tall young man always saved a seat for her right next to him. He opened or held doors for her, helped her into her jacket, walked her to and from classes, and got her drinks or snacks randomly. They were always in contact, and she liked it that way.

Ciara felt blind and dumb for not having seen it before, because at some point over the last semester and this one, they became inseparable.

"You seem exhausted," he commented as Ciara rubbed her eyes, as she traveled into her second hour of studying.

She leaned against the practice room door and sat on the floor with a notebook on her lap as she grunted, "I am, but I blame your playing, it's soothing."

He pulled the bow across the violin in a discordant shriek and inquired jovially, "Did that help?"

Her hands flew to her ears as she whined, "That was horrible!"

Ash laughed and put his instrument back into its velvet-lined case and said, "Let's get home and take a walk before going to the coffee shop for open mic night."

"That's a wonderful idea," she agreed, letting him pull her to her feet, and this time she understood the slight sensation filtering into her skin from their touch. It brought a smile to her rosy lips, and she made sure to hang on longer than necessary, and made eye contact long enough for him to realize it was completely intentional.

"Are you going to sing tonight?" Ash questioned, and she saw the color rising into his cheeks, the way he would glance at her, then glance away as he rubbed the back of his neck.

Ciara pulled her coat on, followed by her messenger bag, noticing his subtle signs of anxiety and realizing that she was the cause. "I might, but I'm not sure if my song is ready just yet."

He led her from the building and out onto the cold sidewalks leading toward the parking lot. "You'll still sound much better than anyone else there, most of the singers screech."

Ciara laughed because, for the most part, his statement was true; there were very few quality singers at the open mic night. For some unknown reason, the instrumentalists were typically better than the vocalists. "I might sing, I don't know, I'll see," she said contemplatively, before the hairs on the back of her neck stood up. She peered into the darkness and saw a deeper shadow slip into a copse of trees.

Ash followed her gaze, his eyes narrowing as he asked, "Did you see something?" Unconsciously, they stepped closer together, and she gripped his hand.

"Felt more than saw, he is hiding behind that clump of trees," Ciara whispered back and shivered, drawing her bag tighter on her shoulder.

"Well, he's back then, if he ever left that is," Ash grunted and gripped her gloved hand in his own. She squeezed his fingers back and, this time, didn't immediately pull her hand away, but let it linger as he said, "Let's keep going and walk straight to the coffee shop. How does that sound?"

"Sounds like a good idea," she replied and took one more glance at the place where Joseph Grendale stood hidden, and intentionally turned her back. She marched off with Ash, pretending to ignore the man when all she wanted was to dive into the underbrush and cuff him.

It was much easier to ignore him once Ash and Ciara ducked into the hushed quiet of the coffee shop where open mic night was already underway. Their friends waved them into two empty chairs, and they quickly obliged, setting their belongings down. On stage, a poet relayed a heartrending memoir of a long ago night while they murmured their greetings to their friends. Ciara drifted over to the cashier, with Ash in tow, to place their orders and waited for their turn at the microphone.

"I already put both of your names down," Nate informed them with a wink as they sat back down in the wooden chairs with their steaming mugs in hand.

Ciara raised a delicate eyebrow at Ash as she stated, "Really?" Then joined the crowd, clapping for the poet who seemed beside themselves at the praise.

The next person's name was called, and they walked through the crowd to the stage, tuning up an acoustic guitar. Ash chuckled and defended himself, "You said you wanted to, so I told Nate to sign you up!"

"I said *maybe*," Ciara corrected him and groaned. "Too late now, I did bring my music at least, but you have to play the piano because I can't do both." She fidgeted with the torn hem of her band shirt, secretly pleased that she wouldn't have to make the decision herself.

"You'll be fine; you practiced it a few hours ago and it was great. Don't be nervous," Ash ordered and bumped his shoulder into hers.

Leah looked over from her hushed conversation with Tyler and stated, "You sing in front of people all the time, why would you be nervous about something like this?"

"That's different, I didn't write it," Ciara explained and shook her hands, trying to dispel her nerves. "It's fine, I'll be fine; it's just like choreographing my own dance. If the people like it then great, but if they don't well, it doesn't really matter."

"Exactly, it's art and everyone vibes differently with art," Jez said and squeezed her arm. "At least you are in the business where people, typically, like what you have to say or do." She smirked and added, "I'm always pissing half the crowd off."

Ciara laughed as she acknowledged the bitter truth behind her friend's words, and it erased the remnants of nerves with the sound. The group lapsed into a pleasant silence as they listened quietly to the poets and performers; there was even a short comedy act. Then it was Tyler's turn on the stage, and the percussionist walked up to the piano, shaking his hands out as he walked. Jared catcalled him, making Tyler's ears redden slightly as he sat under the light.

Closing her eyes, Ciara listened to his beautiful music, letting it take her in every twist and turn. Tyler was much quieter than Jared, but Ciara realized he was one of the most solid of the boys in the group and cared deeply for his partner. When he approached Ciara a few weeks prior, asking if she would help him with a surprise for Jared on their upcoming anniversary, and she readily agreed. The hours they spent together in the practice rooms gave a wonderful view into the confines of the quiet man. Ciara clapped and whistled with the others as the song ended, wishing that it could have gone on longer.

A few minutes later, Leah shakily walked onto the stage, Tyler whispering words of encouragement to his childhood friend. She walked up to the mic and froze, her face a ghostly white under the stage lights and her eyes wide with fear. Quickly, Ash stood and pulled his guitar strap on, letting his long legs carry him to the stage. He sat down on a bar stool just behind her and started playing a smooth melody. Leah took a deep breath in, reassured, at eyes divided between another person, and began to recite her magical words. They wove a tale as old as time, a tale of a cross between two worlds, a tale of Avalon and of Camelot. It was a beautiful interpretation, and the crowd was spellbound. Ash stayed behind as his name was next on the list and, once again, the others were left in sheer wonder at the talent the giant possessed. Even though Ciara heard him play every day, when he performed, there was nothing like it. His shy exterior disappeared, and he stepped into the act as if born to it. The crowd was used to his music by now, but they still sat in stunned silence for a moment before exploding in applause.

The announcer gave Ash a grin and joked, "Want to stay for one more song? Looks like Sierra and Ash are up next." Ash shook his head and said her name for the man who apologized, "Sorry, Ciara, come on up."

As the man stepped aside, Ciara pushed herself out of her seat and made her way to the microphone, steadying herself with a deep breath. She glanced over to Ash and nodded to let him know she was ready, and his fingers began to sail across the keys, letting the folk melody flow through the gathering. Ciara closed her eyes and began a low hum, weaving in the melody to follow with the piano. When she opened her mouth the crowd fell silent, her mezzo timbre pulling the attention of every person in the building. While the song rang with a folk sound, the words were unfamiliar. It was a tribute to her brother and the adventures they experienced, a song of sorrow and of love, like every good Irish ballad. When the song ended, her voice hovered in the air like morning fog. The listeners shook their heads, as if coming out of a waking dream, to whistle and cheer with the rest. Ciara thanked the crowd and walked down the steps and back to her friends. She shook herself as she sat down, dispelling the jitters from her short performance.

"Better than you thought?" Jared questioned.

"Much better," Ciara said with a smile and drained her cup of tea. Without asking, Ash set another mug down in front of her.

>>>

Ciara began to notice The Shadow more often after the open mic night and tried to ignore him, but it became harder as each new day drifted by. At the insistence of Curry, she spoke to her friends and got them to relax security around her.

They didn't like the idea, but they understood her reasoning behind it and realized it was her choice. However, they were worried about her, and they noticed how anxious it made Ash. They also noticed how often Ciara looked over her shoulder.

"Are you sure you want to do this?" Jez questioned one day as they carefully walked down the just-salted steps toward the main buildings on campus. Jez had just finished a presentation and, despite the ice, wore high heels of a bright blue. She held onto Ciara's arm as they crunched over the salt, attempting to perforate the thick covering of frozen water on the sidewalk. "I should have changed shoes in the classroom, but I didn't realize it was so bad out here."

Ciara snorted and declared, "Probably, but I'll catch you if you fall. I'm sure I want to do this; it's the only way to stop it."

Jez sighed and lamented, "If that's what you think, then it's your choice. Do you still want me to go over your Roman Law paper tonight?"

"If you could, I think I have most of it, but there are a few details I'm a little hazy about still." Ciara pulled a bit of her hair out of her face, grateful she remembered her gloves that morning.

"Just let me see it when you work tonight and I will take a look at it there so I can ask questions if I need to." The woman narrowed her deep brown eyes on Ciara, patting her arm as she suddenly changed the topic and inquired, "What's going on with you and Ash?"

"Nothing yet, I don't know why he won't make a move. I thought I was being quite obvious," she said, perplexed as she kept Jez steady on the ice. Ciara thought of all the little things she did to try and let him see how she really felt, but she seemed to have very successfully friend-zoned herself. Over a month had passed since Jared's enlightening talk with her. Ciara confided in Jez about it, who just given her a sympathetic look and admitted that the entire group was aware of the two's awkward predicament. She wanted to take Lex's advice but wasn't sure how to go about it.

"Men are slow sometimes and Ash is too shy," Jez confided and winked at her, before adding, "You realize I'm the one who asked Nate out right?"

"I never knew that," Ciara said with admiration in her voice as she gazed at her friend with a new sense of wonder. "I might have to go that route too, Lex told me I should, but I've never asked anyone out before."

"It's a new age my dear," she intoned as they quickly strode through the center of campus to the warm-looking brick buildings hiding under a fresh powder of snow. "Perhaps you need to be the one to make the first move."

That night, Ciara sat with a stemless glass of wine, scratching her head and wondering how she was ever going to stay on top of everything. She had books stacked in three separate piles and two papers loaded up on her laptop. Jez was reading the third draft of her paper, while Leah munched on popcorn and running a finger down the pages of an old book searching for a quote she had encountered earlier that night.

Despite the academic air in Jez's apartment, Ciara couldn't seem to rein in her wandering mind. All she could focus on was the past. She remembered another night, five years ago with Sean, that had been extremely similar.

"Cia, you can't put this in here," Sean had said as he leaned over and tapped the handwritten line in her history notebook.

Ciara had glanced over and had squinted in the golden haze of light from their tiny lamp. She had been attempting to cook the manager's special ground beef with some broccoli, but the flame on their tiny propane burner hadn't been staying lit. They had needed more fuel, but their money was drying up. She had groaned in frustration and asked, "Why not?"

"This is a research paper, right?" Sean had patiently questioned. He had almost always been patient with stuff like that. Normally, she was grateful for that, but just then she had wanted to stick gum in his hair, like when she was five. Ciara had nodded as she relit the flame for the fifth time, and Sean had scooted closer and pulled the tiny pot from the top of the burner and taken it from her. He had then pumped the valve as he explained, "You can put that in the beginning to set the stage for the point you are making, but the rest of the paper is new information. What you have discovered, how you discovered it, your process."

"But how am I supposed to do that?" She had whined as her stomach growled and her aching head had started to pound.

Sean had set the burner down and had directed her, "Go to the college library, they have more resources and you can always call some people and maybe do some interviews."

As Sean had gotten up and begun collecting wood, Ciara had groaned in frustration and said, "No one else is doing that. Everyone else is basically doing literary analysis papers, history style."

"Are you everyone else?" Sean had asked with a raised eyebrow. "Start clearing a spot for the fire, no more fuel."

Ciara had looked down at the dirt-covered ground of the abandoned barn where they had spent the better part of the last two months and did as he had said. She had loved it there; it was warm and cozy once they had patched up the holes, and the view onto the pasture had been inspiring. After a long moment of silence, she had finally answered his question, "No, I'm not."

"If you half-ass it, you will regret it. I know that and you know that. Help me get some wood and I can help you rework this after we eat, because no good ideas came out of starvation, unless you're The Buddha, which neither of us are." Sean had peered at her with that patient smile again before leaning over and ruffling her hair.

Pushing herself to her feet, Ciara had sighed and helped him bring in some of the wood they had collected. She couldn't help feeling that Sean had wasted all that intelligence because he'd decided not to enroll in school the last time they had moved. Ciara had known it wasn't just a onetime decision, even though they had never talked about it, but somehow she had known Sean didn't plan on graduating high school. Part of her had felt guilty about it, but the other had known it wasn't her choice.

"Why the grim face?" Sean had asked for over the pile of wood in his arms.

"Nothing," Ciara had lied and dropped her pile to begin making a teepee of twigs.

"*Hey, I'll help with the paper and it won't take that long. Once you get rolling, it will be done before you know it,*" Sean had promised, and had wrapped an arm around her and kissed the side of her head.

Ciara sucked in her bottom lip at the memory, wishing she could hold on to that feeling of his hand in her hair, that smile on his face, the absolute belief in her. In a throat choked with sudden emotion, Ciara reached for her wine glass to try to loosen it up. She took a few quiet, calming breaths before looking up at her friends. Jez was still caught up in her paper with a pink pen between her teeth. Leah, however, was watching her with intensity, noting every slight muscle shift as she mouthed, '*You okay?*' Ciara nodded and went back to her pile of books with renewed vigor.

If I could live through that and if Sean dropped out so I could have a chance, then I can't complain. I can do anything, Ciara vowed to herself and closed her eyes. She pulled up the image of Sean sitting in the lamplight, casting his shadow huge behind him, making him larger than life. *But that is how he has always been to me, larger than life,* Ciara acknowledged the truth to her and the total sacrifice he made for her. Ciara smiled, and when she went back to work, it no longer seemed so daunting.

Black Out

Ciara slid around a corner in her jeep and almost lost control before she could slow down. Snow had fallen heavily all through the day, and finally school was canceled for fear people wouldn't be able to leave once night came. With wide eyes, Ciara glanced at Ash, apologizing, "I'm sorry, I'm so sorry."

She put the jeep into four-wheel drive and slowly began moving again, and when they came closer to their apartment, Ash pointed at a car curled around the transformer. Police cars, an ambulance, and a fire truck surrounded the smashed car, still steaming from its engine. After that, they noticed the lack of power in the neighborhood; none of the streetlights were working, and the electric signs hung blank. However, some stores seemed to be running on generators; one being the pizza place a block from their apartment complex.

"Let's stop in and get a pizza before heading all the way home. With the power out we won't be able to make anything," Ash suggested, and Ciara agreed, gently sliding to a stop in front. Quickly, they hurried inside to place their simple order with the harried cashier.

The frazzled high schooler shook her head at them and admitted, "We are so far behind, it will probably be a little over an hour wait. It seems like this entire half of town ordered a pizza and no one else has power."

"A transformer was hit, so unless people have generators or are powered on propane, everything is out," Ciara explained. And remembered that being a part of her life for a long time and how quickly she had grown accustomed to amenities.

"Oh, gotcha," she hummed and glanced behind her to see how the other workers were doing before asking, "Would you like it delivered?"

"We aren't that far," Ash said with a shrug, and Ciara watched as he mentally braced himself for the walk back in the bitter chill.

"Alright, I will put you down for that and it should be ready in an hour. Unless you don't need delivery," she said, ringing up their order as Ash handed his card over to her.

When they got back into the jeep, Ash smiled shyly at her and murmured, "You can bring some blankets over if you want, two people in one room will be warmer than one. And we should probably check on Mr. Durand also."

A few minutes later Ciara pulled into her spot, not noticing the smile as she concentrated on controlling the Jeep in the deepening snow. They climbed the stairs quickly, and she snatched up blankets and more comfortable clothing as Ash waited in the doorway.

Then they went over to check on Mr. Durand, who answered from a candle-lit room and smiled in his wrinkled face. "I'm just fine but come in and we can all play a few games to take our minds off this storm. Ciara, don't you have a little camp stove so we can heat up some water for tea?"

"I do, let me go find it," Ciara exclaimed, running out and came back a few minutes later with a propane stove that she and Sean used to use almost every day.

Ash brought a pot of water over as Ciara lit the stove, and as they settled in, Ciara pulled out the pack of cards and began to shuffle with an expert hand. Without asking, she began to deal a game of poker, knowing Ash had been wanting a rematch with Mr. Durand since last week's enormous loss. She had tried to remind him that he hadn't learned how to play the game until the fall, but Ash had a hidden competitive streak in him. Mr. Durand grinned and settled himself in his chair, spreading the cards in his hand.

Ciara fanned hers out and stared at Ash with a quired eyebrow as she asked, "What's your play?"

An hour and a half later, Ash trudged back into Mr. Durand's with the pizza in hand, having successfully convinced Ciara not to come with him. But he had taken her advice on bringing a blanket to wrap the pizza boxes up in to help keep them warm. After dinner, Mr. Durand pulled out his ancient Scrabble set, and they each drew their letters. In the lamplight, the three played round after round until they began playing with the most childish words for points.

Ash and Ciara laughed and called it quits, knowing Mr. Durand had once again won by a landslide. As they left Mr. Durand to his apartment, Ash hesitated at his bedroom door and muttered, "Stay warm, but if you get too cold just come into my room." Ash paused and bit his lip, appearing uncertain about what he wanted to say next before finally finishing, "You can steal another blanket."

Ciara tried not to let her disappointment show and thanked him as he disappeared into his bedroom.

With two pairs of socks, two sweatshirts, long Johns, and sweatpants on, Ciara curled up on his couch under a nest of blankets. At first, she felt alright, but in what seemed no time she was shivering. Her mind strayed to the warm blankets piled on Ash's bed and how warm it would be if she snuggled up next to him. Strengthening her resolve, Ciara got up with an armful of blankets and slowly pushed open his door.

>>>

"Ash?" Ciara stage-whispered into the dark of his room.

His scruffy face popped up out of his pile as he answered, "Please tell me you came in because you are cold too."

"Yes," she chattered out, her body nearly convulsing with shivers.

Ash pulled the blankets back, inviting her over, his voice rumbling over to her, "Hop in, I'm too cold to give you any, so I hope you're okay with sharing."

Gratefully, Ciara climbed in and through her demanded, "Tell me what your favorite thing about music is."

For a moment, Ash didn't answer as he contemplated her answer, and in the dark, Ciara could only observe the shadow of his profile. But she thought his fingers brushed tentatively against the back of her hand, just before he responded, "I love it when a piece of music conveys one emotion into crowd of people. It just feels so powerful and not many things can do that."

"That's very true," she mused and turned on her side to squirm even closer to him, intentionally seeking his warmth.

"What do you like about it?" He shifted and stared into the bottomless depths of her ocean-dark eyes, and Ciara watched him swallow.

"It crosses cultures and you don't need to know the language to understand the meaning behind it all, because the music speaks for itself." She gazed into his eyes and softly said, "Thank you for letting me come over."

Once again, Ash appeared to be contemplating his words as he bit his lip and finally whispered, "I wanted you here, Ciara." And then Ash leaned his head closer and placed his lips hesitantly on hers.

Ciara's face grew red, and she wondered if steam would start to rise off it in the cold air as a grin spread across her lips. She wrapped her arms around the giant and pulled him closer as Ash murmured against her mouth, "I guess that was okay then?"

With her fingers curling into his soft brown hair, Ciara laughed her response, "Of course, I've been waiting for you to kiss me or say something for weeks." She chuckled and smashed her face against him as she kissed him again.

"For weeks?" He questioned, before admitting, "I thought it would just be added things to worry about."

Ciara rolled her eyes, her fingers tentatively brushing against the scruff along his jawline as she murmured back, "This would have made everything easier, but..." she gave him a sly smile. "We can make up for that," she hesitantly said, before kissing him again with fierce determination.

Within a few minutes, Ciara and Ash no longer needed their double layers, peeling them off without a moment's thought. But as Ash slid his hand along the soft skin of her stomach, he did pause with a question in his eyes and a raised brow. Ciara tilted her head back and nodded her acceptance as she firmly stated, "It's okay, anything you want. Whatever you are okay with, does that sound good?"

He nodded and continued kissing her as he slowly undid her bra. Somehow, she managed to slide out of her shirt, and even in the dark, Ciara could see the heat it brought to his face as she slid her hand down the front of his pants. Time slipped away after that in a tangle of warmth and limbs, mouths and sensation as the two found their rhythm together. Until, breathless, they lay curled against one another in the dark, feeling whole and finally warm in their new cocoon.

>>>

Everything seemed sparkly and new to Ciara the next day, lulling her into a false sense of security as the day passed. The group stayed working in the warmth of the coffee shop until the email came in that the power was back on in their neighborhoods again. She was loath to part with Ash in the hallway of their apartment building, but she needed to shower and needed time to process and, of course, fill Lex in on the current events.

After an excessively long shower, Ciara pulled out her cell phone and called Lex, who was, for once, in her time zone. After several rings, the blonde answered, "Hey!"

Ciara held back her grin as best she could, but she knew Lex would still hear it in her voice as she greeted her, "Hey."

"Oh!" she dragged out the word, and Ciara guessed that she was fist-pumping in the air while demanding, "Tell me every single last detail!"

"So, I know it's been a while since we talked," Ciara admitted and flopped down onto her bed as she elaborated, "But not much really happened until last night. I did try to do as you suggested, but he was just not picking up what I was trying to lay down, if you know what I mean."

"Meaning you were attempting to flirt and were failing epically?" Lex asked, and Ciara heard her crunch into something. "So, what happened last night that changed things, because if this story doesn't end with you two getting together then there is going to be a seriously annoyed Alexis."

Ciara snickered into the phone as she said, "Well, see last night – did you catch the news?"

"The east coast was hit hard with a snowstorm, right?" She questioned after swallowing another bite.

"Yep, but we also lost power," Ciara explained and added, "Car hit a transformer or something and blacked out almost the whole city, it was nuts."

"Things are sounding a bit steamy and I'm picturing candles and serenading, so many romantic things happen when there's no power. It's just so much more sentimental when there isn't all that technology getting in the way," Lex surmised.

"Right," Ciara said with a snort and shook her head at her friends overly dramatic thoughts. "Not exactly what happened, but I like where you're headed. Anyway, it was obviously freezing, and we had been hanging out and then we got to thinking it would just be better if I stayed over at his place."

"It would be better if you stayed over at his place. Please for the love of all things holy tell me you slept with that fantastic piece of male specimen," Lex blurted on a gust of air.

The other woman bit her lip as she tried not to laugh at her friend. Her face had gone bright red, she was sure of it, but more from the memory of the night before than embarrassment. "I told him I would sleep on the couch."

"You did what?" Lex shrieked, and Ciara couldn't hold back her laughter, and then heard Lex's mom calling from her side of the phone. Lex responded, "Sorry mom, Ciara is being dumb, but I'll try to keep my screeching to the bare minimum."

"I didn't stay there for very long, because like I said it was freezing. Well, it wasn't that bad, but I thought it would be a good excuse to at least snuggle," Ciara said as she went on with the story.

"An excellent excuse. You at least made out, right?" Lex questioned with an all too serious tone.

"Oh, we did," Ciara sighed dreamily, remembering the feel of his soft lips brushing against hers that first time.

"And?"

"We got a bit carried away."

"Baby Ciara is all grown up people!" Lex clapped her hands and cheered.

Ciara laughed and rolled her eyes at her friends' antics, but enjoyed the feeling of having someone to share her story with. "Long story short, as I am sure you can guess, we are officially a thing."

"I'm totally taking credit for this, because I encouraged it from the very beginning. Back in September, I knew this was going to be a thing and I told you to start acting more flirtations and to take charge."

"Alright, you can take credit for *some* of it," Ciara snorted, but couldn't deny Lex at least some of the credit.

"Thank you," Lex simpered, before inquiring, "What else is new?"

"Nothing as exciting as that," Ciara admitted, before remembering the other reason she had called and said, "I just read your article. Care to tell me how the rest of your trip in Italy was and how long are you home for?" Ciara let Lex take over the conversation from there and with much relief let her mind drift into sleep a few hours later.

>>>

The next morning, she waved goodbye to everyone in the school parking lot. She had to go to the library for work, and the rest had classes in other parts of campus. She hurried through the stiff wind down a back path to the library. It had been weeks since a real sighting or incident had happened with the Shadow, and she thought she would at least see something before anything happened. She should have known better, should have remembered all those times before being lulled into a false sense of security. She should have reminded herself how dangerous it was to let her mind become unfocused. She should have taken the more crowded path through the main part of campus, where someone, anyone, would have been able to see her. Instead, she walked directly into Grendale as if he knew exactly which route she would take to work, as if he had watched her for months.

"Hello Ciara," he greeted with a menacing grin and covered her face with a cloth. Ciara fell into unconsciousness.

{ 32 }

Caught

Ciara woke to cold metal biting into her wrists, which were bound behind her back, and a heavy cloth pressed over her eyelids. Slowly, she tried to wriggle herself into a better position, only to find her ankles were also bound. Ciara bit back a cry of frustration. The only worse position would be if she were hog-tied. Blinking slowly and taking a deep breath, she immediately regretted it as an acrid and rotten smell infiltrated her nostrils. A bump jostled her, and the sound of gravel kicking up underneath the vehicle told her she was in a car. *This must be where he spends most of his unbathed time... disgusting.* Ciara heard a gruff voice, she recognized as The Shadow, mutter to themselves.

Careful not to draw attention, she tried to get the cloth off, but unlike the last time he captured her, The Shadow was aware of her quick recovery time.

He pulled the vehicle over almost immediately and held another cloth to her face with a cloying sweet smell. Ciara fought him with everything her bound body had, but Grendale wasn't prepared to lose her this time and pushed her onto her back. He held her down until Ciara's body eventually overtook her mind and she gasped in the toxic fumes and fell, once more, into a dreamless sleep.

>>>

Grendale climbed back into the driver's seat and pulled back onto the snow-covered road. He made sure his lights were on and that he was going at the same cautious speed as everyone else on the road, as there was no sense in drawing unwanted attention by doing something unnecessary. His phone beeped several times in quick succession, and Grendale hit the answer button on his phone stuck to his dash and barked out, "Yes?"

"Got her locked tight this time?" Came a rasping, dry reply.

"Yes sir," Grendale replied, keeping his annoyance from entering his voice as best he could. He still struggled to believe a bunch of college kids had bested him and was embarrassed enough without the reminder, and in his circle, he realized his ratings were taking a hit.

"We better not have a repeat because we need that chip and if you don't have it on a plane with you in forty-eight hours, I'm pulling your plug."

Navigating around a cop car, Grendale monitored his voice as he grumbled back, "I will be on that plane with the package secured." He understood his employer wasn't speaking metaphorically when he said he would pull the plug. Grendale had a target on his back, and his timer was running out. If he didn't produce, he was a dead man and eight years was seven years too many, but how could anyone predict just how ingenious the kids would be. The call ended abruptly just as he turned onto a dirt road just out of town, far enough to do what he needed. A few minutes later, he pulled into a driveway and then climbed out and opened the back door slowly, just in case she had woken up again, but she was still out cold. He tossed a blanket over her before picking her up and cradling her to his chest. He didn't need any neighbors asking questions; then carried her into the house already set up with the first step of his plan.

>>>

The next time Ciara woke, her wrists were tied with rope to a headboard, and when she attempted to move, rope bit into her ankles. She didn't like the feeling of helplessness it gave her, especially when a shape loomed above her and slowly came into focus. Taking a shaking breath, she reminded herself that this was what she had been training for the past few months. It didn't make the reality any better though. Being tied up by her family's killer was more real than what she had experienced with Curry's crew.

"Good morning, Ciara," Grendale sneered, leaning over her, grinning, and the scent of stale sweat hit her like a tidal wave.

Ciara coughed and said in the most sarcastic voice she could muster, "Joseph, how are you?"

"I wouldn't be asking how I am; I would be worrying about how you will be in a few minutes, if you don't answer me," Joseph sneered as he pulled out a sharp knife from a sheath located at the small of his back. He trailed the flat of the blade across her cheek, his eyes narrowing at her.

With her rigorous training in torture and scare tactics, Ciara thought it through and realized if she forestalled the actual pain portion of it, Curry might get there before it started. She made her heart race by thinking of the moment she saw her brother fall to the ground. It caused her eyes to water as she stuttered out a response, "But, but... I don't know anything, there is nothing to tell you."

"I'm sure you don't," he snarled and pulled up the sleeve of her shirt. "Of course, if you didn't, then you wouldn't know my name, which somehow you do. They told you something and I told you I'm always watching," he growled and dug the knife point in and twisted. The chip Curry put in popped out, and Grendale crunched it in his palm with a smirk. "I suppose there is a little more time here, let's make it worthwhile."

A gasp escaped Ciara's throat, but she remembered a time when she was young and fell, scraping her knee.

Her mother had picked her up and rocked her, red curls mixing with Ciara's waving dark brown. "Women are stronger and can handle higher pain levels than any man if we put our minds to it. For longer too."

"That's not true," Ciara had pouted, tears streaming down her plump cheeks.

In response, her mother had smiled down at her and firmly stated, "Yes, it is, because we must give birth and sometimes that lasts for hours. We're also better at thinking of multiple things at once, so we can distract ourselves from that pain."

Ciara smiled to herself but made sure not to let anything show to Joseph Grendale. Her mother had given her information and help even after she was gone, and it made Ciara feel close to her again. She bit her lip and blinked, letting her tears fall as she whined, "I swear I don't know anything, all they did was tell me your name, that's all."

"Of course," he droned and slid the knife across her throat. "I could easily do what I did to your brother to you, be careful how you answer." He watched Ciara's pupils dilate, not knowing she thought of other things. He wouldn't kill her right away because he needed her, and she understood that. "Your parent's research, you know something about it and I know you have an idea about where they kept their papers and the chip."

"They had lots of papers, how would I know where they kept all of them?" Ciara pretended to squirm under his gaze as she tried to move as far from his stale body odor as possible. She wasn't able to move far enough, though, and the ropes bit into her wrists and ankles.

"Try again," he demanded and drew the blade down her collarbone. "USBs too, where? What was their research?"

Ciara watched the blade and thought of the time she dislocated her finger, the snapping pain. The heat. Tears formed anew in her eyes, and she panted. "There was a bowl on the counter and a drawer in the kitchen and another in their desks. I have no idea; I really don't."

"Then this is going to get painful," he warned as the knife came closer to her face.

Ciara fell into the abyss of pain and reprieve, never quite knowing what was coming next, but she used the strategies they had given her and, when that failed, she fell into memories. Memories of Sean, her mother, her father, her grandmother. Memories of Ash, Mr. Durand, her old friends, and her new friends. Then there was the black of unconsciousness, until she came to with the sensation of the ropes sliding off, but it wasn't a sense of safety that infused her as her other senses told her it was Grendale.

Steeling herself, Ciara did her best not to react and let him remove her final binding before rolling off the bed and trying to race him to the door. His arm flew out and knocked her to the ground, and Ciara spun her leg out, trying to take his legs out from under him. But he was too steady on his feet, and she was exhausted, her mind foggy. Grendale laughed at her attempt, and Ciara quickly tried to crawl away from him.

"Hiding like a little child? What good will that do?" Grendale questioned as he reached down and gripped her ankle as Ciara attempted to pull herself under the bed.

Screaming, Ciara kicked back at him, getting him in the mouth; Grendale let go of her foot with a curse. She squirmed under the bed, and as he swore and wiped the blood from his now split lip, Ciara dug into the fresh cut on her arm and drew a tiny arrow in the top right corner at the head of the bed.

Ciara had noticed very quickly that Grendale had become way too comfortable living on his own. When he wasn't attempting to dredge information from the depths of her mind, he was talking to himself. The last round, he had let slip that he was moving her over to the house across the street. She realized he didn't think she would hear him, and had stared over her head, letting her know it was in that direction. Her only hope was to leave a sign and that Curry would take Ash with him. Someone else might miss it, but Ash wouldn't, and he knew who her favorite detective was.

Grendale kicked the bed frame into the wall and grabbed the back of her hair in one smooth motion as he pulled a wet cloth from the side table and pressed it to her face. Ciara was under before she had a chance to fight back.

>>>

Ash glanced up from his notes as the classroom phone rang suddenly, and his professor stopped his lecture with a frown and picked it up with a furrowed brow. "Hello?"

"Yes, he's here. What's so important you need to interrupt my class?" He responded with annoyance in his voice.

"Fine," the music professor called Ash over to the phone, not bothering to hide his irritation.

Ash stood with fear binding its way around his chest and picked up the phone and asked, "Hello?"

"This is Professor Austin, Ciara's advisor. Have you seen Ciara this morning?" He asked, knowing how strange he must sound.

Ash's stomach plummeted and his veins filled with ice as he choked out, "Yes, I drove her here today but we split up in the parking lot."

Professor Austin let out a breath as he explained, "She didn't come into work. Did she say she had to go anywhere first? She never misses without letting me know."

"She was headed to the library," Ash murmured, knowing what had happened, but his mind wanted to reject it. "Something must have happened to her, I need to call someone. Thank you, Professor Austin and I will let you know when I find her."

"Ash, is everything okay?" His professor's brow furrowed in concern as he watched the young man's anxious face.

The tall man looked blankly at the classroom and realized the entire class was staring at him. "I have to go, thank you." He hung up and rushed to his desk and shoved everything into his backpack. "Professor, I need to go. My girlfriend's... I have to go, I'm sorry, but I need to go check on her."

Ash ran from the room, not waiting for a reply, as he frantically dialed Curry's number as he went.

"Ash?" Curry asked.

"Ciara's been taken, but must not have been too long ago," he said hurriedly with a slight tremble to his voice. He fought down the rising panic, trying to stay calm as he reminded himself she had been preparing for this. They both had, but simulations and reality were two very different things.

The sound of something beeping rolled over the connection, and then Curry explained, "I started tracking her. He's still on the move. I'll get a unit going, but it looks like there's an accident on the way though. It's going to take us awhile to get around it and then catch up to him."

Ash's jaw clenched in frustration and understood it wasn't Curry's fault. He wasn't able to control traffic or the bad weather, but Ash couldn't stop from aggressively stating, "And if something happens in that time?"

"Ash, I can't control the roads. Some roads aren't plowed or salted yet and there are no roads that go straight toward her. Plus, we are on the opposite side of the city, but someone will be by to pick you up soon. After this is over, I am sure she will need you, but you must stay in the car. You cannot get in the way, do you understand?"

"Yes, Sergeant Curry," Ash stated, breathing deeply and trying to calm down as he grudgingly agreed to his terms.

As Curry hung up, Ash sent a group text to their friends that simply read, "Ciara's been taken."

Texts came flying back, and he responded to their group with the simple, "Going with Curry. Will respond when she is safe."

>>>

The blinds were drawn across the window behind her head in her new room, making it impossible for her to tell which direction her room was in or where exactly she was in the house. Ciara fought against her bindings and tried to scream, but a cloth had been shoved in her mouth and then duct tape covered her lips. She furrowed her brow in frustration but stopped herself from pulling on the bindings; it would only make the knots tighter. Instead, she wiggled her wrists back and forth, stretching and pulling them apart. The ropes rubbed against her tender skin but she ignored the pain. She needed to loosen the bindings while she had the chance, determined not to let him get the upper hand on her. As quietly as she could, Ciara set to work, trying to listen to everything around her.

A voice drifted up to her. *Up, that means I'm on the second floor, if my guess about being moved across the street was accurate. I can't think why else he would have looked out the window like that, though, but I may have just been hopeful.* She shook her head slightly, refusing to allow her thoughts to drift in that direction. *No, I can't think like that. I have to think that I was right and that they are on their way. They must be on their way; it's been at least several hours, and someone will have noticed that I'm gone by now. They can look back at my tracker data, and then Ash will see my clue. Everything will work out okay; just stay positive.*

Ciara closed her eyes and focused on her hearing. They were speaking an unfamiliar language, possibly German or Russian. Scandinavian. Ciara wasn't sure exactly, but she thought she would at least recognize German from her brief stint in middle and high school taking the language, but they were speaking so quickly she couldn't pin it down. Footsteps creaked up the stairs, and Ciara forced her body back into stillness. She heard Grendale bark into the phone a direction before pushing her door open. He grinned at her, yellowing teeth showing starkly against his dark beard as he turned the light on. A thousand nasty remarks came into her mind, and she mentally shouted them at him. It made her feel better, even though he may never hear them with his own ears, but she couldn't afford to make him truly angry.

"Are you ready for the second round?" He questioned, opening a duffel bag sitting on the chair by the bed. "Now that the tracker is out, we have all the time in the world."

Do we though? Ciara wondered, because it certainly didn't seem that way from his conversation. Even if she didn't understand the words, she could at least tell that it was clipped and hasty; usually, that meant time was running out. *What happens when he realizes I really have no idea where this thing actually is?*

Grendale pulled out a nasty-looking device and tapped it into the open palm of his other hand, and ordered, "Let's begin."

{ 33 }

Sherlock

Time seemed to slow as Ash waited for someone to pick him up. Curry hadn't said where to meet or who was coming for him, but when he saw an obtrusive black van pull up, he knew exactly which car to climb into. He wondered at their creativity but didn't think he should chance remarking on it.

"Ash?" someone called from inside, and Ash nodded, studying the person as they ordered, "Climb in, quickly." Ash obeyed, and the back doors opened to show a high-tech environment and two other people crammed inside. "Curry sent us to get you, and we've been briefed on the situation, but you know Ciara best, how long do you think she's been gone?"

"At this moment, I believe," he checked his cell phone for the time before continuing, "Two and a half hours. We split up around one in the afternoon."

"Do you know how it happened?" A lady with her hair tightly braided questioned.

Ash shook his head and described their morning, "We were all going to our classes and she had work, so we separated just past the music building."

A middle-aged man working on a computer glanced over his shoulder at Ash, who crouched in the back of the van, commanding, "Sit here and who is this *we*?"

"Our friends," Ash said, rubbing his temples, as helplessness settled in around him and he clarified, "Nate, Tyler, Jared, Leah, and Jez. We all met up for lunch and walked in from the parking lot, but Ciara realized Joseph Grendale had been following her again."

"Why didn't she warn Curry about it?" The man typed furiously and pictures, maps, and numbers popped up on the screen.

Ash frowned at them, his body tingling as if he had drunk too much caffeine in a short amount of time. He wanted to question why they didn't seem to have knowledge of the plan they had all come up with and been working on for months. Tentatively, he said, "It was all part of the plan; she was supposed to be taken."

The woman nodded and said, "We are just checking the facts, it's simply protocol for us to ask and question."

Ash nodded but didn't do as she said, he was unable to be calm, not until Ciara was in front of him and breathing. They pulled in quietly to a farmhouse another hour later outside of town, where Curry was already standing with other agents.

"One more mile down the road is where her chip is leading us. Let's formulate a plan here, before we head in," Curry then began advising the group of their next steps.

It was another frustrating hour before they decided, and a longer period before they moved into action. Ash kept track of every grueling minute, checking his phone and messaging

Mr. Durand and their friends, and wishing he could tell them something more positive. Curry took Ash into his nearly silent black car and drove him to the other house with the lights off.

The SWAT team quietly maneuvered into place, and at the silent signal, they entered the home in droves.

Curry moved up the stairs and threw open the door where Ciara's chip was sending off the signal and broke it open with his gun ready. He began to curse, causing his closest partner to step in after him to determine the cause.

"She isn't there, damn it!" he swore and punched the wall before commanding, "Search the rest of the house."

They hurried to obey, and the woman who first spoke to Ash came back to the car to report, "She isn't here."

Then through her intercom someone announced, "There is blood on this bed, not much though. She will be fine as long as we find her soon." Curry stroked his goatee, and Ash overheard Curry state, "Regroup and bring Ash in here, he knows her. Perhaps she left a sign that he would understand."

Ash came in with his eyebrows drawn together and an angry, frightened look on his face. "What have you done? You said this wouldn't happen!"

"How was I supposed to predict this?" Curry waved his hands around at the small space and demanded of the taller man, "How, tell me how I could have known he would know exactly where her chip was? He somehow is always just a step ahead of me."

"You are supposed to think of everything!" Ash yelled, pulling at the hair on his head. Then he remembered it wasn't humanly possible to know everything, and he forced himself into a semblance of calm. "What is your plan now?"

Curry paced the living room in his own frustration as he tried to formulate a new plan. "I'm thinking, I don't want anything to happen to her either Ash. Take a deep breath and give me a moment to collect my thoughts."

>>>

Ciara smothered a scream by biting her lip hard enough to make it bleed as Grendale twisted her arm and something snapped. Immediately, she began thinking of the waves behind her grandmother's cottage. She turned the pain into waves and listened to the music of them crashing against the shore.

"Tell me where it is!" he shouted directly into her ear.

The young woman refused to speak as her waves continued to crash, and the salty scent of the sea soothed her. Grendale was getting frustrated. Inwardly, Ciara laughed at him, despite her cuts and bruises, because she was beating him and it was only a matter of time before they came for her. She left them a sign they would be stupid to miss.

"You could make this end whenever you want, it's so simple," he growled at her.

"Make it end? Then what happens? You kill me, right?" Ciara rolled her eyes at him and coughed and wheezed, "Well, kill me now then because I don't know anything; save us the trouble and the time."

He smacked her hard across the face as he snarled, "It isn't that simple, because I know you're lying, you do know something." He scratched his head as he watched the new mark appear on her face as if it were an experiment and grumbled,

"Maybe I am pushing too hard. Here is your reprieve to think about it. You can make it all stop and all you need to do is tell me what I want."

Grendale reached down to answer the phone buzzing in his pocket. His anger and annoyance bubbling up and over, leaching into his next words, "What?" slammed the door shut behind him and, in the growing dark, walked down the creaking stairs.

"Better watch that tone. You still have the girl?" The rough voice questioned.

"Of course, I have her, this isn't my first time," Grendale retorted, clipping his tone back a bit, knowing how dangerous it was to anger his employer. "She is about to crack; I can feel it."

"You can, can you? You have a way of losing your temper with the Fitzpatrick's, are you sure it's not going to end up like it did with her brother?"

"It won't and that was calculated, he would never have told me anything and he was getting in the way," Grendale stated. He strode into the kitchen to get a drink of water, despite wanting something stronger, but that would need to wait until after the chip was in his hands. What he said about Sean wasn't exactly true; his back had been against a wall, and he hadn't had much of a choice.

"Are you still going to make the time or do I need to start working on another route out?" His employer questioned.

Grendale shook his head as he glared at a spot on the wall and said in a measured tone, "I'll make the flight."

The line clicked off, and Grendale shoved the phone into his pocket, pulling the refrigerator open to pull out a bottle of water.

Ciara had watched him leave out of her swollen eyes with her mind clicking into gear. *I need to get out of here, or at least untied.* She wriggled her ankle and felt that one was loose, then flexed her unbroken wrist, but it was tight. Twisting her neck, she realized she could get to one rope now and, mentally crossing her fingers, she bit it and pulled back. Nothing happened the first time, but the second time the rope pulled against itself and release.

Rolling that wrist around, she got to work on the other ropes and looked outside and saw cars at the other house across the road. Praying that someone was looking her way, she went to the light switch and began flicking it on and off. *I hope I got the S.O.S. signal right; I hope someone saw and understood it.* She waited and tried to still her racing heart so she could hear if Joseph Grendale saw what she did, but there was only silence.

Quietly, she left the room to find a place to wait and hide.

>>>

He couldn't stand watching Curry pace back and forth anymore and turned to the lady with braided hair, "Can I see where she was being held before Grendale moved her?"

The lady looked from Ash to Curry as the sergeant waved Ash along, snapping out another order, "Don't touch anything though as it's all evidence and we will need to analyze everything."

The room had drops of her blood on the floor and on the wrinkled bedspread. He saw some muddy boot prints and began trying to recall every detective movie he had ever seen, but what kept coming back to him was *Sherlock Holmes*. And, specifically, his saying about how everything was in the littlest details, it was also one of Ciara's favorite books.

"If he is such a good assassin," Ash began, pointing at the boot prints, before continuing, "Why does all of this appear so sloppy?"

The woman snapped her fingers, and her eyes widened as she blurted, "Something about this seemed off, but he wouldn't have had time to get far... look around and catalogue what you see. I will get some others up here quick, he is trying to put us off his trail. This was all for show and if we can figure out where he was trying to lead us, we will be able to tell where he is not."

A half hour later, Ash jumped and hit his head on the bed frame as he called to the officer he was assisting, "Kayla, look at this."

Tossing her braid over her shoulder, she bent down to study the tiny arrow of blood pointing out of the room to the north. "That fingerprint is too small to be Grendale's and that's Ciara, but it is too light of a mark to have been forced. Come on, let's go tell Curry."

They left the room and went back down to the living room for Kayla to explain their findings. Ash stared outside, feeling impatient. That's when he saw the light flash on and off across the street. "Curry, it's an SOS signal."

The sergeant gazed at the signal in bewilderment that Grendale would have only moved her across the street; it was both brilliant and stupid. He had to realize they were there, though, and Curry's brain stumbled through their limited options. "That's Ciara, it has to be. She must have gotten away from him."

"She is trapped in the house though," Ash said, his heart feeling as if it was beating out of his chest. His body alternating in quick succession from swelteringly hot to bone-chillingly cold. He breathed deeply, trying to stop himself from thinking what may already have happened to her. And, instead, thought about the fact that they now were aware that she was alive and well enough to have escaped. "We have to go save her," Ash blurted out, already making his way to the doorway of the room, having missed half of the conversation Curry had been having with Kayla.

"No, *you* have to stay here," Curry said, emphasizing his words with a stab at the couch. "Kayla, round everyone up. Grendale doesn't get out of this one alive, unless he is in chains."

Quickly, the team assembled and began moving out toward the other home across the street, using the shadows for cover. Curry slowly opened the front door to slip in and heard a roar of anger come from the second floor.

"He must have realized she was missing. I want all the windows and staircases guarded," Curry muttered to Kayla. She gave out the orders behind him before he whispered, "You, with me."

{ 34 }

Charms

Ciara sat huddled in a linen closet, buried under sheets that smelled of mothballs, concentrating on her breathing by singing songs and replaying memories spent in sunshine with her family. She desperately fought against wondering what would happen to her when Grendale found her. As she sat huddled in the closet under the pile of blankets, Ciara's mind began to wander back to an old memory, one of her favorite memories with her mother.

They had lain curled together on the daybed in her parents' study, a book propped on her mother's hip. Ciara had nestled her head just under her mother's. She had loved listening to her mother read, and it was one of those stories where her lilting brogue was perfect for the voices. Ciara had closed her eyes as she listened, creating the fictional world around her like a painting. As time passed, she didn't notice her mother had stopped reading right away, but had snapped her eyes open when she did and turned her head to look at her, asking, "Why did you stop?"

Her mother had laughed, the sound rich in her throat when she answered, "I thought you had fallen asleep."

"*How could I sleep? There is so much action, and I want to know what happens, keep reading,*" Ciara had said, then added, "*Please.*" She had pursed her lips out and begged her with her eyes.

"*Alright, hold on,*" her mother had easily acquiesced and began to reposition herself on the daybed that had gotten much tighter for the two of them as Ciara hit her teen years. "*I just need to shift, much better.*"

As she moved, her charm bracelet had slid along the book's cover and down her wrist a few inches; the old silver had caught the light of high noon. Ciara had reached out a hand and knocked a few of the charms together to make a light tinkling sound. Since she could remember, she had always been fascinated by the bracelet, a relic from the grandmother she had never met. She had traced each one until she came to the piece that never seemed to fit and let her hand fall. "*Just one more chapter?*"

"*One more,*" her mother had murmured and tilted her head down to kiss the crown of Ciara's head before diving back into the land of adventure.

Ciara couldn't believe it as she gently shook her head realizing how obvious it had been and yet left both Ciara and Sean in the dark. *No, Sean had known all along but didn't want to tell me and put me more at risk than I already was.* That was obvious to her now. He was even going to tell her that night, but then Grendale showed up and ruined everything. Ciara felt her anger bubbling up and over.

"Come out, come out, wherever you are," Grendale called, his voice echoing menacingly in the dark. He was trying to scare her again, but the time when he could scare her was long gone. The only power he held over her now was hurting her physically, and she could deal with that, and she would take her parents' secret with her to her grave.

She clutched the charm bracelet to her chest and thought first of her mother, then her grandmother, and finally the original owner – great-grandmother. Though she hadn't been raised religious, Ciara sent a prayer up to whatever god or being was listening that they would get her through this. She took a breath in and let it out as softly as she could, slowing her racing heart as Grendale spoke again, "It will be better if you come now. I'll make it easier on you."

No, you won't, Ciara retorted silently. *Come on, Curry, find me, please find me.*

A creak in the floorboard announced Grendale's arrival outside her closet, but, by some miracle, he opened a different door first. Ciara didn't dare move but knew better than to hold her breath. The other door closed, and her closet opened a crack, but no more than a yell and running feet sounded down the hallway.

>>>

Curry saw Grendale's shadow begin to open a closet at the end of the hallway. "Grendale!" He yelled and ran for him, going for the shock and surprise tactic.

Joseph Grendale cursed and turned to fight off his adversary, but Curry caught him in the jaw with a fist as Grendale raised his knee into Curry's stomach, and both men collapsed. Not sure of what to do, Kayla tried to get a clear shot at Grendale but was too afraid of the possibility of hitting Curry.

The sergeant gripped the other man around the neck and squeezed, but Grendale kicked Curry in the groin, causing him to release his throat. Grendale gripped his wrist and twisted, but Curry moved with it and elbowed him in the sternum. They rolled away from each other and climbed to their feet. Instead of going after her boss, Kayla turned to the closet door, which was sitting open a fraction of an inch.

She found Ciara buried under the sheets, looking ready to either pass out or murder someone, and murmured, "Come on."

Ciara nodded, limping to her feet, and Kayla pulled her unbroken arm around her shoulders to half-drag her to the stairs.

Grendale yelled, "No, she's mine!" He charged Kayla, who was about to take Ciara down the stairs to safety, but Curry dove at the man, knocking him down the flight of stairs. The Shadow hit his head on the hard oak floor and was momentarily stunned. Curry jumped down the stairs after him, and as he attempted to rise, Curry kicked him hard in the head with a booted foot. Grendale didn't try to rise again.

Ciara sagged against Kayla and whimpered, "I can't do it, I can't walk anymore. I want to sit down, I just want to sleep."

"Oh no, no sleeping, not yet," she stated and pulled the young woman up against her side, taking on the majority of her weight. "Besides, someone is waiting for you."

Ciara blinked heavily, unable to answer as the pain of standing on her ankle became overwhelming.

"I believe his name is Ash Callaghan," Kayla explained, while maneuvering her as she spoke and got her to the door. A swat man took Ciara by the other arm as Kayla ordered, "Carry her over. The medical team needs to get a good look at her and start the transport to the hospital with armed men in the back with her. Tell that boy Ash to get in with her before he makes me handcuff him to something." She called for another vehicle to be driven over and helped Curry transport Grendale's unconscious form into the back. There, they handcuffed and chained him to the seat before removing everything from his person and ran a detector over him, checking for microchips and any other hidden items. Curry was not about to risk losing him.

Curry turned to Kayla and, with knitted eyebrows, asked, "You don't have a welder handy, do you?" She gave him an inquisitive look, and he waved towards the chains, explaining, "I want to weld those chains together, so he has no means of escape."

Kayla pursed her lips and barked a laugh as she said, "I will find one sir."

"Good, do that and then get this man out of here," Curry ordered and called after her, "Highest security and I don't want to hear about any slip ups, understand?"

"I will see it done," Kayla shouted over her shoulder and began rounding everyone up as Curry walked with the man carrying Ciara across the street.

Ash saw them coming and ran outside, taking her from the other man's arms as gently as was possible. Immediately, she wrapped her good arm around his neck. She tried to hold back her tears, but in the safety of Ash's arms, she could no longer do it. He kissed her forehead and cradled her against his chest until the medical team began their check as they secured her into the transport van. Murmuring into her ear on repeat, "It's okay, it's over, you're safe."

The medical team transported her to the hospital, giving her a heavy dose of pain medication on the way. She didn't require the sleep aids, but they gave them to her anyway as they began patching her arm where her tracker had been, then moved on to setting her wrist. Ash sat in the back with her, holding her hand as they steadily worked on her, while they navigated the snow-covered roads with ease in the large vehicle.

>>>

As Ciara's eyes slipped closed, Ash reached out a shaking hand and gripped her fingers. He didn't want to let her out of his sight again and felt tears filling his eyes as he looked from her braced ankle and to the mottled bruising along her torso and ribs. Then they shifted to her bandaged right arm where the tracker had been cut out. He dragged the heel of his hand over his cheeks to wipe away the liquid spilling down his face as he glanced to her arm wrapped tightly in a brace. Ash swallowed hard as he looked back at her pale face, which was covered in cuts and bruises.

After several calming breaths, Ash pulled his phone out and, after several attempts, called Nate, who answered on the first ring with concern lacing his voice, "Ash?"

Ash heard a professor yell from the background, but Nate seemed to ignore it as Ash answered. "It's over, she's safe. We're being taken to the hospital on St. Augustine, she's been hurt, but they say she will be okay."

Nate sighed into the phone as he responded, "I will be there just after you. Do you want me to get the others?"

"We are all she's got and I think she would like to see us all," Ash decided gazing into her face as the paramedics monitored her vitals as they pulled into the hospital.

>>>

"Nate, if you don't give me that phone right now, you can leave this classroom," the professor said in a voice filled with steel.

Tyler looked at Nate questioningly as he hung up the phone and answered the professor, "Sorry Dr. Prescott, a good friend was badly hurt and we just got an update. She is being transported to a hospital right now."

"Is Ciara okay?" Tyler asked anxiously as he stood up and began putting his books in his bag.

"Ciara Fitzpatrick?" Dr. Prescott asked, her wrinkled brow creasing.

Nate nodded, knowing that Dr. Prescott, under the gray-steel cap of hair, was really a warm and caring person. "Yes, Tyler and I need to go see her. Can we email you for the assignments later?"

"Of course," she said, putting a hand to her temple and staring at the dark sky. She nodded her head as she looked back to her students and asked, "Tell her to email me when she can and I will excuse her from class for as long as she needs."

Tyler and Nate left the room at a fast trot as he offered, "I'll call Leah and Jared."

"I've got Jez and tell them to meet at the entrance to the auditorium, and we can all ride together. We might want to stop somewhere and pick up food. I'm sure both will be hungry when we get there," Nate added as he called his girlfriend.

Relics of the Past

Tyler reached over for Jared's hand, clasping it in his own at the sight of Ciara with tubes sticking out of her nose, head wrapped, arms and face bandaged, and then the giant cast on her arm. Jared pulled him in and wrapped his arms around his boyfriend.

"She's going to be okay, right?" Leah asked in a shaking voice, and Jared reached over and pulled her into their embrace too. She let her oldest friend tuck her into his chest as Jared's arms surrounded them.

"Yeah," Ash choked out, explaining, "The doctors said she is going to be just fine, nothing permanent." He was exhausted but understood his friends needed to be informed of what had happened.

Nate and Jez came over and wrapped their arms around Ash from opposite sides as they said, "That's amazing news, are you okay?"

"I'm fine," he said, brow furrowed in confusion as he asked, "Why wouldn't I be okay?"

"We mean mentally," Jez said in her slightly stern, yet motherly voice. "You went through a lot too; you were right there the entire time and that's a lot to take in. You were in the van getting a play by play and then were right there when she was brought out. That's some terrifying stuff to go through, I wouldn't handle something like that happening to Nate extremely well."

Ash paused, taking stock of his mental health, but it felt more like digging through a heavy fog. "I honestly have no idea right now; I can't really think clearly right now and I don't even know what time it is or how much time has even passed since we left class."

Jez looked him over and handed him a thermos, describing the contents: "Honey, lemon, and ginger with hot water, all the essentials. It's been almost twenty hours at this point and they didn't let us back right away and then Curry had to clear us. Have you eaten anything since getting to the hospital?"

Ash furrowed his brow and shook his head, beginning to feel dizzy as his mind struggled to focus on the words coming out of Jez's mouth.

"Leah, got the goods?" Tyler questioned, and Leah reached over to the counter to hold up a bag and questioned, "Cheeseburger, can stomach it?"

Ash's stomach responded before his words, "Don't have much choice with that." He reached over and took the burger before beginning to ask, "Any chance,"

Jared handed over a large cup filled with a vanilla milkshake and chuckled, "Know you too well, well, Tyler does at least, I thought strawberry."

"That's Ciara who likes strawberry," Ash clarified as he pulled the paper away from the burger and bit into it, devouring half in one bite.

Nate sat in an empty seat and pulled Jez onto his lap, and the group relaxed into the room, viewing the sleeping girl in the middle of them. It never occurred to them that they had known her for less than a year, because she was a part of them now, seamlessly entwined in their lives.

>>>

Get-well cards surrounded Ciara, along with a stuffed bear holding a flower and a few other bouquets and helium balloons. Lex was going to come and visit the moment she was released, but KT had video chatted with her as soon as he was able. The cards, flowers, and balloons cheered up the room from its off-white color and the shiny-sterile surfaces, while the flowers kept the bleached smell of the hospital at bay. Ciara wanted to leave.

She looked at the cast on her left arm, and even though it was broken with a pin in it, she smiled. Ash had written a song on it and signed it with a heart. Ciara had just been told by the doctor that with a bit of physical therapy, she would have full use of her arm again, despite the damage Grendale had done to it. In fact, she was relieved to find out that nothing Joseph Grendale had done to her physically would be permanent. And the knowledge that he would be in a high security prison for the rest of his life, was simply the icing on an incredibly delicious fudge brownie.

At the memory of her old nemesis, Curry strode in behind Ash, who smiled kindly at her and scratched his freshly trimmed goatee. "You asked me to come by; I was going to anyway; we aren't through just yet. Quinten wants to come and see you as well, if that's alright."

Ciara sighed tiredly and said, "Yes. I remembered something and truthfully, I think I always knew, but the charm bracelet I wear a lot, it has something special on it."

"What kind of special?" Curry asked, perking up with a slow smile creeping under his dark facial hair.

"The chip, or part of it," she explained with a tired smile, and it pulled on the bandage under her lip. "It's in that drawer. My mother almost never took it off; it was a family heirloom passed down for several generations from mother to daughter. It has charms of everything sacred in the Irish culture, but one piece never seemed to fit, the triangle pushed into a case that comes off."

Curry's face seemed to fall slightly, but Ciara kept on smirking at him as he pressed, "That's all? I think you know where the other piece is too though, don't you?"

"Of course, my brother had it and now, you probably have it. Unless he is still in the morgue with every item he had been wearing at the time on him," Ciara said with tears welling up in her eyes but pushed them back.

"All of his belongings are in a lock box in my office," the sergeant murmured and closed his eyes, wishing she would stop leading him.

"His watch always seemed to rattle, but we could never get it to open, to figure out what rattled. Except, since I have been laying here with nothing else to occupy me, I realized this bracelet also has the key, the trinity fits into the back of the watch. If you turn it, it will unlock and, if I am correct, the rest of the chip is inside." Ciara yawned widely and finished, "There you are but I want my bracelet back when you're done, and my brothers watch. Turns out, I was right all along, Grendale really did kill the wrong one. I think Sean knew everything the whole time, well, maybe not everything, but he at least knew about the chip."

Curry sagged into a chair near the doorway. "All this time, right under our noses."

Ash kissed Ciara gently on her cut lips as he proclaimed, "You, my dear, are brilliant."

"I try," she said with a jaw-cracking yawn, dramatically this time, as if being brilliant was boring, but her eyes closed regardless and she fell into a dreamless sleep.

>>>

A few days later, she received a call from an unexpected person. When the hospital phone rang, Ash, Jez, and Nate were all in her room filling her in on the latest details of campus life. It was the first time the hospital phone had rung, and she nervously picked it up and asked, "Hello?"

"Ciara?" the person inquired, pronouncing her name with a lilting brogue.

The young woman's air caught in her throat and tears welled up in her eyes as she exclaimed, "Gram-mamma!"

"Oh, my sweet," the woman croaked back, and Ciara could hear tears in her grandmother's warbling voice. "Where on this earth have you been hiding all these years? Some man named Fredrick Curry called earlier this morning with the most insane story about you and Sean being tracked and hunted and Sean is, dead?"

"It's not a story Gram-mamma," Ciara murmured, drinking in the sound of her only relative's voice. "It's all true but the man who chased us is now locked up, but he did, he killed mom, dad, and Sean." Her voice slipped easily into the Irish accent she had grown up around.

Ash and Jez glanced at each other as they heard the change in her voice and smiled. They had experienced Ciara slipping into it a few times, but this was complete. They hid their grins as Ciara explained everything to her grandmother, and after an hour, she gave the old woman her cell phone number, promising to call when she was released from the hospital.

"I get to see her once this semester ends," Ciara explained, wiping at the tears filling her eyes with happiness. "I can't believe it, after eight, almost nine, years, I get to see my gram-mamma again, and Ireland. Oh, it's the most beautiful place on earth you guys. The thick green hills with the multicolored gray stone fences splattered across the hillsides, it's so wonderful, you should all come visit."

Her three friends laughed at her relief and at the relaxed smile spreading across her face. She had nothing to worry about except things a normal twenty-three-year-old should worry about.

Ash came and sat with her whenever he got the chance, and her friends stopped by every day. Even as she walked out of the sliding glass doors of the hospital, her freedom hadn't quite set in. She would never be normal from all that had happened

to her, but she was free, as she gripped Ash's hand, Ciara reminded herself of that. She had her freedom.

{ 36 }

Epilogue

The emerald green of the grass was interspersed with the fluffy white clouds of the sheep until they turned to show the stripes of different colors to identify who they belonged to. Ash had been very confused by that at first until Ciara explained the reasoning.

Ciara pulled his arm, dragging him closer to her and said quickly, "Watch it."

"Watch what?" He asked, looking down at her as they neared the top of the hill and the ancient watchtower came fully into view.

"Peat bog, nasty to fall into and pretty sure that one still has my blue shoe from when I was five." Ciara pulled the top of her hair up into a ponytail and breathed, "Almost there."

Ash followed her off the trail and onto the grass, avoiding a lamb nursing with her mother as she dragged her hand along the golden yellow and cream-colored stone as she passed it by. A feeling of serenity infused her as she breathed in the scent of the ocean. Ash pulled his phone out and snapped a picture of her. She shoved his arm and snatched the phone from his hand, tugging his arms around her shoulders and took a picture of them smiling with the sun shining down on them.

Leading him over to the cliff edge, Ciara grinned at Ash and exclaimed, "Come on, it's worth it, I promise. Much better than the Cliffs of Moher," she said with an eye roll at the name of the world-famous tourist destination, and Ash took a hesitant step towards her. "Come on, I won't let you fall and it's not quite as high, a little over 700 feet instead of 1,000, but you can get right up to the edge."

"Oh yeah, that's just what I want to do, dangle my legs seven hundred feet in the air. Cia, I don't have a death wish," Ash stated and pulled back as she giggled.

"Fine, stay there then," she sang and calmy walked right up to the edge. And after a deep breath, flung her arms out above her head in the universal gesture of accomplishment. She had made it home.

When she opened her eyes, she saw the blues and greens swirling in the water below and remembered the first time she had climbed up here with her family. Sean had been chasing her the whole way up in an endless game of tag. Her dad had to carry her on his shoulders most of the way down because she had been so exhausted, and her mom and she had made flower chains to put in their hair. When they got back to her grandmother's cottage, low tea had been waiting on the table for them. Tiny cakes, thick warm scones with clotted cream, and tea flavored with lavender and honey.

Ciara looked at Ash and ran at him, throwing her arms around him and gushed, "Thank you."

He looked at her with his yellow-gold eyes, his brows drawn in confusion, and asked, "For what?"

"Helping me find my way home," she said and kissed him deeply.

Ash wrapped his arms around her tighter and murmured into her hair, "Always, and don't worry, if you get lost, I know just where to find you."

Ciara laughed and pulled him down to lie in the sweet-smelling grass and listen to the wind blowing over the cliff edge and the sheep bleating in the distance. Their friends were driving up from the airport in a few hours. They didn't have much time before they needed to get back to the cottage to help with dinner, but just then there didn't seem to be much of a rush. Life would happen in its own time and, in Ireland, no one ever rushed anywhere. They inter-twined their fingers and smiled at one another; they had all the time in the world.

Author Bio

N. Penz writes stories for the underdogs and those searching for hope of all kinds. When she's not wrangling her two children on her paddleboard, she's probably haunting local libraries or coffee shops searching for new characters. Penz is a former journalist and a current educator for special needs students in low-income schools who constantly remind her what empathy, resilience, and perseverance are.

Other works by N. Penz include *Indigo Skye*, a contemporary romance (LGBTQ+) and the *Marked* series, a fantasy epic. Many more stories are coming soon. Follow along on N. Penz's socials:

Instagram: @author_npenz
Facebook: Niki Penz
Bluesky: N. Penz